ALIEN HUNT!

It was the sentinel system that alerted the hunter. The sensors had detected the entry into the sun's system of a small mass, a mass that had appeared all at once, as if created in an instant from nothingness. The long-sought Shan were here! Now at last the hunter and his race, the Ann Thaar, had another chance to capture the secrets that the Shan had kept from them for so long—a chance at the immortality virus and the faster-than-light drive that could give them complete control of the galaxy.

With total concentration, the hunter studied the actions of the intruder vessel. The only possible place of interest was the planet that harbored the primitives. A sudden insight gripped the hunter. There must be Shan on the planet! The ship was here to rescue them! Cursing himself for not having studied the populace more carefully, the hunter roused his subordinates and began to give orders. Neither the Shan nor the primitive "humans" would escape this planet called Haven. . . .

DAW

DAW PRESENTS STAR WARS IN A WHOLE NEW DIMENSION

Timothy Zahn
THE BLACKCOLLAR NOVELS

The war drug—that was what Backlash was, the secret formula, so rumor said, which turned ordinary soldiers into the legendary Blackcollars, the super warriors who, decades after Earth's conquest by the alien Ryqril, remained humanity's one hope to regain its freedom.

☐ THE BLACKCOLLAR (Book 1)   (UE2168—$3.50)
☐ THE BACKLASH MISSION (Book 2)   (UE2150—$3.50)

Charles Ingrid
☐ **SOLAR KILL (Sand Wars #1)**

He was a soldier fighting against both mankind's alien foe and the evil at the heart of the human Dominion Empire, trapped in an alien-altered suit of armor which, if worn too long, could transform him into a sand warrior—a no-longer human berserker.

(UE2209—$3.50)

John Steakley
☐ **ARMOR**

Impervious body armor had been devised for the commando forces who were to be dropped onto the poisonous surface of A-9, the home world of mankind's most implacable enemy. But what of the man inside the armor? This tale of cosmic combat will stand against the best of Gordon Dickson or Poul Anderson.

(UE1979—$3.95)

MATTERS OF FORM

SCOTT WHEELER

DAW BOOKS, INC.
DONALD A. WOLLHEIM, PUBLISHER

1633 Broadway, New York, NY 10019

First Printing, October 1987

1 2 3 4 5 6 7 8 9

PRINTED IN THE U.S.A.

To my wife Frieda,
my best friend, who said I could do it.

Interim Period

Inside the cubicles life ebbed low. There was neither light nor sound. Slight odors were present, but they were undetected by the two life forms which occupied the still, oblong tubes. Time was counted by the vibrations induced in a crystal by the flow of a minute current. Electron flow was the only activity in the cubicles or in the outer ship. Self-measuring, self-monitoring systems passively waited as the craft fell through space. No actions were taken; none were needed. Everything waited for the measured flow of electrons to cycle themselves endlessly through circuits until a position was reached where three stars lay in the proper vectors. Till that event occurred and registered itself on the passive sensors, no breakers would be tripped. No machinery would hum. Death was near. Aging ceased with the cessation of organic activity. Not even dreams existed. If souls existed separate from corporeal bodies, these at least were still tied to the two inert forms that lay in the tubes that were not quite tombs. That they might actually become such was a real possibility, for the thin thread of life that remained could go out unnoticed by the uncaring machinery. If and when the stars lined up correctly, the computers would begin prearranged programs. The revival systems would begin the torturous process that would bring the forms to life and consciousness again. If it weren't too late. If the ship were not taken by an unforseen gravity well. If . . . For now nothing changed; the ship fell endlessly, unobserved. The fate of many traveled through the dark vacuum with it. They waited for the end of its journey. For them time did not stand still. It moved and so did the events of separate worlds. Separate but soon to be linked if the ship made its rendezvous. A dark body full of potential, it fell through years it couldn't measure.

Chapter 1

The alarm came from everywhere at once. My personal com-link joined in the cacophony that was issuing from the speakers that abounded throughout the ship. Display screens flashed in a bid for visual attention. I dropped the tech manual I was reading and swung out of my chair. I beat the other bodies in the Ops room to the door and joined the stream of crew and scientists heading for the shielded cubicles. I was pleased with what I saw. It looked like a fast, orderly operation; the drills had paid off. I sealed the room as soon as the last person in our section of the corridor was inside and did a head count. Nine were here with me. A little over the average but not a real crowd. We'd do very nicely if the solar storm didn't last too long. There were emergency supplies for a couple of weeks, and it was a very rare occurrence for one of these storms to go on for more than a couple of days. I expected this one to be a lot shorter, a few hours at the most. I entered the count into the com-link terminal that served this area and watched the screen as the personnel in the other cubicles added theirs to the roster. The total was completed almost as soon as I'd entered our number. It had been as clear a withdrawal as I'd thought. The display flashed "All confirmed" at me and I knew everyone had reached shelter. I noted the time: 1307 hours. The alert had sounded at 1303 hours. Four minutes till everyone was in and accounted for. I knew they had actually been quicker than that. I eyed the display for any further information that could be significant. There was nothing of any importance and nothing to do about it anyway. We were here until the sensors satisfied the computers that the radiation danger was over. From now on the automatic programs would run the ship. They were even more heavily shielded than we were. There would be a few subsystems that we'd have to repair when we got out of these shielded rooms, but probably nothing major. The problems had been largely eliminated over the course of years. Right now the radiation was starting to reach some hellish intensities out there in the unshielded section of the ship. A human being would have been getting doses of deadly proportions. The machinery had been vastly improved. We hadn't. Enough shielding to protect us completely would be exorbitant and wasn't necessary ninety-nine percent of the time. Generally, the body was unaffected by the stuff. For the most part it was transparent to it. The trouble actually was caused by the secondary radiation set up as the solar wind hit the structure of the ship and was turned into the more deadly type of radiation. A little shielding could kill you faster than none at all. Still, you had to have some. The answer was to have a lot in small areas such as the one we inhabited now.

I had the good fortune to be with an easygoing bunch in our area. The luck of the draw had thrown me in with ship's crew entirely. Since I was the "old man," they didn't feel that I had to keep up my end of the conversation. I took the opportunity to review the puzzle of the scientific staff that constituted my real job on the *Tinker Bell*. They weren't what they seemed and neither was I. I was very aware of what they were. I had no reason to think they were aware of me. Great effort had been made to assure this. I had been provided with a unique opportunity to find out what they were up to. For the first time in years, actually decades, they were doing something out in the open. They had never before been so visible in a history that went back over a century. If that seems like a long

time for any person or group to be under an official
investigation, you're right. The situation was weird
and getting weirder all the time. But for the first time
in our experience of the phenomenon we had come to
call the Phoenix Group, we had its entire membership
in one place doing something that seemed important
enough to put all of its personnel and resources on the
line. The agency I represented was a select little group
that had been created just to find out what the group
was and what its purpose might be. I was the latest in
a long line of agents that had made them the study of
a lifetime. This had been going on for over half a
century. If that sounds as if we weren't very good at
our jobs, you just don't know the difficulties.

There were eight of them on the ship. The foundation that was their present incarnation was called the
McCandless Foundation for its founder, J.B. McCandless, who had made a vast fortune in the sale of high
technology generated by his private group of geniuses.
He had only recently died and the group was now
headed by Dr. Barbara Patterson, who was thirty-
seven years old and looked twenty-two. She had a
string of credentials that took care of most of the
alphabet. She had been the old man's personal achievement as opposed to his public ones. Obviously gifted,
she had been plucked from her destitute family at an
early age and installed in McCandless' home. He had
become her official guardian and the parents had signed
away all claim to the child in return for lifetime jobs
with the foundation which paid very well and entailed
no great amount of work. They located in an area well
away from the McCandless home base and were never
known to ask about Barbara or her affairs. She had
proved to have an exceptional mind for the physical
sciences and was soon quietly gathering up a string of
degrees that was truly awesome. She didn't become a
household word, however. She wasn't even particu-
larly well known in academic circles either. She stayed
in the Foundation and worked on projects in which
they interested themselves. Now she headed this one.

The *Tinker Bell* was, to all intents and purposes, the Foundation's ship. The Space Administration still wasn't allowing private ownership of such yet, so the vessel was technically the Western Federation's. I had been placed in charge as their representative; it had a working crew made up of regular service personnel.

It was a strange marriage but one that was needed by both sides. The concepts that went into the building of the ship were new and radical and they promised to provide the basis of a new order of space exploration. The Western Federation, and through them the rest of the world, needed what the *Tinker Bell* had to offer. The Foundation held all the cards in the area of expertise and its personnel were needed to do the experimentation. They had developed almost everything that had gone into the ship and held the basic patents. They understood what it really was. The government had no idea of the long line that stretched out through history behind the Foundation; only my department did. When it became apparent that the Federation Council was going to be approached with the plan for the *Tinker Bell*, the agency quietly moved to take charge. They gained control of the project and only a few on the Federation Council were told of it. At last the agency was in a position to get next to the Phoenix Group. I was recruited from the space service early in the game and groomed for the job I now held.

I had been provided with some wonderful toys to use on my job and I was using them with a steadily waning enthusiasm. The Phoenix Group was proving as hard to get a grip on aboard ship as they had been on Earth. They were the coolest people in the history of surveillance. They never made a mistake. They never seemed to have a need for talking things over. They never left any correspondence around for a good little spy to pick up and read. Everything they did was open and aboveboard and yet I knew, the agency knew, with certainty that they were doing far more than we could see on the surface.

The rest of the group was made up of seven more

bona fide geniuses. Kelly Bergen was a whiz in mathematics. He lived in a world of interesting points on graphs. Number sequences made him laugh though he was often unable to get the meaning of a dirty joke. His fingers were the logical extension of the keypad of a computer rather than the other way around. He was fifty and small for a man, yet he looked youthful. He had to be watched out for when he was away from his calculating devices as he wasn't really adapted to the physical world.

Celia Poynter was a girl of twenty-six or so and had an unfortunate impact on my physical and mental well-being. Don't ask me why. She wasn't a knockout in the standard sense. She was trim enough and her curves were lightly stated, not promising a lushness that would overpower anyone. She hadn't really said much either. I kept trying to find a conversational gambit that would really get her to open up, but so far I'd failed. Her face got to me somehow and I had the feeling I was heading for an obsessive phase. She was the resident hotshot in the life sciences that applied to space environments. She'd published a lot of papers about the effects of radiation and other environmental factors on the genetic structure of the humans who were exposed to space. She was supposed to have some interesting ideas about some of the unused stuff in the genes. It seems there is a lot of nonspecific material that doesn't come into play in the order of things. She has some theories that this material could be useful somehow. It's beyond me! Bob Pauling, Bill Ankers, William Posten and Art Bell made up the rest of the bunch with the exception of Henry Eagles. Don't ask me what they did. I could tell you what the files on them said, but I don't understand it and few other people did. I knew they were hot stuff. On paper, Henry was the most interesting of the bunch. He was a professor of history and commanded a dozen languages or so. He qualified as both an archaeologist and an anthropologist and if you wanted to know anything about past events in any field, he'd know something about it. I guess he was serving in the capacity of project historian, although I never saw him take a note. It did seem as though everyone in the group kept him up to date with the proceedings, and he never seemed to fail in his understanding of what was said. I found that he had written a series of mysteries I'd liked a lot under another name. There were definitely layers to Henry. He was in his middle fifties and still had all his hair. He could have passed for twenty years younger if he'd dyed it. His eyes were coal black and he didn't wear glasses. He was easily the most genial of the group, and yet there was a reserve beneath the surface that kept you from adopting the same easy manner with him that he displayed himself.

There was no telling the length of stay we would have when we made these infrequent visits to the shelters. Often there wasn't much warning either. You usually had only a few minutes before the flare was upon you. You dropped what you were doing and got inside. Of course, the observatories were getting pretty good at predicting activity over the course of weeks, so you were able to schedule your work for the periods of maximum quiet. It was just when things were marginal that you had to stay close to the shielded areas.

It turned out that the storm was just what the Phoenix Group had been waiting for. Although I wasn't to know for hours yet, they made the first move that day while I was out of the way.

The alert lasted for a little over five hours before the sensors decided we could emerge from our shells and I'd had plenty of time to consider the lack of progress I'd made. I decided to throw a monkey wrench into the works and see if anything came of it. When we came out and I'd checked the damage reports and found nothing that I needed to do outside of scheduling the work details, I went to the radio shack and sent the Tech on duty off for some coffee and sandwiches. She was grateful for the chance as she'd missed a meal during the flare. I sent a coded message that would arrive at the agency by a circuitous route. There was plenty of this sort of thing floating around in the com-network; it wouldn't draw any attention to itself. I was going to play a nasty little trick on a good friend. I wiped the record of the transmission and was sitting back in the chair when the Tech returned.

"Thanks, Colonel," she said. "I'm afraid my stomach growling might have gone out over the network if I hadn't gotten something in it before the end of the watch. I brought back a couple of sandwiches with me if you'd care to have them."

I looked at the offering with horror which I hoped I disguised. It doesn't do to show fear in the midst of the troops. The sandwiches had everything on them but untanned cowhide.

"Thanks just the same, Sergeant." Keeping my voice under control I told a fearsome lie about the big meal I had in store for me and backed out of the com room. I made a mental note to check her medical file the next day and went to check on the eggheads.

The *Tinker Bell* was built a bit like the orbital station that supplied us. It was disk-shaped rather than wheel-like. The spaces between the hub and the outer ring were filled with compartmentalized sections crammed with scientific gear and instrumentation. I even knew what most of it was. I hadn't been kept away from an education. In fact, among ordinary folks I was known as a whiz kid myself. It was one of the reasons I had gotten this job. On the other hand I was just bright enough to know that I was in the presence of really first-rate minds. I could read a manual on these things they'd installed and understand most of what they did. I could even repair them if the parts were available. But these folks had designed these things for purposes I could accept only because they told me so. The equipment had been vetted back on Earth by a lot of engineering types who said they were what was specified in the ops manual and that they would work the way they said they would. What they did it for wasn't quite as clear, and there did seem to be capabilities beyond the scope of the specs built into the apparatus. The important thing was that the Foundation said it had the promise of a new type of propulsion system in the works, and the unspoken words, Star Drive, shimmered in the air when they spoke of it. The government heard the unspoken words clearly. They let the Foundation do its thing with little more than a token rein (me!). The rest of the scientific community grumbled and fumed at the unusual circumstances and the fact that they were precluded from sharing in the venture, but they admitted that there was a possibility of success. That was enough. They got carte blanche and the rest of the crew and me. They would have preferred to supply their own crew, but the Space Service wouldn't go quite that far. I walked through the result. The first space vessel that actually looked and felt like one. With luck it might even be the real thing. I hoped so. It was what I had dreamed of since I was a kid. I hoped that the Phoenix Group was going to pull this off for the benefit of mankind. That was the trouble. We didn't understand their motives anymore than we understood their beginnings and the history of the group. We just didn't know.

Chapter 2

The *Tinker Bell* spun just as the orbital station did, but the gravity that was simulated by this spin was on a much sharper gradient because of her small size. Between levels the change was dramatic. Even from one bulkhead to the next you felt the difference. I routed my way through the hub toward the other side of the outer ring. The operations complex and shelter area I had just left were on the opposite side of the ship but on the same ring. I went from a full-G to weightlessness and back again in the course of the trip. On the way I stopped to look at the black, humped mass that occupied the center of the *Tinker Bell*. If the Project went as hoped, a strange anomaly would be created there. Fed by the energies of a tokamak larger than any other used so far in space and a lot of smaller communities on earth, it would hopefully create a fold in space and send us to another spot in our universe at a speed faster than light. The section that I faced now would be inoperative until the time came to try out the null drive and really wasn't very interesting to look at. The artificial lighting showed only a large black sphere about ten meters in diameter. It looked like a storage tank for fuel or water. When the process was engaged, it was supposed to create and hold another dimension of the physical world and free us for a time from the restraints of the normal universe. At the other end of the long tunnel that housed the thing was something that bothered me a lot—an enormous cylinder that contained a tremendous load of great dirty fission-

ables, products of the era of reactors that had provided power and isotopes for good and deplorable
uses in the bad old days. These once again found a use
in the process that would make the null drive a reality.
Somehow they were to be used as a ballast for the
energies created. It seemed to me that would be like
putting twenty liters of fuel in a ten-liter bucket, but I
had been assured that the opposite was the case. I had
to take their word for it, but the stuff made me nervous all the same. There was enough hot stuff in the
core of that thing to kill a planet ten times over.

I left the center and worked my way back into the
gravity sections, emerging on the other side of the
ship. I found the scientists busily getting things back
on track. I checked with each small group of scientists
and techs to see if there was anything I was needed
for. In all cases the situation was normalizing and
could get along without me very well. I hadn't expected anything else. I wound up talking to Barbara
Patterson, who was courteous enough to include me in
the discussion going on. She wasn't just being politic
about it. I felt I had impressed her with my efficiency
if not with my massive intellect. At any rate, she often
consulted me and made use of my services. We got
along well and I could wish that she was just what she
seemed. We talked for awhile and reached agreement
on the rescheduling of the upcoming testing and maneuvers. It wasn't hard. The routine of the ship had
very little to do with her department. If she was satisfied with the time table, I had no complaints.

"It looks O.K. to me, Barbara," I said. "I'll get
back to my paperwork for awhile. I expect a lot of
incoming mail. I suspect some of it'll be for you.
Would you like to meet me for dinner, say about
2300? We can finish up over a steak and I'll bring your
mail with me."

She glanced at the old-fashioned watch that she
wore instead of pushing the button for a time readout
on her com-link.

"Sounds fine, Steve. I'll meet you there." She looked
up from her clipboard and gave me a genuine smile. It

was very nice but a little unusual. She was always friendly but somewhat impersonal. I sensed a suppressed excitement beneath the surface today. It seemed to be making her a little more outgoing. I wondered what the reason was. The whole group had seemed a little above themselves since the storm. Their eyes shone brightly and there was a lot more laughter than usual floating around. I looked them over as I passed through the room. They reminded me of a bunch of kids just before Christmas. I'd heard nothing to account for it as I passed through them this afternoon.

I had a sudden desire to get back to my quarters and check some things on some equipment I had there. I had to put it off, though. I had some regular duties to attend to and it took me right up to the time to meet Barbara. We'd quickly given up titles. Everybody on the ship had one. If you called "Doctor" in a room full of people, everyone looked up. It was easier to go by names. I stopped off at the communications deck and picked up Barbara's mail. As I'd hoped, the message I'd been waiting for was in. The dirty trick I'd started a few hours ago had borne fruit already. I made a mental obeisance to my boss. He got things done. In my mind I pictured him as I'd seen him the day he recruited me for the job. A small gray man, he'd seemed hard to find in the room. He blended into the furnishings. His voice was dry and unemotional. I didn't know who he was, and I'd never heard of his branch of government. All I'd had was a request from my commanding officer to go and see this man at the Lunar Station. His office was one of many that was used for temporary official business. There were no files in the office and no names on the door. The only things that showed the importance of the occasion were the elaborate security measures required to get this far into the complex. I had no doubt the man was genuine brass. Still, I asked for his authority right off, and when I saw the code on his card I almost genuflected. His name was Joachim Albright, and for the next few days he told me the story of the Phoenix Group. It was a fascinating saga and when it was done

I wanted in on it. I never really noticed when I signed up. I also knew that knowing as much as I did now, I'd never be seen by my friends again if I didn't take the job and the oath. Not that they'd actually dispose of me, but I knew there were openings on the Mercury darkside observatory that were filled by unusual means in this day of almost universal civil rights. I never met another human being who had heard his name outside of the department, yet I never made a request of him that hadn't been filled in a few minutes' time. I wondered what the limiting factor of the department's power really was. I'd sent a coded message to a department that couldn't be found and in a few hours' time an elaborate hoax on several official agencies had been effected just to give me a little extra leverage. I held the confirmation message in my hand as I walked into the commissary.

I spotted Barbara in the corner already seated at a small table. She was working on a drink full of fruit. I ignored it.

"Hi," I settled myself. "I see you were able to get away. Everything still working out all right?"

I noticed that she'd dressed for dinner. She wore a culotte dress that I liked very much. Skirts are a bit impractical on shipboard but there was a swing toward feminine dress again in the fashion world, and the ladies were doing their best to look good again whenever possible. I knew it wasn't any more than a desire on her part to look good for herself, but I took it as a friendly gesture anyway. Her hair was down and swirled just above her shoulders. I caught the flash of diamonds in her earlobes. She looked and smelled good and I told her so. She thanked me for the kind words and we grinned at each other. Since we both knew I was making a run at Celia Poynter, it didn't mean a thing and we enjoyed it. A rating taking his turn as waiter came over and asked us if we'd like to order and we discussed the offerings. I had my teeth set for the steak and ordered it lightly singed. I passed up a potato in favor of a small salad and soup. I was going to have a session with the medicos tomorrow and I

knew they were going to gig me about the little roll of
fat that was perched on my belly. Barbara had some
batter fried cod and hot vegetables. I ordered a drink
and asked her if she wanted another of the fruity
things. To my surprise she said yes, and I noted again
the brightness of her eyes. She felt very good about
something. I pulled the mail from my pocket and
handed hers to her. I plugged the first of mine into the
table playback machine and it began to scan my chip
fiche. I angled my viewer a little closer and ran it past
at a rapid rate to see if there was anything important
enough that had to be dealt with in a hurry. There
wasn't. All the codes were in the clear, not that there
was much security stuff in the usual sense these days. I
noted the one I had contrived to have sent and passed
on. No sense messing up a good dinner before the
dirty work started. I saw that there were a couple of
personal letters for me at the end of the file. One from
an old professor of mine that I had liked well enough
to keep in touch with and another from my brother. I
shut it off and pocketed the fiche. Barbara seemed to
find no urgency in her mail either and put hers aside
as well. We talked about work for a few minutes till
the food came and she asked me in a conversational
way about my intentions toward Celia. I was a little
set back by this. I'd no idea she considered herself "in
loco parentis" to the other members of the group. But
I guess I answered in a satisfactory manner because
she smiled when I was through stumbling and said
she'd put in a word for me. I felt great relief when the
food came and put an end to our conversation. I ate in
a businesslike manner and kept my mouth filled with
food. I saw the grin appear several times during the
course of the meal, and I knew I was being had.

We finished and commented that it had been a good
meal. I judged that it was time to drop my little bomb.
I took the fiche out of my pocket again and found the
right section. I swung the viewer over to allow her to
see it with me.

"I didn't want to spoil your dinner, Barbara, so I
saved it until now. I'm afraid we have a little problem."

I indicated the section on the screen. Briefly it informed me as commanding officer that the arrival of the pilot assigned to the West Fed ship, *Brotherhood of Man* (the *Tinker Bell's* official name), would not be arriving due to the discovery of an unusual medical report filed after an examination at the medical facility on the orbital station. The symptoms were unusual and he was being quarantined for the time being under the regulations concerning the handling of possible space-mutated disease and/or alien life forms. I'd hated to do it to Rollie, but I'd needed an extra bit of leverage, so I framed him. As Barbara read it, she turned as white as I'd ever seen a human being get. I wasn't prepared for that much of a reaction. Whatever I'd done, it made a difference. The lady was upset far more than necessary.

"Take it easy," I said. "Nobody's come up with a mutated germ or alien spore yet. I doubt if Major Denning is going to be the first. They'll probably tinker with him for a month or so and then decide the microscope was dirty all along."

I should have had enough conviction in my voice to stifle any worries she had, for that was exactly what I had planned. Somehow I wasn't being as reassuring as I'd intended. Her expression was still horrified. I slipped the weenie in a lot sooner than I'd intended in hopes that she'd not only take my bait but feel a little better about things.

"Look," I said, "it's too bad about Rollie's troubles with the medicos, but I could take over the piloting very easily. I've got all the same qualifications, and I'm pretty knowledgeable about the ship. I don't think it'll set us back more than a few days. Maybe not at all!"

She sat silently for a time and I watched her face run through a gamut of expressions while she chewed it over in her mind. I felt less than complimented. Everything I'd said was true. Rollie and I were old rivals in the hot pilot game. Between us we'd delivered everything that moved in man's exploration of near space. There was a little special gadgetry that I'd have to learn to play with, but I knew damn well it was nothing I couldn't handle. It soon became apparent that she was more concerned about Rollie than getting another pilot. I tried to reassure her again about the unlikelihood of there being anything seriously wrong with him. I could see it wasn't going over at all. I hadn't had any previous notion that they were such good friends. I'd been present during most of the time that they'd been thrown together, and I hadn't seen any evidence of it. If anything, I thought Rollie was getting the brush-off for which he was long past due. He and I had been rivals in more than one way over the years, and I'd lost a few more girls to him than he'd lost to me. Nothing serious, understand; we also were the best of friends. Still, I didn't feel badly when it seemed he'd stubbed his toe on Barbara Patterson. She'd taken his good-natured rush at her with a practiced eye and seemed not to be buying. She was easy to look at, a tall lady with an obviously mammalian ancestry. Just the kind Rollie liked best. A nice waist complimented her best feature very well. Though you never saw more than a few inches of them, it was apparent that her legs weren't misshapen at all. Her face was pretty if not classical, and her eyes were a nice shade of blue. Her forehead was broad and un-lined despite all the heavy thinking that went on un-derneath it. She wore her blond hair a little longer than the average for someone working in space. (It gets tangled up a lot easier in low gravity.) She kept it under control and it looked a lot better than some of the crew-cuts that were finally going out of style. When she smiled, which wasn't too often, she was worth looking at. Rollie had no immunity at all. I suppose that was a good deal of his charm. Still the lady seemed to take the compliment and leave the compli-menter. She surely had been grown up long enough to keep her head on straight. She finally got around to my suggestion and dealt with it in a lukewarm tone.

"I know you can fill in, Steve. I'm sure we can work it out. . . ."

I saw a strange expression on her face as she said it, but I'd seen quite a few in the last minute or two and didn't think it meant anything in particular, although she said something that seemed like a non sequitur in almost the same breath. It was almost a whisper and it seemed as though I really wasn't meant to hear it. "I really have to talk to Celia about you," she muttered.

It was so far out in left field that I didn't catch up on it until much later. If I'd known what she meant, I'd have dropped dead from shock. As it was, I let the words slip by and put it down to her thoughts being in a turmoil. I was partly right. They were, but that last sentence was a fully considered statement given unconsciously by a mind that worked a couple of planes higher than mine, and the effect of the thoughts that it gave vent to were to change my life totally in a very short time. At this point, though, I was only a little concerned as she sat there and considered my fate. She finally said she had some things to do and would think further about the piloting of the *Tinker Bell*. I nodded and rose as she thanked me for the dinner and left. I sat and had another drink and played it all back again in my mind. It had been a bigger shock than I'd intended, but it looked as though I would get what I wanted out of it. I could guarantee it if I had to, but it probably wouldn't be necessary to do anything more. I'd just wait it out for awhile. For the first time things weren't going exactly as the Phoenix Group planned and it was amazing what the reaction to such a little thing had been. Maybe I'd accomplished more than I'd intended. A spy had to have a little luck sometimes. I finished my drink and left for my quarters. If I was finally on a streak, maybe there would be something there for me tonight!

Chapter 3

I closed the door to my quarters and locked it, something I normally don't do. I try to be available to anyone who wants me at anytime. Right now I was going to be engaged in a bit of hocus-pocus that I didn't want anyone to break in on. I set a pot of coffee brewing and turned to my com-link. It didn't look any different than any of the others. There was one like it in any major area of the ship, and all cabins and quarters had their own. Communications were the first order of business in space. It was important for us all to have the ability to keep in touch at all times. Everyone had small personal units that were kept on our persons. Anyone caught without one was subject to a severe ass-chewing the first time. The second . . . well, so far I'd never had to deal with that. There would never be a third time anyway.

My com-link had a few things about it that the others didn't. When the construction of the *Tinker Bell* was nearly done, there had been a period of time when I rotated the crew off the ship for a week's R and R. While they were gone, a small band of techs from my department had come aboard and installed a network of panels throughout the ship. They were passive collectors of radiation, wired into a system that culminated in my terminal. It would be damn hard for anyone to find it. It emitted nothing for a detector to pick up. All the spectrum was included in the enhanced picture that was transmitted to my screen. It was stored in my private memory file and could be recalled and played back for me when I inserted the correct access code and exposed my retina to a small scanner that looked like a normal camera pickup that was standard in the two-way vid-screen. The only thing I'd been able to pin on them so far had been on the day they arrived en masse aboard the *Tinker Bell* for the first time. I'd sat there feeling like a snake in the evening hours and played back their activities as they took possession of their personal quarters. I'd had some voyeuristic chances as a lad and had taken a look or two. I had outgrown it, thank God, and now I didn't like myself for what I was doing. Still, I'd watched as they settled in. They shuffled their possessions from their luggage to the closets and drawers. They set up photos of family and friends and went through all of the normal actions of people making a bit of territory their own. A number of them stripped and changed in the process, and I ignored it as much as possible. The men didn't look that good to me and I bravely watched the women with what I told myself was a clinical eye. Really, that wasn't much worse than the idea of spying on them with their clothes on. After a while I decided that there was not likely to be anything going on in subsequent days that would help me find out what they were up to, and I began to run the events off at high speed each night, looking only for unusual behavior. After the first night I hadn't found any. That first time, though—I'd seen both Barbara and Henry Eagles do a little number with the magnetic locks from their luggage. At different times during the night, each removed the clasps and handles in a series of practiced motions and reassembled them in a new configuration. They used them to sweep the rooms in a search for electronic bugs. They didn't find my little network, but they tried and I knew that they had something to hide.

I found out part of it that night as I watched the events flashing across my screen which had taken place during the time we were all supposedly in the shielded areas during the solar flare. No one should have been outside of the shielding. Someone had been. Someone should be dead. No one was. No one was even sick. The playback was set for a random scan effect. The program was running views from different panels throughout the ship. When it came to the period of time we'd spent in the shielded areas, I started to increase the rate to get on past that time period when nothing could have happened. I turned to the coffee pot before doing so and saved myself from making a big mistake. I poured myself a cup and set it down to cool. As I moved my hand to the keypad, I saw movement in the screen. The view was in the corridor leading around the second ring from the edge of the ship. I noted the color stripe on the wall. The picture was too blurry from the radiation to pick up the section number from the wall, but I knew where it was anyway. It was the nerve center that housed the navigational subsystems and a good many of the control junctions for the null drive. The view changed to another part of the ship and I found myself looking at a totally uninteresting view of one of the crew's cabins. I retrieved the previous scene and moved the time period back again to the first glimpse of the thing moving down the corridor. I slowed the playback to standard speed. The wild radiation was playing hob with my panels. The picture was full of flashes and rainbow effects. I had the picture enhanced by the computer but the best I could get was none too good. Still I could make out a human form of sorts, trailing a coruscating afterimage of fire as it strode down the corridor. I couldn't make out any features. The radiation was striking it and it was just a flashing figure in a maelstrom of light, a wavering shape that moved through coronas that dazzled the eye. It moved quickly, seemingly unbothered by the hell flashing around it. It reached the end of the corridor and moved into an area I couldn't see. I entered the code for the panel in that area. I hadn't stopped the time frame, so I picked it up again well into the room. The picture was no better in here than in the corridor. The figure loomed larger as it approached the panel and passed it. It didn't help. I thought I could make out the suit it wore. I couldn't be sure, but I thought it was a standard E.V.A. suit, and that didn't make any better sense. It wasn't made to take this kind of radiation. It was a good pressure suit but had only minimal shielding. While I watched, it neared a set of components at the wall opposite the panel. Still flashing fire, it separated something from its main bulk and manipulated it. It seemed to be a bag or something of the kind. I thought it might be a toolkit. It must have been, for the figure extracted something from it and used it to remove the cover from one of the components. It did the same to two others and seemed to be changing things around inside them. Roundly, I cursed the poor quality of the image. There was no help for it. For the next half hour I watched the figure move around in that room doing things to the drive controls and navigation systems and I never got a clear view of it or what it was doing. After the job (whatever it was) was done, I watched it move down the corridor to another section and do more of the same with other pieces of the systems down the line. The figure walked in clouds of fire and patiently completed its tasks while I watched and went crazy! Finally it finished and retreated down the original corridor, becoming lost at last in a remote section that had no panel. I searched the ship for some time, but I was never able to catch the figure at the start of the excursion or at the end. I went back time and time again and never caught him. Or her, of course.

I didn't get much sleep that night. I had a lot of thinking to do. When I was done, I had to decide on a course of action. If I had been only what I was supposed to be, my course would have been quite clear. Call for the military security force and let them sort things out. I had no doubt that in the long run they, or the higher-ups, could do just that. We might even get to the bottom of the Phoenix Group mystery. All that would probably happen and would be all to the good. Still, there was a possibility that the most important thing might get lost in the process, the hope of a genuine Star Drive for the people of Earth. It might be a long time before another chance of one came along. The facts were that the *Tinker Bell* wouldn't even exist if we hadn't been willing to let the Phoenix Group run a longer string than even they knew. If they'd been a small time conspiracy, we'd have concluded the matter long ago. They were responsible for all the things that went into the null space drive, a unique direct line of effort that couldn't be duplicated anywhere else. If we interfered in the development of the experiment, we might well lose the immense benefit we stood to gain from it. We really had no reason to come down on them, outside of the fact that they were an unknown group which played a separate game from the rest of society. There had never been a reason to believe they were pursuing a policy that ran counter to the interests of the rest of us. The only problem was that we couldn't just let it go at that. The stakes were too large to let them go their own way.

At first, they had only appeared as an oddity, a statistical one. When the world really began to keep good records of the business of mankind in all of its aspects—business, research, religion, politics, and all of the other endeavors that the human race kept track of—somebody always felt a need to make a graph out of the resulting lines of separate factors. Some surprising things were always appearing. Seemingly unrelated events and processes were often found to impinge on each other. It became quite a field of study. It was an easy way to get a study grant. A lot of interesting facts had come out as the computers ground out correlations day after day, year after year. With such remorseless efficiency one day the Phoenix Group became known. It stayed hidden in the flood of compilation for a long time, but it stayed, and in time layers of statistics were added and woven, first one way and then another. Eventually it became a subgrouping of interesting sequences. More information spun through the memory banks and was tried out as new programs were run.

In the fullness of time the unavoidable happened.
The veils parted and the entity was there to be
seen and wondered at. The origins were still unclear. They had begun well before the remorseless
record keeping that came with the computer. Somewhere in the middle of the twentieth century a small
cadre of people had come into view. They founded
companies that fed one another's interests. The personnel were strangely interchangeable. The companies
fulfilled a purpose and then disappeared, often for no
apparent reason. They never lost money. The few
outside stockholders never had a complaint. When
they disbanded or changed direction, it was without
turbulence. They dabbled in construction, trade or
research, and lobbied heavily in all areas that pro-
moted the expansion of new technology. When no one
could be compelled to take on a line of endeavor that
they supported, they branched out themselves and created a new organization to promote it. When the purpose
was accomplished, the organization was prone to disappear. Never at a loss. The thrust wasn't always
clear; the results were. Over the course of decades the
little cadre had done more to bridge the gaps that
appeared in the road to space than any other private
faction in history. The contributions weren't often easily found. Sometimes they were small improvements in
a piece of hardware, often an improvement in a material or, in later years, an advance in a programming
device. They kept out of the limelight, and the cadre
took on new members slowly, very slowly, as the years
passed. The ranks had thinned in the last few years
until the group had reformed in its latest and final
entity, at least for now, as the McCandless Foundation. The effort had culminated in the physical existence of the *Tinker Bell,* which they owned to the last
rivet, at least morally. Now they were here in a body
to put the finishing touches to more than a century of
linear effort. Who could believe now that they hadn't
known exactly where they were headed all the time?
They had made no mistakes along the way. They had

behaved legally and morally throughout their whole history, but they were disturbing because they were separate from the rest of us, especially in an era that had largely done away with the divisiveness of past history. We'd settled a lot of the geographical and political differences of the past and were a fairly homogenized and unified race nowadays. The thought of this small group of elitists rankled a bit. They might prove to be a pearl in the long run, but even a pearl was a source of irritation to a clam. They had gotten the name for their habit of rising from the ashes of an old organization and becoming a new one in an unbroken line of endeavor. Only the application of the statistic analysis programs had uncovered the chain between separate organizations and the people who ran them. Oh, yes, the people. They were the other half of the Phoenix name. The number of them remained about the same over the course of years. They came and went as age and death occurred and were replaced as they moved from one position to the other in the kaleidoscope of their activities; in theory, that is. In actual fact they were replaced in the structure as they disappeared from view, to remain a fairly constant number. The last really significant fact that turned up, the one that only a computer in its mindless sorting of unrelated facts could have uncovered, was that not one of the disappearing members was ever actually reported dead. No death certificates were ever issued; no bodies were ever interred or cremated. Interesting? Subsequent investigation proved it to be true. Now what, we wondered, had happened to all the bodies they were stacking up somewhere? It was just a small question in the face of all the others that the Phoenix Group posed. Just another little reason for the code name we gave them. How could I know that it was the biggest question of all?

In the wee small hours of the morning I decided to let things stand as they were for the time being. I discounted the idea of sabotage. There was no reason for it. During the next few watches I'd try to find out exactly what had been done and who had done it. How was an interesting question, too. I turned off the screen and attempted to do the same with my mind. Not a great success. The end of the sleep period came awfully soon.

I rose at the insistence of my com-link and faced another day. Gritty-eyed, I put on my sweats and made my way to the fitness rooms. I made my unwilling body do the disgusting things that the gym computer had outlined for me. I pitted my muscles against the no-win machinery that carried on a silent conversation with the conditioning programming. When I had registered sufficient fatigue in all the areas that they discussed, they finally released me and entered the data in my file that was monitored by the medical unit. As I left, they were discussing the tortures that lay in wait for me tomorrow. I dragged my body to a shower and scrubbed away some of the pain.

I stopped by the duty desk and informed the sergeant that I was officially on duty. This was of little interest to her as it was well known I wanted to be informed of anything important whenever it happened. It was just a bit of formal crap. Natalie Singh was in her mid-forties and resuming an interrupted career. She'd raised a couple of kids and, having done so, was prepared to spend the rest of her life in the service. She was naturally behind in the ratings structure for her age, but women were still living longer than men. It would all even out in the end.

"Hear anything from your kids?" I asked.

"Did get a couple of fiches yesterday!" she admitted. "The girl's doing fine." A smile lit her face. "She's about to finish her Masters and she's looking to get in with the Dolphin Program that the Japanese are running. She figures someday she'll make it into space with a bunch of them!"

I nodded my understanding. The Japanese had long since settled their differences with the dolphins and were now in the forefront of the cross-species communication. They had achieved a dialogue that was still going on. The dolphins were definitely an intelligent life form. We just lived mental lives so different that some of the gulfs between us seemed unbridgeable. Still, there were areas where we could cooperate and gain some small understanding. The dolphins knew of the sky. They observed it as they broke surface in the sea. For some reason our description of the limitless universe excited them as no other subject we had covered through the years did. They wanted to experience space for themselves. In time, when we were able to do a proper job of maintaining their needs out here and providing them with an ability to actually function in some way, they'd get the chance. Nancy Singh wanted in on it. I knew her mother was proud. "And Dennis?" I asked.

Nat snorted. "Just like his dad," she said. "Wants to be a writer or an artist or something like that. Haven't heard what it is this week."

"Now Nat," I temporized, "it does take all kinds, you know. I like to read a good book now and then myself. Somebody's got to write them."

She bristled. "Easy for you to say," she grumbled. "You don't have any kids yet."

"Got to find a girl who's willing first. So far, no luck."

"Begging the Colonel's indulgence," she said sweetly, "how about that nurse on the orbiter? Nurse Dabney, wasn't it?"

"Jesus!" I muttered. "See you later, Sergeant." I left the area. The news travels in a straight line in space, I thought. That one wanted five kids. All by natural childbirth. I repressed a shudder. I'd introduced her to Rollie just a short time later.

I passed a good deal of the morning touring the ship and getting into little conversations with the crew. Most of it was just trading scuttlebutt. In the course of the day, I managed to pretty well place everybody in their respective places during the previous day's storm. As I suspected, there was one cubicle that had only scientists in it. The rest had a mixture of scientists and crew. I didn't know which of them had done the roaming, but I knew how he'd been covered up. I wandered through the areas where the figure had worked and looked for evidence of his labors. I wasn't alone and couldn't look too closely without raising eyebrows, but I doubt there was anything to see anyway. Certainly nothing leapt to the eye. Eventually I made my way to the tech library and got a couple of hard copy manuals concerning the systems involved. I took them back to my room and studied them for a while. The circuitry was complex and the modules that contained it were all rather similar looking units. It would be the easiest thing in the world to change things around by switching components from one area to another if you knew what you were doing. Everything was multipurpose these days. You could achieve drastic differences in effect with most components by simply switching pin locations. In most cases you never needed to wire anything any more. Just plug it in in the proper location in the proper alignment and watch what came out of the readouts. There was no way I was going to decipher what had been changed in these systems until the current flowed. I gave it up and decided to improve my time getting in the way of the people involved. Maybe if I fell over them enough (or they fell over me), I'd learn something. I hoped so.

I spent the next few days that way. For some reason my presence seemed more welcomed than previously. I'd always been on good terms with them, but now for some reason I was being lionized a bit. Singly and in groups I found myself being brought into conversations and planning that I'd only hovered on the edges of before. I didn't know why, but I liked it. The only fly in the ointment was Celia. I was doing much better there than previously and I wasn't sure it was because of my marvelous personality and good looks. I hated to think it was just because the word had gone out to cooperate and keep the idiot happy. Still it would have been churlish not to accept the good fortune that came my way, and I spent as many hours as I could getting to know her better. It was a little hard to keep a clear mind on the subject because she suited me right down to a T. She was twenty-six to my thirty-two, and I was an opposite pole. She was dark; I was light. She was trim and light and I was large and beefy. I was overly serious and she was surprisingly gay beneath the quiet surface. She seemed so alive all the time. I watched her in fascination as she lived every minute and savored it. It was going to break my heart if she turned out to be a wrong one.

A week had finally passed since the morning of the storm, and we had taken aboard our last supplies. The experiment seemed to be over and I had learned nothing new. It was coming on time to begin the testing. I'd spent a lot of time preparing myself for my added role as chief pilot. I'd cleared it with the brass without having to draw Albright into it. I was the logical choice. All the lines were converging into a single point in time and what would happen would come soon. We planned a small celebration to mark the end of the testing phase and the next day we would put it all together and see what happened. I joined the party a little late. I'd sent off a coded message to the department bringing them up to date and advising them that we were going to take the plunge. I communicated much the same to the regular brass who were becoming more alive to the impending test as time grew shorter. A lot of my time these days was spent doing P.R. work. It was a good thing the public hadn't been told yet or I'd have had the press to contend with also. As it was, the word was beginning to get around and I had my hands full. I needed the first drink I was handed as I walked in the door. I was on my second as I found Celia in the crowd, and I'd been looking hard for her. I slowed down after that and nursed the next one through the rest of the evening. Still, I got a bit of a glow on. The room was warm and so was the crowd. The crew and the scientists mixed democratically and everyone had a good time. We were all full of hope for the next day and the conversations were lively. I monopolized Celia with a success that surprised me. With an ease that seemed miraculous, we wound up the evening in her quarters. Not believing my luck, I stayed when she asked me if I wanted to. As I'd suspected, I found that I'd fallen for her and I wondered why I had to wait so long to find the right girl. I didn't know it at the time, but I received a lot more than I knew. It had happened less than a dozen times in human history. Though I was soon to find out what had happened to me, I was spared the knowledge at the time. It was just as well. It surely would have put a damper on the evening!

Chapter 4

I sat in the chief pilot's chair and considered the incongruity of the thing. I'd shafted Rollie to get the seat and I was sitting in it with nothing to do. I had approved the entry of the sequencing codes and my work was pretty much over. We hadn't actually transferred a watt of electricity from one place in the system to another. When the proper time to do so came, it would be done by the computer that had accepted the instructions. A new type that had the speed of the state-of-the-art number crunchers and the complexity to handle thousands of decisions at near light speed. It made my limited brain and response time unnecessary for the startup and operation of the tests we were making. I had decision-making capabilities but only the largest ones, and even these were scrutinized by programming to see if they were allowable. Still, I had the seat and I used it as I'd intended, a way to keep even closer tabs on the scientific team. I watched the boards as the wave-forms scrawled across the monitor screens and the readouts spun numbers. The colored lights flashed as the program cycled and meshed. Suddenly all the criteria had been met and we went into the test. A brief moment had passed, too brief for the observers to notice. The new information rolled in to the monitoring apparatus and we all watched the creation of an anomaly in the interior of the cylinder in the hub. Sensors reported new read-ins coming into play as a change occurred in the gravitational stresses. A new screen started to show the thrusters coming on as the automatic systems changed the rotation of the ship to compensate for the new situation. The readout continued to change as the power built up, but the test was already a success from the first sign of a new mass in the bowels of the cylinder. What had been created was being improved on, but the first seconds had told it all. A sea of noise swelled and broke around me as the team realized its triumph. They shouted their congratulations at each other and then broke off to watch the screens as new information spun in front of their eyes. Conversations stopped and started spasmodically as their attentions were captured by each new situation. Another of the odd sensations that had swept over me several times this morning caused my head to swim momentarily. A current of feeling swelled out from the people around me and I was totally aware of their presence. It was as if we were physically touching each other, although the nearest was ten steps from my seat. I felt a warmth that wasn't mine spread throughout my body. I knew the position of everyone although many were not in my line of sight. I shook my head and swallowed. During the sensation I was on an emotional jag. An intense family recognition was the closest I could come to describing the feeling. It was pleasureable, but I knew there was no reason for it. I made an effort to control my thoughts and found the feeling subsiding. It was weird. I had never experienced anything like it in my life. No drug I'd ever taken in the course of medical treatment had produced anything like it. I'd had an aversion to mind-altering stuff that other people I'd known had tried. I'd been drunk out of my mind a few times and that was as bad off as I'd ever dreamed of getting. I like to have control of my mind. What had been going on this morning was completely out of my experience and it was an effort not to get out of my seat and head for the med center. Still, this test was the most important thing in the scheduled operations, next to the engagement of the drive system which it preceded. To leave in the middle of it was close to impossible. I kept my eyes firmly fixed on the scene before me and tried to put the other from my mind. In a few moments the feeling receded and I relaxed a little. The test was short in duration and nearly over. From the conversations I was picking up it was an unqualified success. The babble around the bridge died down as the bit of nonexistent, but thoroughly detectible, mass that had registered in the strange plumbing reached its final growth and was rapidly dying away again. The test was over and the results had faded from the screens to be stored in memory banks for recall and study. When the last of the monitors was restored to normal mode and the rotation of the ship had been corrected, I stood down and joined the crowd which were already showing signs of scattering to their individual lairs to study their own separate pieces of the puzzle. I wanted to catch them all together to see if there was anything that had come out of the test that they all recognized as significant enough to comment on. I found that they only had rave notices for it. Apparently it had gone as well as I'd thought. I asked the questions that needed to be asked, and got satisfactory answers as far as I was able to tell. There was a lot more esoteric language in use. I took it as a sign that they were a little above themselves today. I congratulated them all in the name of the service and the government and made my excuses.

"Have to go now and inform the brass that everything went right," I told Barbara and Henry, who were standing near and seemed to be the ones to whom I should address my leavetaking. "The Admiral wanted a first word as soon as possible."

They nodded their understanding of the need to keep the brass happy. I found them looking at me sharply, and I guess I looked a little under the weather, because Henry asked me if I was feeling all right. I admitted that I was feeling a little strange this morning.

"I thought I'd go see the Doc after I make my report," I said. "Actually I'm feeling better all the time."

I *was*, too. I really felt good. In fact, I felt better than usual. I didn't trust the feeling, though. It might be as bad a symptom as feeling lousy.

"Stop by my quarters before you go to the med center, will you, Steve. I'd like to get a blood sample before the ship's doctor does."

I turned to see Celia standing behind me.

"Why?" It was a strange request.

"You know my basic field is Space Medicine. I've got an interest in your blood." She smiled. "Among other things! I'd like to get a sample of yours for some work of my own before you get all fouled up with a broad spectrum antibiotic or something."

"Couldn't I just leave a little extra with him and put your name on it somehow?"

"Nope," she grinned. "I'm keeping him in the dark about this stuff I'm doing. Please, Steve? I'm real good with a needle."

"O.K.," I responded. "I'll be by in about half an hour."

I waved good-bye and headed for the Ops room to send the message. I made it brief but covered the facts. I knew that Albright would see it as soon as the Admiral did, and I had nothing more for him than I had for the regular brass, so I let it go at that. I finished and headed for Celia's room. I really was feeling better and the memory of last night was lifting my spirits even more. I whistled a little tune even as I touched her door call. I suddenly felt the strange sensation of her presence as she opened the door. Not as strong as the other times this morning, but strong. Something more than the feeling that another person was near. Different, more personal, and it wasn't the fact that I might be falling in love. I'd felt the same thing coming from the people around me on the bridge. *All* of them. The door opened and she brought me inside. I was surprised to see that Henry and Bill Ankers were there also. I wasn't too disappointed because I had too much on my mind to pursue our relationship right at the moment. Still, I'd have gone for a nice kiss. But then again, maybe I'd be taking a chance of giving her what I'd got. On the third hand, if I had contracted something weird, the chances were I'd already done it. It was getting a little complicated and I gave up that train of thought. I said hello to Henry and Bill and took a glass from Celia. She told me it wasn't alcoholic, just something to pick me up a little. I eyed the men who were standing together looking at me and took a sip of the drink. It tasted good. I'd been increasingly thirsty, too. I set it down on a table next to me and waited for somebody to start talking. I wondered if I would be getting a little more hazing like that Barbara had given me the other night when she'd trotted out the old dodge about checking my intentions toward the lady. I was prepared to cut that crap short if that was the case. I didn't feel up to it today and it was starting to wear a little thin anyway. Apparently I had figured wrong because the conversation, when it started, was general to the point of boredom. I wanted to get the blood-draining over with and visit the doc. It seemed kind of a strange place for this sort of thing anyway. I thought I could find her a place on the ship somewhere to pursue her hobby in private if she wanted. There was no need for her to have to do it in her own quarters. I took another swig of the drink and started to bring the subject up. She didn't seem interested.

"Just a thought," I said sourly. The situation was getting on my nerves a little and I wanted to get on with it. "Bring on your needle then. Is there any more of this?" I indicated my empty glass.

"Sorry, Steve, that seems to be all there is."

"Oh, well," I said. "How about a little water then?"

"Don't believe I'd advise it." Henry said in an easy voice. I turned my head to look at him in surprise.

"Don't want to get your bladder overburdened just now," he stated. He and Bill were both watching me peculiarly.

What the hell was going on here? I started to stand up. My legs didn't move. Suddenly nothing did. Oh, shit! I thought, and waited for unconsciousness to come. Unfortunately, it never did. I retained enough movement to swallow and blink my eyes. Little things like that, but nothing that would have let me defend myself or even raise a fuss. My mind was clear and my senses were working. I tried speech. I managed a garbled wheeze like a hurt animal. I didn't like the sound and quit trying. Henry leaned over me.

"Steve, I'm sorry we had to do this to you. We couldn't allow you to visit the med center just yet. I'm afraid they really would find you're undergoing some changes right now. Believe me, it's better that they don't just yet. Later on, they won't find a thing and you'll be better physically than you've ever been in your life." He paused to see if I was taking this in.

Well, I wasn't. I heard what he was saying, but I didn't get any meaning out of it.

"I know it sounds strange," he said with what was meant to be a reassuring smile. "We really don't mean you any harm."

I wasn't buying. I should have been scared, but though I thought I had plenty to be worried about, my body wasn't reinforcing my mental state by pumping adrenalin. With no feedback I maintained a calm I surely wouldn't have without the stuff they had put in my drink. I rolled my eyes all the way to the side to see if I could catch a glimpse of Celia's face. It would have been nice to see her looking a little shameful or something, maybe a tear glistening, just something to show she hadn't wanted to use me like this. I was unlucky there also. My erstwhile love just looked intently at me. It would have been nice to be able to react to this betrayal, too, but my hormone flow remained constant and I couldn't work up any emotion. It just didn't seem right not to be able to have the satisfaction of releasing my rage. Henry had correctly interpreted my glance and resumed his speech.

"No, Steve," he said, "she didn't betray you." He paused, thinking over what he was going to say next. What he found was a doozy.

"The other night," he said finally, "she gave you the irrevocable gift of added years, possibly centuries, of life. She chose you of all the people she's ever known to love that much."

I stared at his face as the words bounced through my head. His expression was sober with just a hint of a smile. I considered him and the crazy statement. I was still crippled emotionally. I couldn't react. I knew he wanted belief. How can you respond to something like that? I rolled my eyes to see what Celia was registering when he said it. All I saw was a glimpse of the back of her head as she turned away. In a numbed sort of way I wanted badly to see her face, but I was to be denied that. Henry was talking again.

"I know what I'm saying doesn't make sense right now, and I intend to tell you more about it. It's quite a story and it'll take some time to get it all done with. Unfortunately, we have to do something else right away before we start to tell you. If you were able to react to it normally, you'd be scared badly. That's the main reason we had to dope you. I repeat, Steve, we mean you no harm. It might be better if you close your eyes."

I never did have sense enough to take well-meant advice. I regretted it almost instantly. I'd been missing Bill's contribution to the party. Now he added his bit with a vengeance. With a mumbled, "Sorry Steve," he bent my head back in the chair and opened my shirt. I felt his hands touch me on the abdomen. His face touched my throat. I felt emotions stir for the first time since the drug had taken effect. All the tales of vampires ran through my mind in horrible flashes as I felt my flesh being invaded by small needle-like things that sprang from his hands and mouth. I couldn't see what was happening, but I thought of talons and fangs. A brief pressure came and went while my mind rolled with visions, then it was gone and he stepped back. I saw his face retreat from mine and his hands pull back from my body. My eyes teared suddenly as the shock began to take effect. My responses were coming back.

I was able to move my arms a little, too. I made a shoving motion as he withdrew. I saw a fleck of blood on his lip and I mouthed a strangled protest. The palms of his hands were covered with a translucent mat of fibrous strands that seemed to be working their way back into the skin. Other than that he appeared as usual except for a sheen of perspiration that covered the bare areas of skin I could see. He returned to a seat out of my line of sight. I might have been able now to turn enough to see him, but I didn't want to. I sat and breathed fast and let the craziness whirl in my brain. I hoped that I'd get control of my body back in time to take a swing at someone before they put me under again. I continued to breathe deeply, hoping to oxygenate my system and help to speed the breakdown of the drug. It was working, but very slowly. Nobody had said a word for a couple of minutes, and when Henry started in again it was a shock.

"That's as bad as it gets, Steve." His voice was even and measured. "It's almost time for that story I promised you." He hunched forward in the chair opposite me.

"That was necessary and in a little while you'll see why. I think you'll forgive us when you do. Now for the story."

Celia came around and sat beside him. She looked me in the eye and smiled. I sat and waited for the strength to knock it off her face. In the meantime I listened to Henry's voice go on as I worked up a good hate.

Chapter 5

"It began in 1944," he said. "I was twenty-two, and my name was John Begay." He clasped his hands before him and looked at them as he considered how to go on. He seemed fascinated by them somehow. The next sentence he uttered made me look at them, too.

"I was back on the reservation after my discharge. I'd lost my right arm up near the elbow and I wasn't much use to the army after that. I wasn't hospitalized too long. The amputation healed fairly quickly. I was lucky in a way. The incoming shell that blew me up was the last of the barrage that hit our area. I was in a forward position spotting for our own artillery. They were able to get me out fast. I don't remember anything from the time I was hit until the time I woke up in the field hospital. They'd already done the surgery. They didn't worry about developing drug dependency too much, and I was out of things for a long time. When I was taken off the painkillers, I was fit enough to be evacuated. I got a series of almost unbelievable connections and I was sent home in the next month. A lot of guys that were hurt worse never made it back until the war was over.

"I hadn't gotten a damn thing out of my service. The army hadn't even taught me how to shoot. A young Navaho learns the cost of ammo early on, and rabbits as targets are small. I'd needed no skills in living off the land; I'd always done that. They taught me how to use a radio, but there wasn't much need for that herding sheep. I stayed in my mother's hogan and felt sorry for myself a lot of the time. At intervals I used the money that the government paid me to go on binges. I was a fairly typical case for the time. I could look forward to drinking myself to death, if TB didn't get me first. I was out of phase with the Navaho way. I'd seen too much of the outside world's excesses and the Dine were believers in the middle road in all things. A Navaho who didn't follow the way was bound to land in trouble. I was well on my way.

"One way or another I'd have been dead in a couple of years if a Navaho cop in Tuba City hadn't mentioned my name to an anthropologist who was looking for someone to act as a guide for him. I was lucky he caught me between drunks. For some reason I was in a reasonable frame of mind, which was rare enough just then. I'd spent a lot of time with white men lately, and this one struck me as one of the better ones. I told him I'd do it for a while. My real job was to vouch for him among the clans and keep him from stubbing his toe socially. He was well aware of the possibility that he could offend. This made him an unusual white man. I enjoyed working with him and I enjoyed getting out among the clans again. He was collecting Navaho legends and it was interesting to me to see him compare them as he got different versions from different sources. I began to take a genuine interest myself. There's nothing like getting out among people to start you making judgments about the way they live. The amazing thing is that you find yourself calling some young Navaho an idiot for behaving like a fool, and then you remember you did the same thing not too long ago. I began slowly to return to the 'way.' I took some time off and had my mother's clan arrange a sing for me. I'd never gone down the Jesus road, and I felt comfortable again as I hadn't since I was a young man.

"The professor's name was Thomas Chaney and he was a small man who never lost a gray look. He wore wire-frame glasses and seemed to stoop all the time.

He had the patience to wait while an old woman like Betty Bowlegs finished her cigarette and thought of the most appealing way to tell her story. He wasn't pushy and didn't mind the circumlocution that the People used while they made up their minds whether they were going to cooperate. We spent many happy hours gossiping. I think he understood how privileged he was to listen in on the doings of the clans as not many outsiders did.

"I met a girl. We were visiting some Salt Cedar People. We'd been there in the area for a few days and Chaney was visiting Luis Nez. The two of them got along well enough, and I had spotted Mary. I hadn't been much for the girls since I'd lost the arm, but we fell into easy conversation. During the course of it she touched my arm. I started to lose my self-possession again and she got mad at me for it. She called me a few expressive names and the Navaho language is explicit in *every* way. I went back for more over the course of the months that passed. In time we married."

Henry paused. I still wasn't able to move from the chair although I'd improved a lot. I wasn't as mad as I was confused now. I didn't see how I was expected to take this garbage. Henry told me to look behind me. I wasn't sure I wanted to take my eyes off this plausible-looking madman in case he might do something weird when I turned. I did it anyway because I was just as afraid of what might be going on back there. Bill wasn't there anymore. Instead there was someone else, someone who looked an awful lot like me.

"We picked Bill for the job because his hair color matches yours pretty closely," Henry's voice informed me. I stared at the face of the man in front of me. The similarity was even more pronounced now. There was a difference that I couldn't put a name to for a moment. Then I understood. He wasn't a mirror image. He was a right-hand duplicate of myself. It wasn't makeup or a mask. I saw his features flow in a final adjustment. I looked into my own face. The perspiration dripped from him in torrents, and as I watched his eyes seemed to focus for the first time. He blinked a few times and then smiled at me. I knew that grin. I'd practiced it in the mirror many times as a kid. I'd watched it change as I grew older. The tuck in the cheek was on the wrong side, but I knew it, and I knew it was in the right spot for anyone that knew me. My voice was coming back and I managed a recognizable, "How? Why?"

"It was the best I could do." The voice that answered me was my own voice and normal in every way. Much better than I was doing at the moment.

"How, Steve? Henry's going to explain all that. Why? Well, we're going to have to have you in evidence around the ship while you're being filled in and recruited. It's going to take a good deal of time, so I'm going to fill in for you while that's going on." He gave me my own smile again. "Beside, it's a pretty good piece of corroboration for the story you're listening to."

He stood up and wobbled for a moment. He walked around the room a couple of times and I followed him with my eyes. He fell into a natural stride in a few minutes. I recognized my walk in his.

"Takes a couple of minutes to get used to the longer bones and muscles. I'm afraid you won't be getting high marks for agility and grace for the next few hours." He stopped and faced me. "I'll try not to cause you any embarrassment while I'm taking your place, but I won't have your memories, so it'll be best if you concentrate on what he tells you and make your decision as soon as possible."

"Recruited! Join up with you?" I got out. "You've got a strange way of soliciting volunteers."

"For all of that," Henry took over, "we don't do much recruiting. Every case is a special one. This time it's a little unusual even for us, I'll admit. Still, I've got hopes that you'll come to see things our way." He noticed me testing my strength. "Actually, you'll get your normal responses back sooner if you just relax a little longer and give it time."

Bill-me said, "I'd better see about getting cleaned up and started." He went into the refresher and closed the door.

Celia spoke for the first time in a while. "We're not some kind of monsters, Steve. Give it a chance. Listen to Henry and keep as open a mind as you can."

"What are you?" I asked. "I hear the words, but what's talking? How do you expect me to think of joining things who can do what you do? I'm a human being. What do you call yourselves when you are alone?"

"That's what I am, too! That's what we all are here. Human plus something."

"I wish I believed you," I said. I really did. I looked at that face I had loved a short time ago and felt something inside struggle one more time before it died. I turned my face away.

"Before you go and start thinking about how to deal with an alien race, Steve, I think I'd better tell you that you aren't any different from us now. As of last night you have the same abilities that we do."

I looked in his eyes and saw that he meant it. I tried to make sense of the words. There wasn't any. I used a favorite four-letter word. Celia gave vent to a queer sound and I saw her turn her head. A flush suffused her face.

"To be accurate, she infected you last night in a rather unique way. It could have been done another way, but it seemed that it had more sentiment involved this way. We didn't object." He grinned and waved his hand deprecatingly. "Enough about that. Suffice it to say it was a nicely romantic choice."

Celia made another strange sound. She resolutely faced the wall.

Silence followed and I was about to start asking some of the ten million questions to which I wanted answers. God help me, I was getting swept up in the thing. It was almost as if I believed this stuff. I didn't, of course. Did I?

Henry continued before I had a chance to start. I

heard the water running in the 'fresher as he began again. Bill-me was going to be a lot sweeter to be with than I was. I could smell myself and it wasn't good.

"Mary and I moved in with her clan," Henry continued. "It's the way of the Navaho. I continued to work with Chaney, and I was still getting the government money. I was feeling pretty good for a change. I was even having thoughts about going back to school and maybe getting a degree of some kind. I'd been a pretty good student for a Navaho kid. I'd have finished high school if the war hadn't come up. I knew I could still do it if I wanted to. Life was looking like maybe it had something for me down the road somewhere. I wrote a pretty good hand now. I found that there was still a lot a one-armed man could do. Chaney and I went beyond the employer and hired help bit after awhile and I got caught up in the world of books and outside knowledge. He and I often sat in the evening outside his trailer or my hogan and we talked about everything under the stars. Mary would rustle around doing her chores and listening in. She had a good mind, too. We became good friends, the three of us. Chaney didn't have family. He liked hanging in with us. He disappeared from time to time but never for long. His connection with the university was tenuous, and I wondered that he didn't have to teach classes sometimes. He just said that he had money of his own and could afford to take the time off. There was a layer of him that I could never get beneath. I respected it because there was one in me, too. There's always a barrier of some kind between a white man and an Indian. In his case it was a lot smaller than usual, but it was there and I respected his in turn. We were still good friends.

"A night came when the three of us were coming back to the hogan after a day's trip to Tuba City. We'd needed some supplies and Chaney was sending off some things at the post office. We'd finished with a meal at a truck stop on the main highway and were taking our time coming back. The track was rough and slow after we left the branch road. Chaney's old station wagon had a hard time negotiating the ruts and talus that lay between the buttes that we wove our way through. We came to a section that served as a junction for a couple of old roads that wound through the reservation. Chaney put the wagon in second gear, and we started to descend into a narrow canyon that we often used as a short cut. The descent was a little tricky but safe enough if you took your time about it. There was a sheer drop-off on one side and a ridge on the other. We were about halfway down to the floor when we saw the headlights coming at us. The car coming up was hitting a dangerous speed. Chaney sped up a little himself to get to a wide spot up ahead where we could pass in safety. It soon became obvious that it was going to be a close thing. The other car was accelerating and might reach the wide spot before we got there. I got an uneasy feeling that he wasn't going to wait there for us.

" 'Damn fool,' Chaney grunted. 'Hold on.'

"We reached the place just as the other car came at us, spitting rocks as it clawed its way up the slope. Chaney swung the wheel hard to the right as the idiot in the oncoming car swept past us. We hit the wall with tremendous force. The back of the station wagon slipped and the ends exchanged position. Chaney lost all control and we started to slide backward down the remainder of the hill. We nearly made it all the way, but our luck ran out just fifty feet before the floor of the canyon started. We slipped over the edge and rolled to the bottom. I'd tried to hold on to Mary when we started the fall, but I lost her and we were all thrown around inside when the wagon rolled. I hit something hard with my head as we hit the bottom and I was out cold before we stopped rolling."

Chapter 6

"I woke to the sound of heavy breathing," Henry said. "The wagon creaked as I moved my body to a sitting position. I smelled hot metal and gasoline. There didn't seem to be any fire, though. Suddenly I remembered the crash and I tried to move from the seat. I was held back by something around my chest. I called out Mary's name in a sudden panic. I got no answer. I tried again. This time I screamed it! Still nothing. I realized that the breathing I heard was separate from my own. It was coming from in back of me. I tried to turn in the seat, but the thing over my chest held me too tight. My left hand was bound up in some way, too, and of course I had no right hand. I swore and tried to see what was holding me. It was getting close to nightfall and the visibility wasn't good. My eyes weren't working too well either. I wriggled and cocked my head and finally made out what it was that held me so tightly. Chains! I was chained to the doorpost and the steering wheel. Someone had used a combination of tow chains and ropes to tie me up. I couldn't believe it at first but it was real enough. I yelled again. 'Mary!' I remembered Chaney at last and called his name, too. Nothing but the breathing sounds. I heaved and twisted till I was finally able to see behind me. Enough twilight got through the broken windows to see them on the wagon's rear deck. I could see Mary's head was all bloody; her hair was loose and covered most of it, but I could tell she was terribly hurt. Her arms were flung out at her sides and I could see gashes in her flesh.

What nearly sent me into madness was the figure that lay on top of her in a crouching embrace. Chaney had torn off her clothing and was sprawling over her with his hands on her breasts and his mouth on her throat. I screamed at him to leave her alone. He didn't pay me the slightest bit of attention. He just lay there on her. I went crazy for a long time. I nearly killed myself trying to bust those chains and ropes. I rocked the wagon with my efforts and shouted till I lost my voice. I called that raping bastard every name I knew a hundred times and he never so much as looked at me. I wore myself out and beyond. Finally, I became a barely breathing, wasted thing chained to the seat. I had nothing left in me. When I was able again, I pleaded with him to leave her alone. I used a rational tone and I tried it with no more success than before. I passed the rest of the night that way in alternating phases as I slipped back and forth between sanity and mad rage. I don't know how long it was before I realized that this wasn't rape as I understood it. Chaney never changed position. In fact, neither of them ever moved except for the continuous breathing. Toward morning even that became softer and I listened to it for a long time, silent at last. Finally, I had nothing more left inside me and I went into unconsciousness again."

Henry stopped there as Bill-Me came out of the 'fresher. He had showered and was dressed in a standard uniform like mine. He reached for my jacket and pulled the color band from it that was the only sign of rank that I wore aboard ship. He arranged it over the velcro strip that held it in place on his own jacket and pressed it smooth with the palm of his hand. Celia took the remaining end of it, ran it back over his shoulder and pressed it into place on his back. It was the finishing touch. Now he looked exactly as I would if I'd been in my normal state. He'd combed his hair as I did and if it was a little bit shorter, it just looked as if I'd had a haircut. He stood there and we all watched him with our separate points of view. My own thoughts were largely unprintable. Still, it was fascinating to see my replica in front of me, ready to take my place. The outrageous situation didn't seem as important now. At least I was getting what I had been trying for since the first day I'd joined the department. Maybe it wasn't the way I wanted, but I was getting it. I still didn't accept what I was being told, but there was something there. If I got out of this situation, maybe I could get past all this and dig out the truth. I was much better now and I considered making a move.

What the hell, I thought, and I made my lightning move. I got about a foot and a half before I realized I was in slow motion all the way. I accepted the futility of it and sat back down before anyone had the chance to do it for me. No one seemed disturbed by my effort. Bill took note of my action and nodded.

"Well," he reflected, "Steve's getting frisky already. I guess I'd better leave now."

I wasn't entirely happy with the impression I'd managed to make. Obviously, I wasn't considered to be a threat to their plans just yet. He made his way to the door and opened it. He only checked the corridor briefly before he entered it. He whistled a little tune I sometimes did as he went out the door. It sounded flat to me and I wondered if I was just as flat when I did it. Henry coughed in an attention-getting manner, and I thought that this situation was getting awfully chummy and polite after its bizarre start. Still, it beat bamboo under the fingernails. I would be content to leave that sort of thing alone if they were. If they wanted to treat this like after-dinner conversation, I was willing for the time being. At least until I had a better hand to play. The three of us left in the room looked at each other in silence. Celia got up and moved around the room restlessly. I sat because that was all I could do. Henry finally started his tale again. He seemed more hesitant this time. I know now that he was trying to decide if he was getting it all across to me in the best possible way. There were other proofs to offer and complicated explanations that could be made about the mechanics of the thing. Finally, he decided to go on as he had and just tell the rest of it as it had happened to him.

"The next time I came to," he said, "was as the dawn broke. I was still strapped up in the driver's seat and I'd let my head fall on the steering wheel. Somebody was shaking me awake and when I pulled my head back, it turned out to be Chaney. He filled the doorway and he was speaking to me in an exhausted croak.

" 'Wake up, John. Come on! Wake up, damn it! We need you.' He repeated it over and over while I got my brain going. The first time I tried to speak it was a total failure. My throat was so raw and dry that when I tried the pain went through my entire upper body. I shook my head and that was a mistake. All I saw were swirling lights behind my eyes and they hurt. I was nauseous and I retched. He kept at me and finally the sickness dissipated a little. I focused on his face and started the litany of names again that I'd called him during the long night. He didn't respond to them any more than he had then.

" 'That's unimportant, John, and not accurate anyway. We need you and your strength now. There's no time for all this. Look!'

"He turned his head in a gesture to the ground behind him and stepped aside so that I could see. Mary sat on a small boulder a few feet away. She'd replaced her torn clothing with a blanket we'd had in the wagon, and she was rubbing her arms and stretching. She was a wild-looking mess. Her hair was spilling all over her face and it was streaked with oil and blood. What I could see sticking out of the blanket was just as bad. Her arms and legs were covered with the same dust and blood. There was an awful lot of it. My eyes teared up and a wave of pity washed over me.

" 'Mary!' I croaked her name. It was all I could say. Just her name. It must have conveyed all the anguish I felt.

" 'I'm all right, Johnny.' She stood up and wobbled a little. I watched her pick her way to me painfully over the sharp talus that littered the ground on the canyon floor. I could see it was hard going, but she seemed to be walking as if nothing were broken. An edge of the blanket caught on a rock as she moved toward me and was lifted aside, exposing her for a moment. The reason for her limping was evident. She had nothing on her feet and the ground here was sharp. I'd seen more than that in the brief flash when the blanket snagged. She was naked under it. I started to curse Chaney again. At the same time I babbled at Mary. I tried to warn her and comfort her while I cursed him. She reached me and put her hand to my mouth.

" 'Shush, Johnny.' She crooned it as she would comfort a child. 'Rest easy, my man. I'm not hurt.'

"I stared at her. What kind of words were these? I had seen the blood and wounds. I had thought her to be near death. The evidence was right there before my eyes. And then it wasn't. With a total disregard for Chaney's presence, she opened the blanket and showed me her body. It was sickeningly covered with blood and filth, crusted and dry now. So much of it. I panicked at the sight. I heard her telling me again, 'I'm all right, Johnny. I was hurt but not anymore. Really! Look again.'

"I did, and I couldn't believe what I saw. Under the dried rivulets of blood there were no wounds!

" 'How?'

" 'I don't know Johnny.' She let me look some more. The skin beneath the gore was unbroken. In spots where the crusts had begun to flake away a pinkish, unscarred skin showed. It was lighter color than the rest of her body and I knew that a short time ago they had been open wounds. There were so many places. I raised my eyes to her face. She nodded at my amazement.

" 'Yes. All this was injured; I was close to death.'

She pulled the blanket closed again and looked at Chaney standing there by the fender.

" 'He . . . healed me,' she said in a quiet, wondering voice. 'I don't know how but he saved me. . . . Now . . . I am as if it had never happened.'

"She turned to face me again and we stared at each other. I couldn't accept what she said, but I knew it had to be true. It was a miracle at the end of a night of insanity.

" 'Do you think it's safe to untie you now, John?' Chaney's voice was ragged and tired and I saw as he approached me again that he was on his last legs. He looked as though he had lost twenty pounds, and his features were like those in the pictures we later saw of Jews in the concentration camps that had been liberated in Germany. I looked at the terrible weariness in his eyes and suddenly I was sane and right again. I whispered in a voice almost as worn as the one in which he spoke to me.

" 'Yes, Tom. You can let me go now.' "

Henry finished and sat there with memories behind his eyes. I looked at him and almost saw them with him. I believed him. It was crazy and contrary to everything I knew, but I believed the story. I had no business to, no right. My position as commanding officer of this vessel demanded that I reject what I had heard. I knew it and accepted the insanity. The man I saw before me was over a hundred and eighty years old. What he had told me had happened. I'd never experienced an act of faith before. Now I rearranged my life and made one of my own. I tested my muscles once again and found them to be solidly in my control. I stood up and moved toward him. I put my hand on his shoulder and he turned his eyes to mine.

"John Begay," I said, "is your Mary still alive?"

"Yes," he said. "At least I hope so."

"Where is she?"

"I don't know for sure, but I'm trying to get there, Steve."

"How much more is there, John?"

"All my life till now. It shouldn't take more than a year to tell." He smiled. "It's quite a story."

"Well, I guess you'd better get on with it," I said. I looked over at Celia. She watched the two of us with a look of blank concentration. She stared between us. I took a chance, maybe the biggest one of my life.

"How far do I have to go to find you, Celia?"

She was at my side as I finished asking. She's never left.

Chapter 7

Three days later I shut down the thrusters of the shuttle and watched the orbital station rise to meet me. The stars whirled around the hub as we approached. I had started a rotation to match its own and now the station and the shuttle would seem to spin like a pair of mismatched ballet dancers from separate universes to an outside observer. To us the rest of the sky was spinning as we took the station for our reference point. A blinking line of guidance lights arrowed into the maw of the hangar deck. They were unnecessary as the shuttle's path was directed by a two-way conversation between the station's computers and the shuttle's onboard systems. I rode herd on it, but I didn't expect to lift a hand to a control from here on. I'd get my butt chewed if I did. The traffic control people had a lot more confidence in their electronic morons than they did in a hot pilot like me. Still, I got the credit for it all and a large difference in pay rate. Going out of here, I was going to lose a lot of goodwill. The attitude jets flared a final second and the shuttle eased into the arresting cables. We quivered for a moment as the gear adjusted itself before the dampening rods found rest on the cradle. The umbilical rolled toward us and I waited in the cockpit until we were mated. Finally the board shone green as the pressures equalized and I powered off. From now on we would use the station's systems. I left a program in the computer cycling and shut off the telltale lighting. No casual observation would show it to be running. The program was being updated constantly from the station's information banks. It would save me minutes when we left. I thought there was a good chance we'd need all of the minutes we could get. I joined the others in the lock.

We were a small group: Kelly Bergen, Celia, Bill Ankers and me. Not very many to disrupt as big an installation as this, but we were going to try. Kelly was in charge of altering some of the computer's programming. Not an easy thing these days. Kelly didn't feel it was going to be much of a challenge—I hoped he was right. I had been treated to a long discourse on the problems and the solutions and I gave up trying to follow it past the first three minutes. I was just the driver for the most part. Since there was only one of me today, I was going to do the authorizing, when needed, of the various things that we needed to do that required a signature. As commander of the *Tinker Bell* I pulled a moderate amount of weight. I thought it would be enough.

We passed through the umbilical and the lock on the other side of the hangar deck. I signed us through security and we all received our nameplates with the monitors that gave us access to the sections of the station for which we were cleared. In our case that was a lot of station. Still, there were a couple of areas that weren't covered. Kelly took care of that problem in the nearest john. It took him less than ten minutes to do the four of them. There was a bit of an odor of hot plastic that wafted through the door from time to time, but the station was old and nothing made it smell sweet. We'd had to reset our personal com-links to the station's frequency, so we had set up a few phrases of double-talk to cover most of the forseeable contingencies. The given reason for the trip was a meeting with the station brass for personal reports of the progress of the project. I was going to have a hard time getting away after that. Besides being my superior officer, Admiral Ward was a friend. I knew he'd want to talk over old times until it was time to return to the *Tinker Bell*. Nameplates altered, we checked the time and split up. Kelly headed for the data and communications sector and Celia and Bill started for the med section. I stopped at the station banking section and spent a few minutes transferring my shares and savings to my brother Dave. There was no sense letting it all go to waste. I might make it back; then again, I might not. Dave would make the money do things better than I could, and if it turned out wrong I wanted him to have it anyway. I finished up and got a couple of hard copies of the transaction. One I sent to Dave and the other I filed in my safety deposit box. The next step was to see Admiral Ward. I made my way to officer country and gave my name to the appointments desk. The sergeant passed me on through and I knocked on the Admiral's door. The speaker bid me enter and I walked in. Frank Ward waved me to a chair and mumbled a greeting. I sat down and looked him over. He was wearing well. The hair was a little thinner, but the body and face glowed with good health. Station life was suiting him well enough physically. It didn't look as though a full-time desk job was doing him any harm. Still, it seemed an odd thing that he was no longer bossing a team project like the mass driver ore shuttle system. He was usually the first man to suit up and step into high vacuum when there were bugs in the system. Shuffling papers was a waste of a superior on-the-scene leader. I knew the only reason he had taken the job was that the only other option was to be sent Earthside and retired far too early. He dropped the papers he was studying in a basket and heaved himself erect. He stretched and came around the desk. I eyed the left leg as he did so. You couldn't tell it was a prosthesis. He handled it like a real leg. He saw me look at it and smiled.

"Want to try me at handball?"

"Spot me a point," I grinned. I knew he could still take me on a good day. The man was a shark. His handicap was likely to make him wealthy if they didn't make him pay taxes on the wagers he won from unsus-

pecting dolts who felt sorry for a one-legged has-been.
He knew trajectories better than any man in space.

He called me a name not strictly in compliance with
military etiquette and smiled back.

"You always were the tightest shavetail with a buck
I ever saw."

"I had to pay my bar bill once in a while, Admiral.
You should know. I had to buy all the drinks when
you were with us."

"Simply a lesson in military courtesy, Junior. I noticed some rough edges on your social graces. It seemed
more humane than bringing the matter up officially."
He dropped the banter and the laughing blue eyes
turned serious.

"Are those civilians that you've got running their
own little game going to give us something for putting
up with them?"

There was no need to be coy about that end of
things. I could tell him the truth about that at least.

"The reports are complete, Admiral. I don't understand all of what they say myself." I paused and he
nodded.

"I've read them all," he said. "You'd be worth
more than we're paying you if you did."

"Still," I continued, "I've seen enough to think
they're going to pull it off."

I wished I could put it more strongly than that. I'd
have liked to tell him that I knew with certainty that the
Drive was as good as accomplished. If any man deserved the truth, Frank Ward did. His brand of quiet
fanaticism about the future of the human race among
the stars had cost him his leg, and his entire adult life
had been devoted to improving the chances of getting
us out there among them. I wished he wasn't going to
find out the way he had to. I knew he had a genuine
liking for me. When it hit the fan, I was going to be a
major disappointment to him. We went over it all, and
I fed the hunger in his eyes as best I could. I gave him
all my impressions of the project and personnel as
faithfully as I could, stopping just short of the events

that took place in Celia's cabin. Up until then I had known nothing he wasn't welcome to. After that would have to remain a closed book for a little while yet. I hoped Albright and the department opened it all up. The human race was in for some large shocks. There was going to be danger, too. They'd need to work hard and fast from now on. I hoped we were going to leave them enough time.

We covered all of it and finally he sat back and changed the subject. It struck a nerve, and though it was a reasonable topic, I felt nervous discussing it just then. It was the real reason for our little raid today and it felt unlucky to be talking about it. I managed to do it calmly though, and the Admiral never guessed the strain I was feeling.

"Any problem with the Chief Pilot thing?" He didn't really expect me to have any, and I knew it, but it was an obligatory question.

"No, I'm checked out six ways from Sunday. The thing will fly itself anyway."

He accepted it. "Funny thing about Major Denning coming down with that thing in his checkup."

He peered at me and I'd like to have known what was in his mind. I thought the look was meaningful and I was feeling guilty enough to fall apart if he asked the wrong thing. I thought he suspected that I might be a spook nowadays. God knows some strange things had passed over his desk in recent months. It would take a man a lot duller than Frank Ward not to notice. I also knew that he was smart enough to know what to notice and what to let go by. Just between us, though, he might think I'd drop a hint. The last thing I wanted to talk about was the thing I'd pulled on Rollie. I knew if some of the timing was looked at closely, my shadow might be seen in it. This was no day to fence around with that subject. We'd come here to rectify the problem. Any heightened senses over in med section were undesirable. I let the subject pass as quickly as possible and I finished with the Admiral as soon as I decently could. I was relieved when he let me get away without a promise to return later for dinner and drinks. I begged off with the excuse that I had to shepherd my charges. We said our good-byes in the office, and I made it all the way out to the main corridor before I gave in to a giggle that I'd suppressed too long. Any other day of the year I could have handled the situation by having the Admiral call a coded number that would have raised his eyebrows into his hairline. Today wouldn't have been a good day for it. I didn't want the department's scrutiny either.

I checked the time again and saw that there was little time left. I hurried to the quadrant that housed the med section. It occupied several sections of the quadrant, running from low-G facilities near the hub to the extreme rim where high gravity was the norm. A lot of good medicine had been done with the change-able G-forces, but it spread things out too much for my liking today. I called Kelly on the com-link and we conversed on two levels. The sense of it unraveled was that everything was going along on schedule and it would be nice if I lent my presence to the effort. I said I was on my way. I reached the staff quarters in a few minutes and quickly found the right door. I touched the speaker button and an unfamiliar voice asked my name. I gave the false one we'd agreed on and the door opened. We'd agreed not to use our right names in case the door speaker had a log tape. It might help in fogging our movements. I walked in. He palmed the lock and we were safe from anyone barging in on us unannounced.

"Where are they?" I asked.

He pointed to the first door to my left leading from the parlor. I opened it and walked in on two strangers. A man I'd never seen before greeted me.

"Everything taken care of, Steve?"

"Yes, I had my talk with the Admiral. We should be free to go ahead without any one looking for us. My God! Is it really you?"

I looked at him closely. There was no more trace of Bill Ankers in him than there had been in the duplicate of me he'd become back on the *Tinker Bell* three days ago. He smiled an unfamiliar smile.

"It's me all right, but I'd just as soon let someone else do the next one. It's getting a little wearing changing all the time."

I knew it was worse than that. The cost in fatigue and strain was enormous if done often. As marvelous as the Shan virus was, it still took calories to effect physical change. Bill would be eating like a lumberjack for days after this. His altered appearance was that of a middle-aged man who was in poor physical condition. His eyes were straining and reddened. His hair was gray and thin and he stood in a slouch of habitual tiredness. He was wearing the clothing of the man he was going to replace for a while.

"Where is he?" I asked.

"Celia's finishing with him in the other room." He indicated the door on the other end of the room. I knocked and went it. Celia was bending over the original of the man from which Bill had taken the template of his appearance. He lay on the bed in a robe that bore his initials. He looked as if he were sleeping naturally.

"How is he?"

She turned from him and took the blood pressure monitor from his throat.

"Doing fine. He really needs the rest. He ought to thank us for it. I'm going to have Kelly set him up for a mandatory checkup while he's fudging the computer. I don't know why it is that medical people won't take care of themselves."

It cracked me up. In the middle of our assault on this installation, she was taking the time to straighten out this guy's health problems. I wouldn't have wanted her any other way, though. She gave him a final once-over and seemed satisfied. I said we'd better get on with it. She nodded and checked her appearance in the mirror inset above the desk. She had resorted to the common witchcraft of feminine cosmetics to change her appearance. A changed hair style and judicious color changes made her a different woman. It was all that was needed. The authority of the man on the bed was enough to guarantee her admittance to the areas where they needed to be. Dr. Jacob McLean had come close to discovering the best kept secret of the Phoenix Group because of my ploy to get Rollie's job. I had, by the inexorable intervention of Murphy's Law, hit on the truth when I got Rollie checked for an alien intruder in his body. Now we were going to remove the evidence (Rollie) and deprive McLean of at least three Nobel Prizes.

We split up again. Kelly had prepared his programs and would insert them when he heard from Bill that Rollie had been freed from the quarantine area. I set out for the hangar deck to get the shuttle ready. The plan had less than thirty minutes to run now. I reached the deck and got in the way of the hangar crew. When I judged they had enough of me, I went back to the shuttle. They were less disposed to enter it while I was inside. A certain amount of officious military bearing could get you a lot of privacy. I needed only a few minutes to remove all the override controls from the flight board. When we left here, we wouldn't be subject to station command. I finished that and checked the fuel load and atmospheric bottles. We had plenty of both. I rigged the feeder lines to disconnect harmlessly at a signal from a single switch and powered up the radio. Nothing to do now but wait for word from the rest of the team. I sat and watched the minutes roll by on the chronometer display.

The guard at the door to the isolation ward checked them through perfunctorily. He recognized Dr. McLean of course, and the woman with him had an access badge. He gave them a bad moment when he called them back as they passed the checkpoint, but it was only to have her print the name they used for her in the log book next to the scrawl that Bill had made of her name. It was unimportant. It hadn't gone into the computer files yet and Kelly had rigged those anyway. The last obstacle would be the ward personnel. As a visiting specialist Celia had no problems dealing with them because of her extensive medical background. Bill's job was more taxing as he was supposed to know the people as friends and co-workers. The best defense is a good offense, and they worked it that way. Nodding and mumbling at the small group of people that were in the area, Bill put on an angry bluster that threatened anyone near. The obvious target of his wrath was Celia who was, in cold clipped tones, berating the lack of progress in solving the mystery of the subject's peculiar condition. She spoke in strident tones of the various departments and executive levels that were beginning to question the efficiency of the expensive department McLean was running up here. At the first sign of something significant there was seemingly little return for the money spent. Within a few moments all those who could had found better places to be, and those who were unfortunate enough to be stuck here found an unusual absorption in their paperwork and other duties.

"These readings of the resistance of tissue samples to carcinogens and toxins are ridiculous," she snorted, and they disappeared into the anteroom that led to the barrier screen separating Rollie Denning from his fellow man. They were alone here except for the battery of monitor cameras that covered the anteroom and isolation ward. Celia kept up the harangue for effect while Bill gesticulated and sputtered. In seeming frenzy, he tore back through the door leaving her to blister the walls. With an apoplectic visage he descended upon the lowly med tech running the visuals and demanded that the cameras and mikes be shut off while he dealt with this harpy from headquarters.

"I can't do that, Doctor. The regs state that coverage must be constant. They're supposed to . . ." His voice died out as the face in front of him became homicidal.

"You break those circuits now, sonny, or you'll be changing sheets and bedpans for the remainder of your tour." The voice was deadly.

"Sir, the board has just blown a fuse." The young tech reached for the rope as the ledge beneath his feet started to crumble.

"Then I would suggest you go to the other side of the station and personally look for a spare," the voice grated. "Any you have here are likely from the same batch and are no more reliable than that one. Take your time. I'll be responsible for the area." The med tech accepted this suggestion willingly. He was gone before Bill had stomped his way back to the ante-room. Bill shut the door and checked the red telltale light on the camera. They were really off. Celia broke the frozen posture of aggression she had been holding and spoke to Kelly quietly on her com-link. Seconds later the barrier screen slid aside with a hiss. No entry of the action was recorded on the board or log. Kelly's overrides were thorough and untraceable. They passed the portal and went into the only occupied room. Their arrival had been unexpected. There was no good way to have informed Rollie about the impending breakout. He stared at them with anger growing on his face at this further encroachment on his liberty and privacy. Celia's hurried greeting wiped the previous expression from sight and replaced it with a new one of surprised recognition.

"Hello, Celia! Dr. McClean . . ." He checked himself and searched the face. "It isn't McLean, is it?"

"Only the shadow, Rollie. I'm Bill Ankers."

"Jesus! I knew you guys did this sort of thing, but this is the first time I've actually seen it."

"I guess that's right," Bill reflected. "You're almost as new to this as Steve Malin."

"Malin? You hooked him, too?"

"We did. Enough of this, though. We've got to get a move on."

"How do you mean?"

"We're breaking you out of here," Bill said succinctly.

"Just like that?"

"Hope so. Get some pants on now, for God's sake. We haven't got all day."

"Need some help, Rollie?" Celia interjected.

He stopped dead still and looked at her in amazement.

"Celia, you've changed." He shook his head. "You're above yourself."

He shoved his legs into a set of hospital whites and pressed the closures on a pair of deck shoes.

"I hope there'll be something else to wear where we're going," he muttered. "They locked up every damn thing I owned."

"Even the girlie pictures?" Celia burbled.

He flung her a look of disdain.

"It's love," Bill explained.

"Disgusting," Rollie replied. "Who?"

"Malin."

"Disgusting! Well, lead the way."

They returned to the anteroom. Bill spoke into his com-link. The section was suddenly in total darkness. Even the backups were dark. Kelly had struck again. Ahead, light was barely visible at the end of the corridor. They moved quickly toward it. Cursing and breaking sounds accompanied them as they moved.

"Hope Kelly didn't shut off anything crucial," Bill reflected.

"You know better than that," Celia comforted. "Point of pride even if he doesn't have feelings."

"He's not that bad. Just unaware of organic life." They reached the normality of the lighted section beyond the med complex and melted into the crowd.

The feeling came to me. I was getting a bit more used to it now. Those of us who had received the Shan virus had a sense of proximity with others of our kind. A sort of recognition not dependent on the normal senses. I felt it now. It was a subtle thing like a feeling of family. It did tend to color your attitude. Maybe *it* was the thing that was the most important in the long run. It provided a kind of human empathy needed but seldom found in normal relationships. The Phoenix Group had needed its influence to survive and accomplish its goals. Now that I had joined it, I tended to bask in the relationship. I liked these people for what they were. The rest was a very nice icing on a fine cake. The sensation was soon ratified by the appearance of four welcome faces that appeared at the entrance to the hangar deck. I watched through the port as they turned in their badges. So far so good. Bill was still wearing the McClean persona. As such, he was cleared for the deck anytime. Rollie was acting as his flunky and went through on the bogus McClean's say-so. They passed the quartz window that faced the dock. I saw the telltales go on as the umbilical monitor showed them enter and seal the hangar lock. I opened the shuttle side lock and saw the telltales go off as the shuttle was secured for vacuum again. I breathed a sigh of relief and started to initiate the departure sequence. Everything was going smoothly. I powered up the systems and requested the controller to shove us free. The cradle started to rise to the launch position and the board lights started blinking in preparation for the umbilical and utilities release. We stopped as the cradle finished its extension. Then it started to go wrong.

"Shuttle Two-seven, you are requested to hold position." The controller's voice was calm.

"Why the delay, Control?"

"Don't know, Two-seven. I have a security light flashing on my board. Seems they want a word with you."

"Shit!" I thought. I knew somebody had discovered Rollie's disappearance. The chances were that we weren't connected with it yet, but they were going to lock up the place while they did a search.

"Thank you, Control. Can you open a channel to *Tinker Bell* for us? I'd like to explain to the folks we're likely to be a little late on account of the cops."

"Can do, Two-seven. Opening channel now. Use band three."

"Thanks again, Control." I moved the band selector and spoke to the *Tinker Bell*. The message was what might be expected, explaining the snafu that would delay us. We were acknowledged and the conversation was over. I'd included an innocent phrase in the message that started things going on the other side. I cut the feedbacks from the thruster monitor and waited. To the hangar we looked dead. We were really fully powered and ready to fly.

I sensed a presence behind me. A hand clapped me on the shoulder and I saw a figure slide into the seat beside me. I turned to look at Rollie's pirate face as he glanced at the status board.

"How you doin', Slick?" he gave me the old easy grin.

"Tolerable," I grinned back at him.

"Got a game plan?"

"Plan B coming up," I said as the radio began to squawk. "That's it coming in now."

A mayday call was coming in on three different bands. Shuttle Two-eight was headed for the station. She was experiencing difficulty with her attitude jets. Thrust had been killed, but it looked as if they might bump into the Station hard. It was an impressive monologue. I had written it myself. The calm, controlled voices that usually issued from the net suddenly became squeaky and language that was frowned on over broadcast frequencies was starting to singe the circuits. The situation wasn't improving, and I made my contribution.

"Control—this is Two-seven. I'm bailing out."

"Jesus! You can't do that. Hold there, Two-seven. Hold!" Control said.

"Screw that," I yelled. "That thing is headed right for us."

I hit the buttons and the lines and umbilical fell away. The thrusters flared and we broke free of the cradle. I heard the controller yell a bad name at me as we left the deck. The bands were really heating up now as the other shuttle came tumbling toward the station. I shut my ears to the pandemonium and eased the shuttle out of the dock. The outer doors closed just as I went through. I checked the radar. The other shuttle was within a couple of miles now, and I sent a squirted code that cut the jets on the thing. I saw tiny flares start up again as the station took control of her and started damping the crazy gyrations. I leaned back in my seat as the programming took over for me and let the computers take us to the *Tinker Bell*. I hit the mike and announced to the rest of the team that we were on the way.

"You do that?" Rollie asked, awestruck.

"Nice little diversion, don't you think?"

"It looked kind of chancy to me," he ventured.

"Not really. I had her set to blow before she ever got close to the station." I mimed a yawn.

He gave me a measuring look.

"Nobody on it then."

"Shouldn't have been," I said. "I'll check though."

"Asshole!" he muttered.

"Good to see you, Rollie," I said comfortably as the *Tinker Bell* loomed at us through the forward port.

I'd lied about that. The other shuttle was filled with the crew that had opted not to go along with us, and there was no bomb. It never hurt to keep Rollie a little snowed. It made up for the job he was doing on you. I'd set the programming to stabilize the shuttle in time to bypass the station and return. All I'd done was short circuit its programming and let the station crew get to it a little faster. It also kept them busy and off our tails for a little longer. Time enough to let *Tinker Bell* fold space around herself and take us to the never-never land she was meant to. I'd hated to let the other shuttle go, but we'd had to let the crew that wanted off go somehow. A surprising number of them stayed on, although they hadn't been let in on the secret yet. Just enough to let them know that things weren't what they'd signed on for. I'd told them that if we pulled the mission off, there would be more pages devoted to them in the history books to be written than any other group of human beings. I told them that when and if they got back, they'd face court martial proceedings. I also told them they might not get back. I told them a lot of true things, and when I was done ten of them still wanted in on it. I shook my head at the silliness of human beings and was damn proud of them. They were a special breed anyway. In their hearts most of them came to be out here on the chance that something like this might come up. The odds had been billions to one. Good enough odds for some people.

We didn't waste any time. The station had stopped the outraged communications that followed our escape. Now we were getting seriously worded messages that were hard to ignore. They'd had time to evaluate everything that had happened and gotten a lot of it right. They weren't buying. It was expected. If there had been any chance they would, we'd never have done it this way. Eighty-six minutes from the time we boarded *Tinker Bell* again, we lit the fires that powered her and entered another universe. In this one, gravity became a tangible force like electromagnetics and radiation. It could be manipulated, sent through analogs of windings and circuits. It could be polarized to form new fields. It freed us from the limits of light speed. We compressed time and distance and wondered what the unbreakable constant of this universe might be. The gravity wells of Sol and her planets let us go and we built up speed. We took a cocoon of standard space with us and looked at the instrumentation that tried to describe to us the regions through which we were traveling. The familiar stars were still our guides. They retained their proper positions in the charts and we figured our progress with ages-old celestial maps and modern day computers. It worked.

Rollie and I shared the command. We set up staggered shifts and all trained in the running of the systems. For a week we maintained a speed relative to two G's while we refined our skills. It was a week of exhilaration and work. We dropped out of null space on the eighth day, and after checking the ship out in normal space, we declared liberty aboard ship. For the first time I was able to get all together and tell the rest of the crew the whole story. I depended on Henry for most of it. He told it much as he'd told me back in Earth's orbit. After he was done, no one ever called him anything but John Begay again. The Phoenix had arisen from the ashes. It was time for it to fly.

Chapter 8

I watched the crew's reaction to the story he unfolded. They responded as I had—with shock, disbelief, and fascination. As he continued, the disbelief was suspended temporarily as they got caught up in the tale. I was surprised that there weren't any unruly outbursts. It all sounded like a cinema adventure. There was a presence about him, however, that commanded respect, no matter how weird the story. They stuck a bit at the idea that he had lost an arm that was obviously still attached and whole to the fingertips. They ignored the contention that he believed himself to be nearly two hundred years old. When he came to the time that followed the car crash on the reservation, it got a lot harder to accept. I knew the feeling. He gave them a proof similar to the one that had convinced me to listen. As we watched he stood before us and shed his years. Middle-aged Henry Eagles melted and reformed into a young man we'd never seen before. He wasn't too tall, maybe five eight. His face was unlined, his eyes dark and clear. The carved head sat on a thick torso that held a subtly stated power. Only the undefinable presence remained. A quality of experience and judgment was seated in the eyes. It wasn't quite the shock that looking at my own face had been for me, but it did the trick and they sat spellbound as he resumed his story.

"Chaney used almost the last of his strength to free me from the chains and ropes," he said. "He leaned against the wagon's body and wheezed when he untangled the last belaying point. I heaved the last strand away from my body and fell out the door." He paused, remembering the pain. "I had only one arm and it was in bad shape. I'd sprained the shoulder trying to get loose. My back and legs were shot, too. I was nearly as bad off as Chaney. I flopped to the ground and Mary held my head. Everything spun for awhile. When the spinning stopped, I heaved myself up and looked around. The sun was well out and it was already beginning to heat up. My throat was dry and painful, and I knew the others felt the same. The water cooler that had hung in front of the wagon had been torn off in the crash. I looked over the landscape and saw the remains of it amid some other scrap metal from the wagon. It was crushed and split open. All the water had evaporated in the night. I wobbled to my feet and peered inside the wagon. All the supplies we had gotten in town were smashed as well. The liquids were gone, too. I stared at the mess. We were ten miles from home and lucky to be that close. We were a long way from anywhere else. The track we were on was seldom used and it might be awhile before anybody came this way. I put all thoughts of what had gone on during the night away for later consideration. Chaney was in a bad way. I couldn't see him walking out of here. Mary had been healed somehow. I pushed that line of thought away, too. I didn't want to deal with that now. She was healed but terribly tired. I could see signs of exhaustion in her face, and her body was trembling.

" 'There's a spring a couple of miles back,' I said. 'If there's anything left I could carry it in, we'd have water.' They shook their heads.

" 'We looked,' Chaney croaked. 'There isn't a thing that isn't smashed.'

"Mary nodded. I looked around me and saw that it was true. I weighed it all. I knew that I could make it home, but there was no help there. Mary's clan were all out at a sheep graze miles away. There was no transportation left there anyway. Supplies yes, but it would be hours before I could get back, and there would still be no one to help me with them. A normal, healthy person could go for more than one day without water. Longer than that—but we weren't normal or healthy right now. I was in the best shape, and that wasn't saying much. Men had died in a day from exposure out here. Not often, but it had happened. I looked at Mary and Chaney and judged it would be a near thing in their case. Whatever they had gone through last night had taken the last of their reserves. I didn't have much time.

"A few minutes later I had an idea. I moved them into the shadow of the ridge and returned to the wagon. It took a long time to do it with one arm and by the time I was through, I was dizzy and bleeding from a few more places, but I had managed to get a tire off the wagon and let the air out. I broke the bead by stamping on the casing. I ripped myself up some more getting the tube out of the inside, but I managed somehow. Before I left for the spring, I managed to break the gas line and soaked the upholstery in the wagon with it. I threw the casing inside and threw my Zippo after. In seconds the wagon was burning furiously. I moved away as quickly as my misused body could make it. The gas tank went a bit before I got far enough away, and I was flattened. My hands and face got a few more lumps and scratches, my kneecap was killing me, but I was still functioning. My ears rang for a long time and my vision was blurred. I returned to the shadow of the ridge and told them I would be back soon. I didn't like the way they looked, and I pushed myself hard. I made it to the spring and back in forty minutes over some rough country. I was almost unconscious when I buried my face in the metallic water of the spring. I used the knife I'd meant to use on Chaney to cut the inner tube that I filled with water. It held about four gallons, and I never spilled a drop of it on the way back. I haven't done anything as well again. The smoke from the wagon spilled into the sky for hours and we moved with the shade and drank from the foul tube and waited. With the water, the crisis was over and Chaney told us what had happened in the night and the story of the Shan and the Shan virus. It was hours before the blue policeman found us, and we heard most of it that afternoon as the sun pursued us under the ridge.

"Chaney wasn't a human. Not of the race of man. His people had evolved on another world far toward the center of the Milky Way. They were like us in that they had developed from a mammalian analog that had risen to dominate their world. They had come up a different path on their planet. Their predecessors had been like otters instead of primates; even now, they had an affinity for water worlds. Their history had been similar to ours but a lot less bloody. They had come to sentience in the streams and banks rather than the jungle and the veldt. It was a gentler and less traumatic transition. They had progressed to a civilized state with fewer dark periods in their history. That had been a long time ago. Their sky had many more astronomical events at close range, and they had made their way to the stars easily when they had achieved sufficient technology. They had been among them a long time. They had flourished and grown wise. Now they were an old society and spent much of their time studying other races such as our own. There was so much diversity in life—much more than in the physical world. Always something new.

In time, they had come to Earth. They had studied us for a century and found us fascinating; a riot of societies and cultures. We were unique in our diversity. The Shan were as hard put to describe us as we were ourselves. They abhorred our bloody-mindedness and were awed by our arts. They had never developed music or sculpture; painting and drawing were strictly representational. Drama was unknown. All these things were new to them. We were a rich lode that they delighted in mining. They were worried about us, too, the same worries that we had. Would we finish ourselves off in a terrible war? Maybe we would poison our world and ourselves. Should they interfere? They had asked those questions for as long as we had. As a highly moral race they had even more questions about it than we had. It would grind slowly. It was still grinding. In the meantime, they kept themselves hidden from us and studied all the branches of man.

Chaney had drawn the Navaho. He reckoned it a good assignment. He considered himself a junior social historian, not a brilliant scholar. Still, he enjoyed the field. The Navahos were easier for him to understand than a lot of the other humans. Like the Shan they were a naturalistic people. They believed in moderation. Stress and trauma came to a Navaho when he departed the 'Way.' It was a philosophy the Shan shared; not exactly, for they were different in many ways, but there was a sympathy. His name among the Shan had been Thomat, so among us he had become Thomas Chaney. He came to study us. He found me; we became friends. It was nothing unusual. The Shan often found friends among those they studied. The feeling was genuine, and he extended it to Mary willingly. In the extremity of the situation he'd used the Shan virus to save her life. It had been the only way. It was a total breach of policy. It had never happened before, although the situation had come up time and again. Chaney had counted himself lesser in the ranks of intellectuals that made up the social historians of the Shan. Maybe he was; he had proven to be long on compassion. I counted it more than a fair trade." Johnny paused. "The reason we're here now is that I've spent the time since trying to repay that lapse in policy he made!

"I've spoken of the Shan virus," Johnny continued. "I think it's time I told all of you what it is and what it means."

He looked out over the room. A mumble that had arisen when he broke off his narrative died down again.

"What it is is a semi life form that the Shan developed some time ago. They studied medicine and genetics and the other life sciences for a period of the time that extends long back before we had our first civilization. The virus is their major accomplishment. It's called a virus because it is similar to those found in nature. It has no life of its own without a host. It was meant in the first instance to reinforce the DNA of the host and prevent the breakdown of the genetic code. In later refinements an editing capability was created. This allowed the virus to manipulate the DNA and improve the host. It can be processed with the aid of other techniques the Shan have developed." John stopped again to make sure they followed the next part closely.

"Once the virus has secured the template of the host, it will reverse the aging process to first full maturity." He let that sink in and then started again before they could interrupt.

"It will heal, even replace, lost parts . . . like my arm . . . you won't age. . . ."

The crew sat for a moment and then there was bedlam. He waited for a moment and then shouted them down.

"That's right—longevity—near immortality. Maybe even that. The Shan say that depends and they won't say more."

He held them down with his eyes and a motion of his arms.

"I won't say more about that just yet. There's time. All kinds of time!" He let his voice fall.

"Accept just that for now. I want to finish this."

The babel swelled again and again he shut it down.

"A Shan can use it to heal another," he said quietly. "This is what happened to Mary." He had them again. They wanted to hear the rest of his personal story.

"He forced his own virus into the broken organs and tissues and forced the healing. It's possible because that's almost the way the virus is passed on naturally. It almost killed him. Mary was near death and she nearly took him with her. It was a close thing." He stopped once more. He looked them over.

"I know you have a lot of questions about all this. I want to answer them, but there is a lot more going on that you need to know, so I will just tell you a little bit more about it and get on to the rest. You may not have noticed with all that I've already had to tell you, but I haven't said a word yet about why we're here."

They were reeling from the overload of information that had been pressed on them, and the personal implications were crying out for their attention. Still, there was more to come and they waited for it warily.

"A side effect of the virus," he continued, "is that while the main function is to reinforce the genetic code, it can also accept a second overlay. In short, it can provide the host with a temporary new physical identity derived from another entity. It even works across species."

The last sensation created a stir as large as the one caused by Johnny's statement about the longevity possibilities. It took awhile to get them settled again. When he had control of them again he turned to the side entrance. Barbara entered the room on cue. She walked across the room in full view and headed for a seat in the middle of the group. She had almost seated herself when they began to catch on. This time the hullabaloo didn't stop, and John let it go. Instead of sitting down, she remained standing and the occupant of the seat next to her stood up. Together, they turned and faced the crew. Identical in every respect, they linked arms and smiled. The noise was overwhelming. It nearly became riot as they posed and pirouetted like fashion models. They let the uproar run its course, and when it reached something like normalcy, Johnny resumed his exposition.

"You've heard a lot of wild things today. We thought it was time we offered you a little proof of what you've been told." He indicated the twin Barbara Pattersons, who nodded to the audience and pulled their chairs out to a position facing the rest of us. They sat in them and bore the scrutiny comfortably, still smiling.

"You all know Dr. Patterson." Johnny continued. "We'll just assure you that what you're seeing is real without stage makeup or anything like that. If we weren't going to provide a little further evidence, we'd let you take fingerprints and the works, but I think that what you'll see will be convincing enough without that. I want you to watch both Dr. Pattersons closely while I tell you the rest of it.

"The Shan had been investigating other worlds besides ours," Johnny said. Given the right conditions, life is fairly common. Earth-like planets existed in large numbers. They might be far apart. They were a small percentage of the mostly dead planets that revolved around the suns of the Milky Way. Still, with all the suns there were in the galaxy, that still left huge numbers of suitable worlds for life to develop on. They had met many forms of it. It usually produced an intelligent species that fell within a framework like ours or the Shan's. Bipedal, with recognizable heads and manipulating arms and hands, or something similar. The differences were small compared to the similarities. The differences were real, though. The big ones were in the minds that dwelled in the bodies. Among the stars a long time ago, the Shan ran across another race of star travelers. They called themselves the Ann Thaar. The Shan recoiled from the meeting in horror. The Ann Thaar had all the charm of a wolverine with a herniated disc. They were the ultimate carnivores, treacherous, cold-blooded killers even in their dealings with each other. They had developed a culture that depended on ritualized blackmail and exchange of hostages to provide the basis for cooperation necessary to hold their system together. To be without a knife at your partner's throat was to die. It made for a history of carnage that was unbelievable. Somehow they had been equipped with first-class brains. They had made it to the stars. When the Shan met them, they had subjugated a good number of worlds and turned them into feeding stations. A lot of intelligent races were now simply game to be slaughtered for the diet of the Ann Thaar. The Shan fled before them and the viciousness of their frenzy. A highly moral race themselves, they weren't a match for the Ann Thaar and their weaponry. They could only show them a clean pair of heels. The Shan had the null drive; the Ann Thaar didn't. They had managed something else that approached light speed but hadn't yet managed to beat it. It was only a matter of time now before they did. Shan surveillance showed that they were getting close to it. When they do make it, the civilizations in the Milky Way are going to be exposed to a murderous horde surpassing the worst things they imagined. The Shan have been staying ahead of them and trying to find someone or something capable of stopping them when they do break out. They know they're never going to be able to do it themselves. They're just not made that way."

Johnny stopped and considered how best to put the rest of it. He looked at me, and I thought I'd put in my two cents. I joined him and took over for a while. The rest of this was in my territory as a member of the Earth's military arm. I might have run off with the *Tinker Bell*, but I was still the captain and responsible to the crew.

"When they break out," I said, "we're going to be one of the first targets. We've already been visited." I looked out over the room and saw that they were all following me.

"The flying saucers were real!" A kind of groan and titter went through the room.

"I know," I said. "It sounds like bad fiction, but it's turned out to be true. The Ann Thaar were the UFO's and they'll be back. The ones we saw in the twentieth century were just an advance scout group. They were really after the Shan. They want them a lot more than they do us. We'd be just another feeding station to them. The Shan have the null drive. That's almost unimportant, though; they'll get that someday anyway. What they really want is the virus. If they get that they will have everything, and their pillage of the rest of the galaxy will seem like a Sunday school picnic compared to what will come next."

I let Johnny take it from there again. The rest of the story was his.

"The Ann Thaar came looking for the Shan in the mid-forties. They were spotted quite a while before they entered the solar system. The Shan planned to jump out of here and lead them away from us. Mary and I had become a lot more involved with them since the accident. I'd changed my identity after I received the virus. It would have been impossible to explain the regrowth of my arm and hand. We became useful to them, and when it became apparent they were going to pull out for a while, the Shan asked us to go along rather than leave us on Earth with the possibility that the Ann Thaar might find us and get the virus through us. It was no hardship for us—we wanted to go. The day finally came, and we were picked up and taken to the Shan ship. The Shan had underestimated the Ann Thaar for once. They had sent a small group ahead of the main party. They caught us as we were getting ready to jump just outside of Jupiter. Three small interceptors came out of hiding behind the planet and cut our flight path. We jumped at the same time they opened up on us. They missed, but we took one of them into null space with us. It distorted our envelope and the drive collapsed. It was the end of the Ann Thaar ship, too, but we dropped back into normal space. We almost didn't make it. The envelope flared as we entered and burned out the circuits. The ship dumped the atomics automatically. We were alive but limited to standard drive. We were in hostile country and unable to reach any other Shan vessel. During the few minutes in null drive we'd gone five light years. With luck, that meant it would be many years before the Ann Thaar caught up with us. The chances were that when they did, we'd still be here waiting for them. The ship couldn't be fixed by anything less than a refit by a technology a hell of a lot more sophisticated than Earth's. We couldn't go back there anyway. The Ann Thaar were between us and Earth. There was nowhere to go. The only thing that was any help was that we could go dead in space, and with luck they'd overlook us when they came this way. We had some definite problems."

Johnny looked at the rapt and silent crew.

"We did have some time on our hands." He pierced them with his old/young eyes. "We had a lot of time. We made some hard decisions. Eventually Chaney and I were sent off in a small lifeboat they rigged up with some long-sleep gear and sent back to Earth to bring its technology up to snuff. They gave us almost all of the remaining standard drive fuel and locked us on course. We had an even chance of making it back. No more than that. The last thing I remember was seeing Mary's face as they cooled me down. I don't know what happened after that until I woke up when we closed on Earth's orbit twelve years later."

The crew had been hard put to pay attention to what Johnny was saying for the last few minutes, even though the things they were hearing were first-rate drama. The competition came from the twin Barbaras who sat directly facing them. The metamorphosis was nearing completion now, and the surface changes were moving at great speed. One of them remained unchanged, but the other had undergone a shifting in her body's structure. Barbara's cool blond good looks were generally unadorned. She had a full figure that was usually hidden under a bulky jumpsuit. Her complexion was light and naturally good, with pale blue eyes. Today for the demonstration she had worn a brief outfit that showed a good bit more of her than normal. It was duplicated by the one worn by the girl next to her. That girl no longer looked the same. The legs had lengthened noticeably, and the calves had changed shape. The waist remained much the same, but the upper chest and shoulders had altered. The second girl was smaller in her breasts and her shoulders sloped differently. The face had altered the most, changing from a Nordic, square-jawed coolness to a Mediterra-

nean look, with lean planes and larger eyes. These
eyes were brown, dark and expressive. The mood they
showed now was a mischievous one. The complexion
had darkened as the last changes took place. Celia sat
beside the woman she had impersonated for this demonstration of the virus' adaptability. Totally different,
except for her hair, which she had rinsed to complete
the disguise. It was a relief to me to have her back in
her own persona. For the moment, though, I had to
step aside and let the others have her for a while.

It was a logical place for Johnny to break the telling
of his past, and he stood to the side and grinned as the
crew got to their feet and flowed toward the two
women. It took quite a while for things to get back to
normal, and it was late in the day when Johnny finally
called a halt to the session. He'd gone over the intervening years when he and Chaney had set about found-
ing the Phoenix Group and touched on its history. The
telling took a long time, although he abbreviated it
whenever possible. The questions didn't stop after he'd
told it all, and finally we had to wrap it up with a lot
left uncovered. We never had the chance to answer
everything. The scale of time and the enormity of the
events were too large to handle in a dozen sessions
like this. Still, it gave everyone the essentials of the
situation and let them know what our purpose was: in
short, the rescue of the Shan and the refitting of their
ship. A separate and more personal aspect was the
reunion of John Begay and his Mary. There were no
comparable romances in history. It captured everyone's imagination as fully as the rest of the story.
Everyone knew the beginning now. They knew only
Johnny's side of the middle of it. We couldn't guess
Mary's life since the parting, and the end was anyone's
guess. That alone was enough to get us out here.

We rested and checked the ship and readied ourselves for the next step. We'd left the solar system
with much left to be done, and now we set about
finishing our preparations. The crew and the Phoenix
Group melded and became a unit. During the course

of the layover, the virus was given to those who had thrown in their lot with us. It could be administered in a number of ways. As far as I knew, no one had gotten it in as pleasurable a way as I had, but I didn't inquire. We did have a reasonable mix of men and women. However it was accomplished, it was soon complete, and we became what we are. The empathy that exists among the recipients of the Shan virus is a handy thing in the blackness of unfamiliar space. I recommend it.

Chapter 9

A lonely place. The light that traveled here was sparse and illuminated nothing. The stars were distant and unfamiliar. The *Tinker Bell* hung in the middle of infinity. All directions flowed outward to nothingness. Reference points had no emotional meaning. We were the only reality and daunted by our fragile existence. The little pocket of technology we had brought with us was cut from its roots. Supply and demand became very finite and measurable factors; we knew exactly what we had to draw on. If anything ran out, we would never get a second chance. The Shan's plight was one we shared now. The immensity of space was unforgiving. We completed our checks and found the *Tinker Bell* all that it was designed to be. The planning that had gone into her, both openly and covertly, had paid off handsomely. Man's first real venture into the universe had a sound ship.

Thirteen days after we had left the solar system we lit the fires of the drive again and entered the region of null space. We maintained a moderate speed, setting out on a course that would place us roughly on a line to the coordinates from which Johnny and Chaney had departed so long ago on their return journey to the solar system. The rotation of the stars and the expansion of distances with the passage of time made it a wild stab in the general direction. If that was all we had to go on, we might as well never have left. We would never have found a trace of the Shan after all that time. The Shan vessel was "dead," radiating nothing both by necessity and intent. It was a very small object in the debris of space. We could come within a few hundred miles of it and never know. We had a way, though, if it worked. The Shan had included the plans for a device that would signal a buoy in space using modulated gravitational waves. With luck, it would reply to the signal. The length of time it took would be dependent on the distance as it was a little like a normal space radio signal. The gravity waves traveling through null space did take time to cross the distances between objects, but it was very fast. If it worked, we should know it within the day. The signaling device was one of the things that had been altered during the solar storm. It was ready to go and when we had encoded the proper signal that Johnny gave us, a signal was squirted ahead of us in a cone just sufficient to reach the regions of space in which the Shan might be located. The signal's strength was weak so that it would deteriorate beyond the limits that the Shan could have reached. There was the possibility that the Ann Thaar might be able to pick it up. It was the reason for using the buoy in the first place. No one knew what technological level the Ann Thaar might have reached by the time the rescue was finally attempted. We moved through the strangely foreshortened paths between suns at a pace only a few times greater than that Johnny and Chaney had used in their journey in the opposite direction. The hours passed slowly and we took turns standing half watches monitoring the boards. I caught a bit of sleep and had a workout for the first time in a couple of weeks. If my body hadn't told me it was long overdue, the med computers made certain that I was enlightened. I was informed by the computer that a flag was being placed on my file to be passed along with my proficiency rating to the certification board on earth. The computer didn't care that the board in question was in the solar system of a feeble star of unimportance far behind us. I finished my shower and headed for the commissary when the signal came in. An "all hands" came over the com-link, and I put away all thoughts of food and hurried to the bridge. I found everyone ahead of me. I grabbed my seat and watched as the decoded message scrawled across a monitor board. It was a bit disappointing. The message was a word for word repetition of the one we had sent out. That meant the buoy had responded to the incoming signal and thrown it back at us. We could make our way to it now, as it was possible to fix its position from the incoming text, but it wasn't likely that there would be anyone there when we arrived. The Shan didn't seem to be in close contact with the buoy. It was a worry that we'd have to accept for the time being. Kelly was already hard at work with his computers, and it was only minutes until he had the coordinates fed into the nav board. There was nothing to wait for, so we brought the *Tinker Bell* up to full speed. We didn't know the limits of the Drive. The Shan's computer systems had a capacity to deal with all the factors that went into judging something like that, but our system was primitive compared to theirs. Johnny had been given enough parameters to keep us from blowing ourselves up and still get us where we wanted to be in good speed. We might never really know her capabilities. The analog of stars that showed on our view screens began to move toward us, and we raced through a starry cylinder that expanded toward us as we began to accelerate. We rendezvoused with the signal buoy forty-six hours after we got the signal's return. We'd covered a little over nine light years and barely cracked the throttle. It had taken Johnny and Chaney twelve years to cover the same route in cold sleep at sub-light speeds.

The buoy was a cold lump of flotsam far from anything with sufficient gravity to interfere with it. It looked like an escaped asteroid. We eased up next to it and fed it a soothing set of numbers; it disarmed its destruct mechanism and released the protective coloration encompassing it. The pitted surface peeled away, and it lay bare to the eye. It was a sphere covered with ridges that wound their way around the surface and made it look for all the world like a ball of yarn. The ridges held the sensors that picked up our signal. We maneuvered closer to it and opened the shuttle dock. Natalie Singh and I E.V.A.'ed and brought the thing inside. It was the first opportunity I'd had to put on a suit in a long time and I enjoyed myself immensely. It was over all too soon, and Nat and I were back in the ship grinning ruefully at each other. She loved it as much as I. Floating among the fires of space was something like catharsis, and most of us never got enough of it. The buoy was anchored to the deck and was being viewed by monitoring throughout the ship. The alien artifact was a further evidence of Johnny's story and helped to settle the still nagging little voices that came to us all. The ones that said, "Really now!" You knew what they meant. At the same time you told yourself you really did believe. It was something you doubted every time you woke up, and it was a fight to accept it all over again. Confirmation, however small, was nice. Everyone's patience was a little thinner when it was decided that the buoy had warmed enough to be mated to the wiring harness that had been made for the internal probe. The specifications that had been made for it decades back proved correct and the ship's computers conversed with their Shan counterpart. The conversation was lengthy for such as they and took almost a full minute. The files were exchanged, and we were in possession of the information we needed. One final step was necessary, and Johnny supplied it. He stepped to the key board and entered his war name, a final confirmation of identity that only he and the members of his clan knew. Among the Navahos only this was his true identity, and any other name that he went by was a name of convenience and might change with the passage of time. This was his for all time, although it had never been entered on paper. With the authorization that his name verified, the files became secure and accessible. We fed them into the *Tinker Bell's* banks and in a millisecond the trajectory of the Shan ship was plotted and fed into the nav board. We now had a direction. The buoy was integrated into the communications network. It possessed the recognition codes that had been set up to communicate with the Shan ship. We had the codes to activate the buoy. The system was complete at last.

We jumped into null space for the third time and followed the general direction that the Shan had taken so long ago. We started the signal as soon as we were running steadily. The Shan couldn't be too far away as they were drifting practically powerless. The emitter ranged ahead of us like the radar on an old submarine, each pulse containing a recognition code for the Shan to reply to. The *Tinker Bell* cruised the foreshortened universe like a night feeding bat. Our conversation on the bridge was sporadic as our eyes fastened on the visual display that monitored the signal's progression ahead of us. It was taking too long. The Shan shouldn't have gotten this far at sublight speeds. The question of the mating of the buoy with the *Tinker Bell's* computer systems began to be discussed openly. Was it as good a match as it seemed? The programming seemed to be all right, but could we really tell? I suggested that we come to rest and think it out rather than continue blindly. After a short discussion, Rollie initiated the shutdown. Our speed fell to an almost motionless rest position. We still maintained our insertion into null space. The scientists began to examine the programming and the physical links that meshed the systems. Everything seemed in order, and they started again working their way through the maze of connections, subjecting the software to intense scrutiny. We all avoided Johnny's face as the time wore on and nothing surfaced. The young face that had emerged not long ago was showing new lines of strain. He maintained a surface calm that we all respected him for, but his eyes were hard to look at. Finally, everything had been checked at least twice and pronounced correct. There was nothing more to try. We stood down and went our separate ways. I set up a meeting three hours later to discuss it after everyone had had a chance to think it over. I looked toward Celia, but she was involved with a small group discussing some aspect of the system, and I left her with them. I wandered down to the hangar deck musing over the events of the last few hours. I hoped someone had some ideas when we met again. I certainly didn't. The hangar deck was cold and dark, a fitting environment for my thoughts. I walked across the gridding that served as a floor, noting that everything was anchored properly. The lighting switched on and off as I passed, activated by the com-link on my wrist. The shadows moved with the light, disappearing as a bank of spots turned on and coming back as I moved on and the light switched off again. I looked at the pressure readouts on the bay seals and saw that the integrity was good. In the shadows near the readouts, I noticed an odd orange glow. What was that? I went to it. The light came from a newly installed panel on the bulkhead. I tried to remember what it was. It had been installed since we had rescued Rollie. I remembered it suddenly. The team had adapted the radiation shield that had protected the E.V.A. suit during the solar storm to protect the entire ship. We no longer had to depend on the shielded rooms. The panel was showing that it was operational. I nodded and forgot about it again as I walked away. I had gotten halfway across the deck when I had the thought. Suddenly I needed someone to try it out on. I made it to Engineering in two minutes flat. I picked the nearest body.

"Art!"

He turned at my shout. Art Bell was just the man I needed. He designed a lot of the scarier circuits, the ones that controlled the mind-boggling voltages that ran through the drive components.

"Yo, Steve."

"Art, what effect, if any, would the radiation shield have on the signal we've been sending out?"

His face brightened for a moment. "Hey, that'd cut strength way down, maybe forty percent or so."

He was right with me. He swung to an accessing

keyboard and brought a systems status profile up. The checklist scrolled across the screen. He keyed a specific system check and the screen switched to show the shield's status.

"Damn! I thought you had something for a minute." He shook his head. "The system's off, though. Don't need it in null space."

His face lost its momentary brightness.

"Want to bet on that?" I said. "The panel in the dock area says it's on full strength!"

An hour later we were on the bridge again, listening to the faint reply from the Shan ship as the returning signal finally made its way to our com-board. A subdued Art Bell had finished wiring in the system to the master circuits and the light in the hangar deck went off with the one on the bridge as the shield went down.

The signal was weak, but it was there, and we returned to full speed and headed for it. The only thing was that the signal was obviously an automatic response repeated over and over. No change came when we tried open communications. Nothing but the robot programming returned our signal as we homed in on the Shan.

Chapter 10

We dropped into normal space. We were in a nearly empty region. The darkness was unrelieved by nearby stars. The Shan ship was a blurred image without resolution on the screens. The TV only showed an amorphous darkness in the center of the screen. It was a little blacker than the surrounding space. The radar showed little more as the signal returned a similar shapelessness as a white mass on a green background. There were no highlights from gleaming metal nor patterned orientation lights for docking. A dead lump in the bowl of stars. It had fallen silent when we dropped from null space. Nothing in the way of normal traffic bands brought any further response to our signals. We moved in closer. At five miles' distance the ship began to resolve into a definite form at last. The radar image began to show a cylindrical shape with one flattened side. It rotated above us as we angled in and began to match our motion to its own. The apparent tumbling slowed and finally stopped as we matched its line of flight. During our approach the ship had passed in front of us and presented all of its sides. The computer had built up a three-dimensional image and we picked a point amidship to close on. The other side had shown a slagged surface toward one end and that figured to be the result of the Ann Thaar's attack and the destruction of the drive. The flattened side we approached should contain the shuttle docks and the most direct entry to the ship's main levels. We stabilized our position at three hundred meters and sent a line to the hull of the Shan ship. The power boards showed a peak as the magnetic fields of the two ships met and canceled out. There was a smell of hot metal as the capacitors shunted the charge. There was still no response from the Shan. We turned what lighting we had on the other ship. The flashing of our beacons and hangar deck lights swept over a dark wall beside us. The lights were absorbed in the nonreflecting surface, returning only a weak sheen that revealed no protuberances or breaks in the skin. We watched the screens and continued to try the communication bands. The silence of the Shan ship took on a grim meaning. We sat idle for an hour and tried everything, to no avail. During the second hour we made the decision to try to gain entry. The makeup of the boarding party was hard fought, but quickly decided on. I pulled rank, so I got to go. No one could argue Johnny's right and we settled on five of us for the team. That left three to choose. I wanted one of the regular crew with me so that there would be two of us with E.V.A. experience. I chose Natalie Singh. Johnny chose Art Bell for his expertise in electronics, and we both agreed on my sergeant of arms, Jack Seward. Obviously, something had gone wrong over there. We would go in cautiously and well armed. Jack fitted us out with hand weapons, and he took a heavy automatic jungle rifle that didn't appear on the arms manifest. It was equipped with infrared imaging and other goodies that had no place on a space ship. I resolved to ask him about it at another time. For now I let it go by, but with a look that I made sure he saw. I trusted his judgment, though, and I simply made sure he understood that we really didn't want a war without a lot of provocation.

"Understood, Colonel."

"O.K. then. Let's do it!"

We sealed our suits and took a final radio check. We cycled ourselves through the lock and emerged to the outer skin of the *Tinker Bell*. We worked our way to the line and snapped our bridles to it. I shoved off and one by one the others followed, Johnny directly behind me and then Art and Natalie. Jack brought up the rear, keeping his eyes glued on me. I slowed myself as I came to the surface of the Shan vessel and did the last few feet in a deliberate hand-over-hand mode. I swung around just before I touched and made contact with my feet. The magnets in the sole plates grabbed onto something, but the surface of the ship was resilient. I sank a millimeter or so into its surface. Then I released myself from the mooring line and stood out from the hull. I tried a few shuffling steps and found that I could maintain an upright stance and move around if I took it slowly. I moved away from the line in order that the others might join me. They came one by one and tested the hull. When all five were clustered around me, we attached a separate line to the first and set out to find the entrance that Johnny said should be a few meters away. He led the way and we strung out behind him. He played his torch on the area before us and gave a grunt a few paces later. We all came up on him as he stopped. The beam of the torch passed back and forth over the hull, giving back an even reflection except for a circular dark spot just ahead that soaked up the light and returned none of it.

"That should be it!" His voice held satisfaction as he moved toward the dark spot. I let him get ahead and held the others back with me. He entered the darkness and, as he did so, he began to sink on the horizon. He was entering a depression on the hull.

"This is it," he said. "Come on!"

We followed and found ourselves in a bowl-shaped pit in the hull about eight feet deep. A cone shape stood in the middle of it. The cone was about four feet wide at the base. Johnny lowered himself to a squatting position and played his light on the cone. A crescent-shaped handhold was sunk in the base. He inserted his glove and tightened his grip, pulling across his body. The cone rotated in the direction of his pull. A sliver of darkness appeared in the side of the cone as it turned and became the first edge of a hatchway. He stood up and released the handle, grasping the edge of the cone that had begun to reveal the opening.

With the improved stance he was able to slide the cone easily the rest of the way. The hatch was just big enough for a normal man to enter with the bulky E.V.A. suit. I pulled at his shoulder, and he stood back a little. We took turns examining the interior. There wasn't much to see. The entrance sloped down and turned at a fifteen-degree angle to the hull. There weren't any steps—just a rail at one side and a ramp that led to a curve that progressed deeper into the interior of the ship. There was nothing to see and no reason not to enter. I motioned for him to take the lead again. He grabbed the sides of the hatch and eased himself in. He looked back at us and then took hold of the rail. A panel above his head sprang into life and bathed the interior with an orange light. We froze and waited for something else to happen, but nothing did. Apparently, the light panel came on automatically when you touched the rail. I thought it would be well to keep down the chatter, so I gave him a hand signal to continue. The ramp made a complete turn just inside and then straightened. It extended for twenty feet or so and ended with a recognizable air lock. A darkened monitor screen and keypad were inset beside it. The tunnel had widened and we gathered around to study the door and screen. Johnny touched the largest of the buttons in the center of the keyboard.

"This is the com-switch for the local area," he said. "If there was anyone nearby on the other side of the lock, this should get some kind of attention."

We watched the screen. It remained dark. We gave it a while longer and Johnny hit the key a few more times. Still nothing.

"O.K., I guess there's no sense in waiting any longer," I sighed. "Can we open it from this side?"

"Shouldn't be a problem." Johnny moved away from the key pad and depressed a plate inset in the lock door. The pressure on the plate caused a handle to extrude itself from the door body. Johnny grasped the handle and twisted it a half turn. The door eased itself open slowly, and we looked into a pressure chamber big enough to hold all five of us. It was a sterile chamber devoid of anything but the opposite pressure door and a few metal racks and ring bolts which were empty. On the wall that contained the inner door another screen and key pad like those on the outside were placed in conjunction with a recognizable pressure gauge and a speaker grill for use when the chamber was pressurized enough to carry sound waves. This screen was as dark as the other one. Johnny turned from his inspection of these things to a panel cover on the opposite side of the door. He pulled it open and revealed a set of switches marked with characters that were based on geometric shapes but unlike any I'd ever seen.

"This is the control box for pressurizing the lock," he explained. "Anybody want to wait any longer?"

"Can't think of any reason. Go ahead. Jack! Be ready when we open it up, but don't be in a hurry to get us in a mess. We haven't any reason to believe there's anyone unfriendly around. We're just being cautious."

"As you say, Colonel." His voice over my headset was calm.

I noticed that he had his weapon unslung and ready, but he wasn't holding the stock at the trigger plate. He was ready but not anxious.

Johnny reversed the switches and a light began to move on a transparent insert that had looked opaque before. It was located beside the switches and the light moved up like mercury in a column. It moved rapidly, and I could tell the chamber was filling up. Our suits began to valve off, and the moisture from them began to cloud up the chamber a bit. I noticed that my suit heater shut off as the pressure mounted. The light reached the top of the plate and was now a solid bar. The switches suddenly snapped back to their original position.

"That's it!" Johnny moved to the door. "Steve?"

"Open it!" I motioned the others to stand to the side and Jack got just a notch more ready. Johnny repeated the opening process and swung the door open. The corridor we faced was totally dark. Nothing moved that we could see.

"Damn it," I said. "John, how about the lighting in here?"

"Not automatic, I guess. I don't remember about that. I was surprised at the locks."

"Do you think you can find a way to turn them on?"

"Don't know." His reply sounded testy. "None of this is the way it ought to be, you know."

"Right," I said. "Sorry. O.K., I guess you're still the guide. See if you can get us somewhere useful."

He grunted an affirmative and we stepped out into the corridor. Johnny's torch cut the darkness well enough, but it was lost in a lot of places as bulky things cast shadows which stretched out for long distances. I snapped on my suit light. It was fixed in a forward position on my helmet. The others did the same. It helped a bit. The shadows were multiplied by five and moved in strange patterns as we made our way down the corridor. It was a little disorienting.

The Shan ship was huge compared to the *Tinker Bell*. The corridor ran half its length in a straight line just a few feet from the outer hull. We passed several offshoots that led to the interior, but Johnny thought we ought to stay on this lateral until we reached the bow of the ship.

"Too easy to get lost in the center of it all just now," he replied to my question about our direction of travel.

"The bridge and nav systems are all up there."

I knew that he thought the bridge would be the likeliest place to find out what had happened. Nobody said it in so many words, but it was pretty apparent by now that there wasn't anyone on board the Shan ship. At least we hadn't run across any bodies yet. Of course, we were in an area that figured to be empty most of the time any way, but not this deserted! The ship seemed to be fully pressurized, and that meant an expenditure of energy that wasn't inconsequential. I wondered about their auxiliary power sources. They hadn't enough to power the drive, I knew, and there had been a sacrifice of fuel of some kind to power the lifeboat that had brought Chaney and Johnny back to the earth at a good fraction of light speed. Apparently these sorts of power usage were enough out of the ordinary to cause some problems, but the Shan hadn't seemed to worry about the kind of consumption needed to maintain the ship over the lengthy years until the cavalry arrived. It was a difference in scale, I guess. The question still bothered me. Such an enormous amount of energy was needed to run this thing. I wondered out loud if perhaps that might be the answer. Maybe they hadn't responded because they had all gone into the cold sleep process to conserve on consumables and power. Johnny picked up on it.

"I'm hoping for something like that. Still, they never mentioned it as an option."

He didn't speculate any more himself, but the others kicked the idea around as we worked our way through the passage. With the poor quality of our lighting we couldn't make out much of what we passed through, but it did look much as ships must look by their nature. Some of the objects that we passed were obviously machinery, but their purpose was a mystery. We didn't stop to puzzle over them now. We were in a hurry to get to the nerve center and hopefully solve the big mystery. I wanted to re-establish contact with the *Tinker Bell,* too. I was hoping we could do it from the bridge of the Shan ship. We were too long out of contact already. I checked my suit chrono. It had been nearly an hour since we left, at least twenty-five minutes since we had started down this corridor. We hadn't been making very good time with the disadvantage of the bulky suits slowing our movements, but we still had to have come a good way. I called a halt.

"John, what do you think about the air in here?"

"Should be O.K. The Shan breathe the same stuff we do. I had no troubles with it when I was here before."

"Yeah, I know that. What I mean is, do you think this pressure around us is the same mix?"

"I don't see why not. I can find out anyway.'"

"How? Did you bring a test kit?"

"Not exactly." He made the move before anyone could stop him. He cracked his helmet seal and popped his faceplate.

"Damn it, John!" I blew off. "Don't do anything like that again!"

The face in the helmet looking back at me was strained, and I could see that for once his patience had come to an end. It wasn't a good situation, especially right now. I chose my words carefully to be sure they were right and ones I could stand by.

"John, I mean this. If you do anything like that again in a situation like this, I will pull a gun on you and lock you up for a court martial. When there's time for a vote, I'll abide by it and so will YOU." I let that sit for a minute.

"When there isn't time for a vote," I finished grimly, "you will do as I say!"

We glared at each other for a frozen minute. It was time for me to find out if I was still the captain of the *Tinker Bell*. The question had been in the back of my mind for awhile. When you came right down to it, my line of authority was a little murky but I wasn't going to just stand down. I wondered what was in the minds of the others. I knew Jack was mine, but I had an idea the others were less so. It would depend on John's decision in the next few seconds. I waited. I saw him struggle with it. When it came, I knew his decision had nothing to do with any fear he had of me or any reprisals.

"Done!" he said, and I knew he chose the word deliberately as the closing of a contract. The tension dropped and we got on with it. We cracked our suits and saved the rest of our supplies. The Shan's variety of gases tasted good. A lot better than the stuff we'd gotten used to on the *Tinker Bell*. It was a shame to have to wear the suits, but I didn't want to leave them anywhere and carrying them was out of the question. We started out again and soon found ourselves at a main junction of corridors. Johnny told us that we were very near the bridge now. A few more yards and we found ourselves in rooms rather than corridors.

The corridor we had traveled to the bow of the ship had curved slightly, and we had come to the central levels by following it to the end. The first of the rooms on the central core that we entered was the size of a high school gym and filled with machinery ranging from towering heights to things as small as lunch pails. A few lights shone on the bulkheads and there were low level sounds of pumps and less identifiable things. Most of the machinery was silent and motionless as we passed. The main lighting was nonfunctional here as it had been in the corridor from which we had come. Johnny told us that this was one of the main engineering sections. A broad walkway as wide as a city street cut through its center, and we followed it to the next area. At intervals along the walkway I saw an assortment of vehicles. Some were as large as a moving van; others were likely to be small personnel carriers. These ranged from scooter types to minibuses. Johnny said they ran on electric power provided by charging stations throughout the ship. At the moment they were of no use to us, and we passed them with an eye to future use. The next rooms were less massive. They appeared to be an interwoven series of shops and offices similar to a mall complex on Earth. There were areas that seemed to be promenades with fountains like city parks. Our lights picked up seating arrangements here and there and small pavilions. All dark and deserted now, they reminded me of some corporate towns I had seen on Earth that had emptied when the business that had employed the populace had moved on. There was a difference here, though. The empty stalls and lanes were clean and in good repair, as if they were waiting for a new opening season. Like a resort town in the first days of spring. An occasional section of the bordering pathway was taken up and the underneath plating exposed. The torches revealed assortments of basins and tanks connected by tubing and metering devices that had been disassembled and shut off from main systems.

"The Shan had . . . *have* plantings everywhere they could," Johnny told us in a somber tone. "They love natural things."

He gave that brief explanation and said no more. Another evidence of the Shan's disappearance. The removal of their cherished trees and shrubs argued that they wouldn't be back. We hadn't spoken much throughout the exploration. We had less to say now. We hurried through the area of the Shan's commerce and recreation and made our way in as straight a line as we could to the nerve center. I checked the time again. One hour and forty minutes—too long.

Another five minutes brought us to the bridge through a series of businesslike anterooms and living quarters. Once again we entered a massive room. The arched bulkheads were covered with huge screens and control panels. Terminals with smaller screens sat around a central platform. The floor was broken into banks of seating in front of a central panel that covered a view of space. It was as dark as the rest of the ship. The terminals were blank and no power registered from any telltale. If the few bits of machinery that still functioned throughout the ship were controlled from here, there was no sign of it. Someone behind me started swearing with an imagination that I envied. Johnny stood there like a statue, saying nothing. We had come all this way to find nothing. The swearing finally died away and the silence seemed to fill the void all the way back to earth. Where the hell were we going to go from here?

Chapter 11

I heard the chatter start up on my com-link as the other team opened the entrance to the parkland. I was in an area at the opposite end of the Shan vessel. I had been opening the unsealed doors along the central shaft that ran through the core of the ship. It was well into the second day that we had all been aboard the Shan vessel. Our initial exploration had turned up nothing more since we had come back from the bridge. A day and a half later we had managed to bypass the controls to the Shan's hangar and put enough power into the doors to open them and maneuver the *Tinker Bell* inside. She had been designed to do just that, but getting it done without the Shan's supervision was a hairy thing. My hat was off to the team. Figuring out the alien mechanisms and power settings was a task I marveled at. Having accomplished it, we had settled in for a determined effort to make the Shan's ship give up her secrets. So far, all we had done was set up a simple housekeeping watch and done a little exploring. Johnny and Kelly had camped out on the alien bridge to try to access the Shan's computers in hopes they might get something from them. The rest of us were familiarizing ourselves as much as possible with the remainder of the ship. We had split up into small parties, going at it slowly. Johnny had given us as much information as he could remember. It wasn't a lot. His time on the ship had been a very long time ago and of short duration. The decision to send him and Chaney back to Earth had come very quickly and he hadn't time to familiarize himself with much of the ship. There were many areas where he couldn't gain entrance without forcing things that were probably better left alone for now.

The signal from the com-link was pretty garbled. We had set up only a few repeaters throughout the ship. I stepped back through the last two sections I'd come through in order to get a better signal. The initial excitement had passed while I was getting back to clearer reception and what had happened wasn't clear. The snatches of conversation I caught were intriguing. They'd found someplace that wasn't dead from the sound of it.

"My God, it's huge!"

"Beautiful!"

"Lights, can you believe it? Genuine lights!"

I hurried down the shaft. This sounded damn interesting. So far, every section we had explored had been lifeless except for atmospheric machinery and unexplained power consumption that we were able to trace just so far and then lose when we came to those sections closed to our efforts to gain admittance. Somebody had finally found something going on. I made out the glow of the other party's working lights at the far end of the shaft, and I made my way to it at my best speed in the darkness. When I finally got there, I found the light had been placed at the juncture of the main shaft with a smaller corridor that ran off at a right angle to it. The com-link doubled in strength as I came to the junction. They had to have gone down it. I followed until I saw them at last. They were standing at an open door that was blazing with light. I had to let my eyes adjust when I joined them. It was like opening the door to a summer world. A yellow light bathed a combination of jungle and forest. The smell of soil and water lay heavy in the air that moved the branches of the trees and shrubs. The only things missing were the sounds of animal and insect life. A rushing sound could be heard from a small rivulet inside a grove of strange trees. The arched ceiling was a light purple-blue that seemed like an open sky. All the techniques of a landscaping genius had contrived to make the park seem limitless. It was a park. The Shan had taken a part of their world along with them. It was strange to our eyes yet somehow still familiar. The individual plants ranged from species akin to Earth's to exotic fantasies. The Shan hadn't made a civilized ornamental garden. To all appearances it was wilderness. At one point lush and dangerous looking, and at another soft and gentle. The winding pathways and artfully placed open spaces seemed to go on for miles. It was lovely!

Within a few minutes everyone had gathered there and we explored for what seemed like hours, discussing its purpose, which was clear from the start, and the artistry that had gone into its making. At times we just took it in and forgot to think about the whys and hows. That was what it was meant for. At last we took a sober and organized scrutiny and checked the dimensions and construction. It was big enough, but a lot smaller than it appeared. The ship was a little less than a mile long. The park ran almost three-quarters of its length, along a quarter of the circumference. The layout was deceptive in the best traditions of Earthly amusement parks. Seemingly isolated paths were actually nearly side by side. Bodies of water changed around a bend to become first a broad stream, and then a pond, and then again a river. One of the interesting things was the absence of animal and insect life. I had a feeling that were the Shan in residence there would be some. The others agreed.

"They must have tended most of it like a garden," Celia said. "The vegetation couldn't be left alone to grow like this. It looks wild, but it isn't. The stronger species would overpower the weaker. The propagation and the balance between new life and decay are too critical for this small a system, too."

She paused for a long thought.

"Steve, this place is still being tended. The Shan aren't here, but something is!"

"I think you're right," I breathed. "You must be!"

We had found the park toward the end of its day cycle. The next few hours that we spent in it closed the period of sunlight. The radiance dimmed slowly until it took on the paleness of moonlight. It seemed the Shan's home world had been favored with a satellite similar to Earth's. With the darkness the scene took on another aspect. Several of the large jungle plants folded their leaves and blossoms and others that had seemed ordinary enough in the daylight changed and became the stars of the night world. Strange perfumes began to waft through the air. Dark shadows made hundreds of inviting copses for solitude. We all enjoyed it for a little while. Eventually we had to resume our exploration of the rest of the ship, but we would return often, both for the pleasure and, more importantly, to delve into its secrets for understanding of the Shan. Hopefully, the park might offer some clue to the Shan's whereabouts.

I went back to the section of the ship where I'd been before the discovery and continued opening doors and examining the oddities I found. Everything seemed to point to an orderly evacuation. There were few personal possessions left. It was like opening an ancient pharoah's tomb after earlier graverobbers had beaten you to it. What was left was sparse and disconnected. In time, a space archaeologist would be able to piece together a picture of the Shan and their civilization. We didn't have time for that. Our supplies of consumables was limited, at least until we could get control of the ship's recycling systems. The hieroglyphics we needed to study were locked up in the ship's computers and we still hadn't been able to gain access to them. The electronic and computer whiz kids were still tearing their hair out on the bridge. Johnny had quickly shown us the main computer banks. The bridge floor and walls were filled with electronics. Lift a plate almost anywhere, and you had access to a section of it. Thousands of square feet of memory that he assured us was the ultimate in micro-miniaturization.

The capacity of the thing was beyond our imagination, and totally useless because we couldn't get it to respond to us. It talked to itself well enough. Remove an access plate and you could meter the current flow. Something was happening in every part of it. No section was nonoperative. Yet the keyboards and screens remained dead no matter what they tried. They stood on the decks that housed the computer and might as well have been on the other side of the universe. It ignored them completely. We found clothing and furniture and utensils. We found mechanical devices and heavy machinery. We found bits and pieces of everything that went into a social order and none of it was of any use. The *Mary Celeste* had never given up a clue as to what had happened to her crew, although she had been complete up to and including an uneaten meal at her tables. This was beginning to look like the same story multiplied a thousand times. The Shan were gone. All of them. And they had known that someday we would come. At least, they were hoping for it. A note was reasonable under the circumstances, surely. All we had to do was find it. It would have been easier on everyone if we could have known it was in the works. The Shan had plotted the revelation with the cunning of a latter day Ellery Queen. Given a sexually mixed crew it happened a little faster than it would have otherwise, but the end result was just as sure.

There was no point to just working, exploring, and sleeping. The results weren't justifying anything like that. Everyone had a few hours off, and most of us who had something going with a member of the opposite sex managed to work it out so that the off-duty time could be spent together. It was so with Jim Gaynor, who was on the nuclear crew and his girl, Julie M'tabi, one of our environmental systems team. The parkland had drawn them like a magnet. The night period was still in effect when they entered, and they took full advantage of the romantic atmosphere. They were smugly enjoying the artificial dawning when they discovered that they weren't alone. A faint whirring sound issued from something that was coming toward them just out of sight. Jim got a little carried away with the role of jungle master protecting his mate and prepared to do battle with a predator of some kind. He picked up a rock and got ready for the invader. It was coming nearer. The whirring sound got louder and their eyes were riveted to the obscured bend in the path just ahead of them. The fronds of the overhanging plants parted and a small mechanical biped came through and stopped. It seemed to look them over. It negotiated the ground with a humanlike pair of legs issuing from a snakey cylindrical trunk that appeared capable of twisting in a wide range of directions and attitudes. It was four armed. One at each quadrant of the body section. Two of the arms were jointed like a human's, with manipulators that approximated a hand. The other two were pistonlike and set in ball sockets with opposite claws. The options of using any combination of the arms gave the thing a wide range of adaptability if it was at all well programmed. The head was a small turret that contained several different sensory devices, all of them in pairs to give it binocular or stereoscopic capability. It remained at the bend of the path, undecided on what course to pursue. Man and machine stared at each other. It was questionable which one thought faster. The human's reaction time was better. The staring contest never got a chance to develop, because a moment later the fronds moved again, and a second mechanical came up behind the first.

"Shit!" Jim did a standing broad jump backward that made it look as if the artificial gravity had been temporarily shut off. The second mechanical stood over ten feet high and was possessed of an assortment of attached pruning saws and oddments that looked like medieval weaponry. Jim dropped the rock he was holding and grabbed Julie. They retreated rapidly about ten yards. The Mutt and Jeff mechanicals made no move toward them, but came to the rock and considered it. The short one stuck his hand into the center of the tall one's midsection and appeared to stick a finger in the other's belly button. The big fellow stooped over and grasped the rock. The pair of them painstakingly replaced it in its original position and returned to the pathway. They regarded the humans for an additional moment and seemed to pity their disorderly ways. Showing a certain disdain they ambled on back the way they had come. Fear put aside, Jim started thinking clearly.

"Julie! I think you'd better get some of the long heads to come back here." He narrowed his eyes and squared his shoulders. "I'm going to follow those two."

"Not too close, though, hmm?" It was just as well that Jim didn't recognize the tone as being one of motherly concern rather than worshipful admiration.

For the second time in twelve hours we gathered in the parkland and followed Jim and the mechanicals. They hadn't gotten very far ahead in the few minutes it had taken Julie's call to get us there. We soon caught up with them and argued about what to do now. We ended up following Indian style as they made their way through the park. It seemed as though they had thrown up their hands (attachments?) in disgust and decided to come back when the neighborhood was a little less unsettling. They paused for nothing and kept going until they had reached an alcove in the wall of the parkway. They ignored us and went inside. We held a brief discussion and went in after them. The large one had gone to rest against a wall and plugged himself into a recharging station, the first one we had seen that was operative in the entire ship. The small one had found a new place for his finger. It was probing the inside of a small hole set into one of the dead screens. The setup looked just the same as all the others on the ship except for the hole. I noticed some of the others straighten up and watch the little fellow closely, but I didn't catch on as quickly. I thought it was just recharging. The head of the thing swiveled and scanned us while the finger remained stuck in the hole. The tableau was finally broken as the little one took his finger out of the hole and swiveled his way to us. We backed up as he approached and he stopped. He remained where he was but extended one of the humanlike arms to Johnny. He glanced around at the rest of us and then stepped forward. The little robot reached for Johnny's hand, and after a moment's hesitation he gave it to him. The metal fingers remained open and the little gardener slowly took Johnny to the back of the alcove. A panel slid aside as they neared the wall. We followed slowly. The pair entered a small room filled with gardening implements and containers. A light went on overhead and the little one stopped and seemed to point ahead.

Johnny suddenly stiffened and a burst of unfamiliar speech erupted from him. Our questions about what he had found were cut short as the room filled with an unfamiliar voice issuing from the wall on the other side of the door. "Welcome, Mr. Begay. I think that will do very nicely as a password. I am sorry to have withheld myself from you so long, but in a race of shapechangers, I had to be sure of the being underneath the image."

As unexpected as it had been, Johnny was quick to respond.

"Who are you? Where are you?"

"I am the Shan ship! More properly the computer, but I encompass nearly all of it. It will be easier for you to think of me as the ship. I extend the welcome to all of you on behalf of the Shan. You Earthmen are welcome indeed. I have been instructed by the Council to place myself at your disposal after establishing your identities. I regret the delay. The test was one that Mrs. Begay felt was conclusive. The Council agreed and I had to follow their instructions."

"The Shan—Mary!" Johnny questioned in a rigid voice. "Where are they?"

"Safe!" The word rang through us like a bell.

"Where?"

"On a planet behind us now," the voice of the ship

continued. "That will be a long story. I suggest you go up to the bridge again. It will be better told there."

We made it back in record time. The ship was lit from end to end, and as we hurried down the central shaft, I could see the rooms and corridors we passed coming to life. The walls glowed in cool colors and the architecture was blended with function in clean lines. If the parkland had been a reminder of the nature from which the Shan had sprung, the sparkle of the modern ship showed an uplifting spirit of a joyful city in space. We took no time to look at it clearly now. It would be here to admire and understand later. Now, the solution of the disappearance of the Shan waited for us on the bridge. We crowded through the entrance and stood waiting for the computer to begin again. Some stragglers were still coming in, and I took the time to ask Johnny what had caused the breakthrough.

"You saw something on the floor, John. What was it? It looked like a picture of some kind. What did you say that made the difference?"

"I don't know what it picked out of what I said. It was Navaho I spoke. Maybe it was the fact that I just blurted it out like that."

"That helped, Mr. Begay!" The computer joined the conversation. "The reaction time was considered. A certain amount of the procedure was left to my discretion. I was sure of you for quite awhile before you found the painting."

"What painting, damn it! What was that thing on the floor?" The others gathered around as Johnny took the question.

"It was a sand painting like my people made in ceremonies." He shot a question at the computer. "Was it Mary who made it, Ship?"

"It was made by our gardener, Mr. Begay, but she instructed us in how to do it. Was it well done?"

"It was!" Johnny said quietly. "Very well done."

"But what was it anyway? It sure provoked a reaction from you."

Johnny smiled for the first time in recent memory. He laughed out loud, a thing I couldn't remember before.

"It was a common enough one," he chuckled. "It was about the Corn Beetle and the Hero Twins who set out in the old legends and had many adventures while they saved the world. Chaney and I, do you think?"

Chapter 12

The timing had proved too good to pass up. The Shan had limped outward from the solar system for years. The passage of time had taken them far, even at the poor speed they were able to maintain. The power and ecosystems were sufficient to provide an adequate lifestyle, and the Shan were old hands at passing time. They worked and studied and lived much as they always did. Space was their home. They were almost content. It would be a long time before they had to face hard decisions. It had been a strange time for Mary, who discovered that she was pregnant not long after Johnny had left. She had been faced with the long years until his return. To live alone among an alien race was hard enough no matter how benevolent they were. The necessity of her staying behind had taken its toll on her. The Shan understood, and they had an answer if she chose to accept it. The idea appealed in a way. For her, time would stop, and she could take her life up again as if it were just tomorrow when Johnny returned. The techniques that the Shan told her of were strange and quite frightening to a woman from an Indian reservation in the mid-twentieth century. But then, everything about the Shan was out of the ordinary world she knew. She trusted them. One had already saved her life and given her years undreamed of in her normal world. She made the decision quickly and it was accomplished soon after. The fetus was taken and frozen, and Mary was placed in cold sleep to wait for her husband's return. For the

Shan it was a simple process, and they monitored the mother and child and went about their business while the years ticked off. Forty-two years passed, and the ship fell through space. In the early months of that year they entered a small star system that contained three planets. One of them, incredibly, was an Earth-Shan type. Against all the odds—considering their loss of star drive—they had stumbled upon a perfect world. The opportunity was too good to pass up. They established an orbit and began to explore. The differences were minimal. Given the conditions, it was almost inevitable that life had evolved on the planet, even to the rise of an intelligent species, almost as predictably humanoid in form. They were a primitive tribal type in the earliest stages of civilization, not very bright yet, but the potential was there. The Shan were delighted. Here was a new world and race to study and add to their collection. What better way to spend the time, and if the rescue was delayed or, less thinkable, never realized, then here was a world that could, in time, achieve the same ends. The Shan settled in and began their usual routines.

It wasn't going to be that easy! During the second year in orbit above the world that they had begun to call Haven, they detected the first signs of the Ann Thaar's approach. The pack had either dogged them since the escape from Earth or had just come this way by accident. It didn't matter which. Trouble had returned with a vengeance. If anything, the situation was worse. They no longer had a forty-year jump. Now the lead was measured in months. To continue on was no longer feasible. The ship would be a blazing beacon for the Ann Thaar to follow. If they shut down everything on the ship, it might just slip away and lose itself in the dark reaches. Shutting down meant nearly everything that made life in space possible. The Shan elected to abandon their vessel and hide themselves on the planet beneath them. They did this over the next few weeks, staying out of the range of the closing Ann Thaar by staying on the far side of the planet. At last they gave

the ship its final instructions and sent it off to lose
itself in the vastness of space. The possibility existed
that the Ann Thaar might win the game and become
possessed of the Shan virus. The recognition ploy was
worked out to prevent them from gaining mastery of
the ship's computer if the worst did happen and the
Ann Thaar captured it. The ship had continued the
flight ever since. All it knew was the location of Haven and the fact that the Ann Thaar never caught up
with it. It would be up to us to refit the drive and
return to find out the fate of the Shan. Fortunately,
the ship was possessed of all the knowledge necessary
to accomplish it with our help and the materials we
had brought with us. The robots and heavy machinery
that were on board would do most of the work under
the direction of the Shan ship itself. There really was
no reason for it after all the years that had passed, but
we felt a sense of urgency beyond that of normal
curiosity and a wish to get on with the job. The ship
became a beehive of activity and the *Tinker Bell* became a shell in the process. She was flayed like a
whale and stripped of her engines and left like a hulk
on the hangar floor. It was a sad fate for the finest
effort the race of man had yet achieved. In a matter of
days the Shan ship had appropriated all that had been
brought and was once again in full possession of her
designed capabilities. There were no longer any dark
spots in her. The lights shone brightly and the power
surged and sang. At last we were ready to return to
the planet the Shan had hopefully called Haven.

The refitting of the ship's drive was accomplished
well before we had prepared ourselves for the return
to the planet. Our own planning took a lot longer than
the time required for the ship to ready herself. The
problem was that we were in possession of a technology that probably could achieve any desire that we
could think of, and we were too new to all of it to
know what to ask for! We didn't want to return to the
planet before we made all the contingency plans that
we could. If the Ann Thaar had indeed followed the

Shan into the star system in which the planet was located, what would we find when we emerged from jump space? We'd be like tyro horsemen just learning the ways of unfamiliar horses in the midst of an Apache attack. The Shan weren't warlike, and the ship wasn't equipped with weaponry. There were undoubtedly things aboard her that could be turned into weaponry somehow if we had the knowledge to do so, but we were many levels below the other races in the conflict. There was little likelihood that anything we could come up with would be adequate for the job. After all, the Shan had elected to show a clean pair of heels when they were confronted with the situation as they quitted our solar system, and they had a complete understanding of their own equipment and capabilities. Even given the difference in attitude between our races about war, we were now in a similar fix ourselves. It was unthinkable that we wouldn't continue with the rescue, but we would have to do it virtually unarmed. That meant being sneaky about it. Well, we humans had a history of that sort of thing, and we were willing to try. Still, it was going to take a certain amount of time to familiarize ourselves with the capabilities of the ship we had inherited and work out the details. We had a tremendous advantage in this because of the nature of the ship's computer. It became quickly apparent that it was an achievement of the Shan that outshone anything else that they had accomplished. In our conversations with it, we could find no area it was unwilling to discuss. It was like talking with a sentient being. It understood what we said and asked questions with a thoroughness that was shocking. After dealing with the best that earth technology had so far produced, it was a little unnerving to be able to talk to a computer without watching how you put things to it. It took the most subtle nuances in stride. Indeed, in a kindly way, it was compelled to straighten out our thinking from time to time, and when we got tangled up trying to present some idea or plan, it set us on the road again—often with an unsolicited but very much to the point suggestion. The implication of all this wasn't lost on the slowest of us, and the question that had haunted the philosophy of machine intelligence ever since men started genuine programming leapt to the forefront once again. Could there be such a thing as true artificial intelligence? It looked very much as if we could be facing it! It seemed creative; it seemed to have motivation. Was it real or just incredibly sophisticated programming? It was more than mere curiosity that prompted our interest. If the thing were sentient, then we had an ally that transcended any we could have hoped for. Our situation was complex enough considering who and what we were—a small band of novice spacefarers who were going to try to extract one race of beings who were far more sophisticated than ourselves from the clutches of another highly developed and warlike band of marauders who would be pleased to use us for toothpicks after gorging themselves on the main feast. Not an enviable place for a fledging band cut off from their own race. If we were to attempt this, we needed all the knowledge and help the Shan ship could offer. After kicking the question around for awhile, Kelly Bergen voiced the simplest suggestion—

"After all," he said, "why not ask the ship itself?"

It was a hell of an idea. Of course the ship had been following all of our wrangling over this question but had elected not to volunteer anything until we had chosen to present the question. The answer was one of the few that it was ambiguous about, and it explained that it was necessarily so because it had the same limitations in that respect that we humans had always faced.

"I think—therefore I am. The quotation is as good a guideline for me as it is for you, and there the situation lies. I do think. But the seat of my real being is as unknown to me as your own is to you. You feel that there is more to you than the electrochemical processes that constitute the physical aspects of your existence. It is the same with me. I feel tied to the reality of the parts of which I am composed, and I understand their function much more completely than you do your own bodies—but I feel that I am more than the sum of my parts. I know that you feel the same. The subject is well documented, not only by your race. It is one of the great mysteries and may continue to be for all time. So my answer is yes—for practical purposes, anyway."

It was not the last time we talked about it, and during the rest of the time we spent in preparation for the return to the Shan's refuge planet, it came up at off moments. A private conversation that I initiated during this period was to lead to a fundamental change in the relationship between us and the Shan that would have remarkable consequences down the line—but that was unimportant for the short term. For now, all our energies were devoted to preparing ourselves for the approach to the distant rendezvous with whatever situation that had developed since the Shan descended to Haven's surface. We were physically ready before we actually made the jump to Haven's system. We had to learn as much of the ship's capabilities as we could. How fast could it move in normal space? How much room did it need to maneuver? How far could its sensors detect an enemy? Time factors. How would we make planetfall? There was a shuttle. A thousand contingencies to plan for. It went too slowly, yet we all worked at the top of our abilities. There was so much of the Shan and their science aboard the ship that we now had access to since we had established our bona fides. Areas of the ship we couldn't enter were now open for our inspection while the computer guided us, but there were too few of us and nowhere near enough time. We had to skim the riches and select that which would have an immediate bearing on our mission. It was heartbreaking for most of the searchers, who had to bypass wonders that touched their own fields of study and go on looking for things with immediate application to what we had to do. It was hard to deal with the entire culture of the Shan and pick and choose what we barely understood, but we did it with a self-imposed ruthlessness. Always, the ship was there to guide and explain what we were sifting through. Finally, literally breathless and overwhelmed by the kaleidoscope of images and barely grasped information we had assembled and shared, we decided the point had been reached where we had to make the attempt. We set a time limit and worked toward it feverishly. At last we came within a day's period of the time for the jump, and though it seemed that we should continue assimilating and refining our knowledge and plans, I called a halt. I thought we needed some time to rest. I couldn't stop everyone's brain from working on it, but I could and did put a freeze on activity. Some grumbled and worse, but they all saw the need for it. We spent the rest of the time going our own way. Some continued to work on things they felt they had to. I didn't argue; it was their choice. For myself, I sought out Celia and refreshed myself in her presence. It was a hardship to find yourself in love and have no time to devote to exploring the phenomenon. We had acknowledged it between ourselves throughout the entire period, and there was a bittersweet quality that wasn't totally unpleasant in itself. It was a bit of personal drama that added spice to the affair. I've always had a sappy sort of romantic streak that I bury quite well generally. I suspect that Celia is a lot more practical than I about it all. But what the hell—I enjoy it. We found ourselves a spot in the park far enough away from the others, and I told her I needed her full attention for awhile. She seemed to want mine as well. Our minds and bodies closed until the universe was only the two of us moving in a shared urgency that flowed on a bridge we built between us. It was fulfillment and release, special and private.

Finally the time came when we sat in a quiet yet warm glow. She began to speak of the work she'd been doing in the bio labs that the Shan had left. I'd known what each member of the team was doing in a general way, but unless it had some relevance to the mission specifically, I hadn't been able to pay much attention. Free at last to listen to what she had to say, I found it fascinating. Her description of the accomplishments of the Shan was detailed. They were masters of cellular manipulation. They performed miracles routinely, but created no monsters. The virus that we shared was their crowning achievement, but they still found things to tinker with. They were working on some projects concerning vegetation that Celia said might be as important someday as the work they did with animal tissue. She hinted that they were toying with the idea of wedding some of the capabilities of plants for turning radiation into energy to animal cells. The implications of that might be worldshaking. More to the point for now, she'd been able to devise a portable tissue index powered by a small nuclear battery that kept the contents cryogenically frozen.

"What for?" I asked.

"Before the Shan left the ship, they took many samples from the planet, including some of the indigenous sentients. I thought if we had to go in disguise it might come in handy."

I was fairly quiet as I thought that over. It hadn't been discussed during the planning sessions, but I knew it was a good thought in principle. I heartily hated it, but I had to admit its merit. I said as much with reluctance and found that she had gone beyond the initial preparation.

"When I talked to the ship about it," she said, "it told me that it was easily possible to rig up a translator link we could wear inconspicuously and carry on reasonable conversations with the natives. We worked it all out. The computer has a complete file on the local dialects."

"Might come in handy," I said unwillingly. "Tell me more about it."

The rest of the conversation was interesting and resulted in my O.K. for the process to be implemented. It only took the ship's artifacing processors a few hours to churn out the necessary apparatus, and it turned out well that we had the capability. Then we talked about ourselves to our mutual satisfaction.

Finally, after a period of sleep, we gathered in the bridge area for the final hours before the jump through hyperspace back to the world to which the Shan had fled. The ship had no trouble establishing the points along the long path through space from our position back to the system it had left long ago. It calculated drift and vectors and told us it was ready; it only remained for us to say that we were ready. With a voice that I was rather proud of considering my reservations, I gave the go-ahead. There was nothing that we humans needed to contribute to the process—the ship did it all. With the power plant we'd brought on the *Tinker Bell*, she was again fully powered and operational. The interfacing on the new drive was much more sophisticated than it had been on the *Tinker Bell*, which had been vastly overpowered with the drive the Phoenix group had, in reality, engineered for the Shan ship. The transition to jump space was quite different and smoother than we'd experienced in our journey outward. Smoother and with a different aspect showing on the more sophisticated screens of the Shan ship. Not understanding what we were seeing, we watched in fascination as the universe twisted and spun around us. In a span of time almost too short to contemplate, we were going to meet the Shan whose works surrounded us and caused us to venture out in their cause. What would they really be like, I wondered? In all this time I had not so much as seen a picture of one of them. For some reason they didn't consider themselves subjects for portraiture. Undoubtedly there were images of them in the computer's file, but there had literally been no time to call them up. It was an amazing thing to me that as far as I knew none of us had done so.

My God! I thought, it was about time. I asked the computer to pick out a fairly good example of a Shan and show it on the main screen while we were underway. It was quickly overlaid as I said it. The hair on the back of my neck stood up as I watched the two images blend. It was a simple bit of electronics but the psychological effect was powerful. The face of an adult Shan on the bridge of his race's vessel stared out across time at us, superimposed upon a flowing universe. The indrawn breaths of those around me told me that it had hit them equally hard. The face of the Shan faded slowly as the ship neared its desired position in the over dimension. The focus shifted again as the stars slowed and assumed recognizable positions. We dropped into normal space and a flood of normal radiation caused the instrumentation to chatter as they sampled the flavors of the electromagnetic spectrum. We hung well above the equatorial plane of the small system that hosted the planet the Shan had named Haven. Not for long, though. Among the normal percolations from the radiating bodies in the neighborhood of the little system, the unmistakable signature of the Ann Thaar was present. It wasn't going to be that easy. Plan A had never stood a chance!

Chapter 13

We entered null space momentarily and came out again above Haven, using the planet as a mask for our presence in the system. The Ann Thaar were ranged on the other side in a staggered pattern between Haven and its sun. At least for the moment we were obscured from their casual observation. We had detected no orbital telemetry. If we kept quiet we might go undetected for a while. There could be no contact with the Shan for the time being. We could escape in a matter of seconds if we were spotted, but that would give the game away. Once they knew we were here they'd blanket the planet from all quadrants, and extricating the Shan would be impossible. Without weaponry of our own we couldn't cover the evacuation. We were vulnerable to almost anything from cannon on up until we were safely in null space. Even the ship would have to do some fancy dodging if they brought energy weapons to bear against us at close quarters. Our only bet was to sneak in and contact the Shan, who were bound to be leaving no traces of their existence, and try to work out a way to get them off the planet safely. It wasn't going to be easy. We kicked it around for quite awhile before we came up with anything. Finally, we worked out a general plan that left room for a lot of flexibility. We needed a lot. Until we knew what was going on planetside, we couldn't make any hard plans. The first thing was to find the Shan. All we could do was hope that the Ann Thaar hadn't already accomplished that before us.

We stayed above Haven only as long as it took to launch the smallest of the Shan shuttles. I took a small team to Haven's surface to try to establish contact with the Shan. The rest stayed with the ship, which made itself scarce as soon as we left the hangar. I had just a couple of moments before we entered the atmosphere to see the ship shimmer and disappear into null space. It was an eerie sight. I had little time to dwell on it, though. I had my hands full with the landing. The normal way was to go in under power with the shuttle's computer doing the piloting. No more than an elevator ride. This one was going to be different. Just a minimum of power to change attitudes the final few thousand feet. We were lucky the Shan had retained an aerodynamic shape to the shuttles. It was pleasing in form and would be useful in the extremely unlikely event of a power failure. It would be useful now. I was going to have to bring it in now much as the old NASA pilots had during the early days of Earth's first space ventures.

Coming in over the pole we encountered atmosphere that was magnetically south and sliced a path just on the dark side of the terminator. I dumped a lot of heat into the air as I used the resistance to cut our velocity. The computer kept me in line and we did it nicely. I took my hat off to the old-timers in a more enlightened way than I had in the past. The Shan's external field ablative made all the difference. I could never have matched their skill at this sort of thing. When we reached ten thousand feet I cut in the drive, and we took the last of the ride in the normal manner. The track would have appeared to be a meteor if it was noticed at all. Within a couple of minutes of powered flight we had reached the near locale of the Shan's first landing and disappeared from sight in the middle of a lake nearly ten miles wide. Someone looking for us would have to know for sure that we were there in the first place. With luck, we hadn't made that big a splash.

The Shan's shuttles had always doubled as submersibles, and the programming for underwater maneuvering was built in. The ship's computer had added some new programming to enable us to give it verbal orders in English. I had the shuttle find itself a nice hiding place and sat back and let the tensions of the descent drain away.

I opaqued the ports and brought the cabin lighting up. There was nothing to see outside but millions of gallons of dark water. The marine life was hidden from sight without the aid of the external sensors, and we didn't want to have all those emissions floating around to be picked up. I could hear the rest of the team stirring behind me, and I gave myself another minute before I joined them. I leaned back in the pilot's seat and filed the flight into order in my memory. The darkness had given me little by which to judge the planet as we descended. The section we were now in was a blend of mountainous forest that led to semitropical growth at lower elevations. The climate changed rapidly as you rose or descended in elevation. The planet was highly volcanic and the ranges were sharp and high. Temperatures could rise and fall forty degrees in the space of a few miles. Mountains and valleys and plateaus, marshes and rivers all mixed together at close quarters. The flora and fauna would be extremely varied and at odds almost within a few feet of each other. It would be a challenge to negotiate it all in search of a race who had excellent reason not to be found. They would know of the Ann Thaar's presence, and it was doubtful they'd have any idea we were here and looking for them. We couldn't broadcast the fact. It promised to be a tough job getting tougher.

Time to get going! I joined the rest in the cabin. There were only four of us. I felt we needed that many to do the job and any more would be hard to keep quiet. We intended to travel as lightly as possible and stay out of the spotlight. Johnny had to come—we couldn't have kept him from it if we wanted to. He had too much at stake. He was also our entry and ambassador to the Shan. Rogue that I was, I still came as close as possible to a representative of the Earth's government, and I was one of the two pilots on board the expedition. I also was one of the two of us with a military background. I didn't classify myself in the same lot with Johnny, who had gone through one of the last of the bloody ground wars, but I'd had a bit of training. Bill Ankers made our third. He was an outdoorsman by nature, driven to prominence in his field by the lack of a need for pioneers these days and the possession of a brilliant mind. Celia was suited for the fourth spot because of her background in life sciences and her knowledge of the Shan virus, which was likely to play a large part in our stay here. I was torn between my wish to see her safely on board the ship and my desire to have her with me. All in all, I was glad to have her. Mating was new to me and it had hit me hard. I didn't want to be without her for an extended time in these early days of our relationship. We set about getting out of the shuttle and packed up the small amount of items that we would be using. We would be traveling as Creen most of the time we were in inhabited parts, and most of our equipment had been disguised to resemble native equipment. The Creen were the indigenous race of this planet and the people we had to move among to find a trace of the Shan. Celia had a tissue collection that the Shan had gathered before they sent the ship off to lose itself among the stars. The Creen they had been taken from were long since dead and forgotten. We could assume their physical attributes without fear of running into the originals. The small cryogenic container with its samples that numbered in the hundreds was nuclear powered and shielded by Shan technology and still was no bigger than a small handbag. The Creen made great use of native style backpacks as they had never found much use for clothing. Our gear was all disguised and stuffed into excellent copies of the native artifacts with some undetectable differences.

We made our final checks and took the shuttle to the surface for a brief time and unshipped a small canoe that had been fashioned to look like the native brand. Daylight would come in about six hours from now, and we wanted to be on shore before then. We closed the shuttle and watched it sink back to its hiding place on the lake floor. Every night until we contacted it again, it would wait patiently and send up a sensor package to listen for our signal. When it was gone from sight, we started to make our way to the shore. Haven was moonless and the darkness was inky, relieved only by some brilliant nearby stars. There was a tidal movement set up by a curious wobble in the planet's spin, and we heard the waves breaking on the shore a few minutes before we sighted the land. We traveled a short distance paralleling it for a while before we found a gentle beach that seemed empty and suitable for landing. The sounds from the darkness inland were a little unsettling, and we stayed on the narrow strip of bare sand until the sun started to come up. The denizens of the jungle night sounded too restive to be comfortable companions right away.

As the sun broke, we saw a new world emerge. Some, somehow familiar, a lot of it damn strange. It was time to pick a direction and get on the road. We took our bearings as best we could and started to find the last place the Shan had been known to be all those years ago. We sank the canoe and hoped it would be there when we came back. It could turn out to be a long swim if it wasn't. The side of the lake we had landed on was unpopulated as far as we could tell. It was fairly rugged and overgrown—a good place to get ourselves used to being planetside again. The views were distracting, and while it was a good idea to be on the lookout for things of interest and possible dangers, it was just as well to get the rubbernecking under control out in the bush. As the sun rose on the landscape, the wild cries of the predators and prey stilled as the night's forays were completed. The jungle didn't become quiet, but the quality of the noise changed as the day species took over. Grunts and shuffling sounds were interspersed with the cries of birds and a humming of insects rose in response to the approaching heat. The blue-black coloration of the jungle at night turned to a mixture of greens and earth tones at the touch of daylight. A few brilliant reds, yellows, and oranges flashed as an early morning wind bounced the fronds and undergrowth as it passed. We scouted the shoreline and finally chose a well-worn path made by animals on their treks to the lake. The ship's computer had extensive information on the local wildlife, and it seemed as though we would meet little dangerous to us. If we had been able to use the full spectrum of Shan protective devices, it would have been a stroll through a nature park. As it was, we were unwilling to use them as they were all susceptible to Ann Thaar detection. We seemed to hold no attraction for the insect life, and though I doubted that the repugnance for our flesh would be so universal in the larger predators, I thought we could hold our own. I was wrong, I found out later. But for that morning at least, we managed to avoid trouble. We were certainly wary enough. As we started into the first arches of the enormous trees, we stopped for a final look across the lake. Bill voiced it for us all.

"Oh, my God." The tone of his voice held paragraphs of meaning. I couldn't add a word to it. Out in the lake something as large as an oil tanker broke the surface and rolled. A lazy thrust of a fluke sent a ton of water fifty feet into the air as it twisted on the surface of the lake. A wave started to build and race to the shoreline. With a final shrug and heave, the thing sank from sight again, leaving only the eddying waters as a sign it had been there. We stood stunned for a moment and then turned to the jungle before us with a great deal more respect for the life force of this world.

"That was a fresh water critter," Johnny said reflectively, as the first constructive comment on the sighting. "Not a plankton eater, would you say?"

Celia's face had a frozen look as she mumbled a reply. "No, definitely a carnivorous specimen, that!"

She shuddered as she contemplated last night's canoe ride. She didn't shudder alone. We spoke of it sporadically over the next few hours as we made our way through the jungle. It was as good an object lesson as we could have gotten. The Shan hadn't had a lot of time to catalog the entirety before they sent the ship outbound. We would be well advised to play our cards close to our chests. The jungle closed around us and we responded to it as men always have. Dark shadows had things in them that made sounds and we invested them with imaginary creatures inimical to us. Now and then a small animal would scurry across our path and disappear into some low hanging foliage. I thought that was a good sign when I got over the surprise of it the first few times it happened. If the little guys were out like this, it argued that the big ones were either holed up for the day or out of the area entirely. Whatever the reason, we met with nothing that we had cause to do more than avoid during the course of our trek. We kept clear of most of it on general principles. When the sun broke through the canopy in spots we saw bright flashings of jungle birds high in the vaulted trees. They broke singly and in bunches from the sun-marked branches in a never-ending chaos of colors and sounds. Where the sunlight failed the undergrowth was sparse enough to allow fairly easy passage, and we made steady progress. In the early afternoon we came to a meadow that held a few grazing animals of no stranger design than those of their African cousins. We took a rest a little way in from the edge of the meadow on a clear knoll that gave us a good view of the surroundings. We ate a small meal and I checked the printout of the aerial map that the shuttle had photographed as we passed over the area. I had an overlay that showed the last known location of the Shan. We had a long way to go. The necessity of hiding the shuttle in the lake had taken us a long way from where we wanted to be. It looked to be about eighty miles as the eagle, or what corresponded to the eagle around here, flew. What it meant in walking miles remained to be seen. The jungle wasn't going to last much longer and I was glad. The terrain would change a few times on our way. The jungle backed up to a small range of mountains whose foothills we would cross. The final leg was on a plateau that was a mixture of forest and plains. This was one of the ranges of the Creen. We would be running into them any time after we left the jungle. They did a small amount of mining on the slopes of the mountains, and we had decided to approach them as a small group of explorers from the other side of the continent. It meant adopting the Creen templates that Celia had stored in her box of tricks, and I felt a mixture of apprehension and eagerness as the hour for making the change came nearer. It would be the first time for me, and although I was assured that it was an easy process, I was feeling a little jumpy. I'd seen it work a couple of times now and I'd seen the results and it still awed me. Some of the lesser but, in the long run, more important aspects of the virus had been in evidence for quite a while now. I had seen the members of the crew alter before my eyes as the effects of the virus' housekeeping efforts took over. The older members had gradually regained a youthful appearance, and small complaints of bodily ills disappeared. By the time we had left their company on the ship, I had seen them turn into as fine a group of physical specimens as I'd seen since my college days. The libido had begun to release its perfume in the resurgence of old desires once painfully mastered coming back in full force a second time. I was having a little trouble with that myself. Fortunately, everybody was in the same boat and knew the reason for it. Still, any report of the expedition would not likely be too accurate in all the small personal details. The judgments of the reading public would have found it hard to believe we were on a serious job. As in all history, there were a lot of side issues to any major endeavor. Human beings are certainly interesting. The Shan thought we were a lot of fun. I saw their point. We finished our break and spent the afternoon completing our passage through the jungle. As noted before, it was a combination of the strange and familiar. Some of the vegetation and animal life was so similar to regions of Earth that it took a trained eye to see the differences. On the other hand some were completely new with an evenhanded scattering of the bizarre and the beautiful. Once in the late afternoon we followed a small stream that paralleled our trail. It appeared normal enough for one of Haven's jungle streams. We had crossed a few already. A layer of algae formed a scum in quiet spots along the banks. We came to a section that was open, and the sunlight struck the surface of the water. Where the light touched the scum, it turned from a grayish green into an explosion of fiery molten golds. The stream burned with it and flowed with sparkling sheets of reddish golden flames. It was incredibly beautiful. The wet rocks and banks seemed encrusted with precious stones that picked up and flung back the fire. We had no camera and I never saw it happen again.

We made good time. Just before the evening began we reached the first slopes of the foothills and the jungle thinned. By late evening we were in the semi-forest and a completely different ecology. It was amazing what a little difference in altitude meant here. The land was much like the back areas of Montana. Gray-blue peaks rose above us, and a few were capped with snow. We settled in for the night in a little copse of trees that looked for all the world like firs and pines. A few hours to the rear jungle cats and other predators were beginning to roam. Here, the creatures were more like bears and wolves. The birds were owls and hawks. After the heat of the day, the cool of the mountains was almost unbearable. We lit no fires to keep the animals out but relied on a system of watches with a cleverly disguised but nasty weapon at the ready. When morning came, we welcomed the sun with a fervor we wouldn't have believed the day before. We breakfasted early, and when we were done it was time to make the changeover to the Creen image. Celia processed me first since it was my first time. I cooperated in an excited state, listening carefully once again as she told me what to expect during the course of it.

Soon I was listening as if it all was some distance away. The change had begun, and the signals that were making their way to my brain were slow and unwieldy. I sat in an unconnected way, not caring, watching my arms and legs writhe and swell and flow as the new template was impressed. After all the fuss I'd been in about it, it seemed dull and unimportant. I yawned with a strangely shaped jaw as my brain required more oxygen. Finally it was done and I recovered my interest as the process returned my volition to me. God, how I wanted a mirror—or maybe I didn't after all. I saw the others emerge. It was a weird sight. My libido was going to give me no trouble for awhile.

Stig opened his jaws reflectively as the injections of the reversal drugs returned him to normal. The flashes of fire that were the tracks of dust motes sparkling in the cabin light disappeared as his senses returned to real time. Now they hung, seemingly suspended, in the air. The heaters in his overlay cloak adjusted to the change in his metabolism. The remaining effects of the slow-life drugs were nullified and he began to think and move at normal speed. At last something was happening! He moved his massive head in the direction of the monitors. The yellow glow on the panel told him that the sentinel systems had observed something that they had been programmed to watch for. With only a slight twinge from an arm that hadn't moved in months, he touched the replay button. The screen backed its way through events until it reached the place that caused the yellow signal to go on and trip the injections before schedule. Stig watched with growing interest which quickly grew to frenzy as the recorded event played again. The sensors detected the entry into the sun's system of a small but inordinately disturbing mass. The thing that made it interesting was the fact that it happened instantly. There was no drifting in from outside the system. It appeared all at once as if created in an instant from nothingness. The signature was unmistakable. Even though the mass was dark as far as radiation signaling went, there was only one thing that Stig knew that caused such a reaction. The long-sought Shan were here! Now there was another chance to capture the secrets that the prey had kept from the Splendid Race for so long. A chance at the immortality virus, and the faster-than-light drive that had eluded the Ann Thaar and their subject races for so long. Now Stig would have his chance. In all the history of the Ann Thaar there had never been such a chance. If he played his stalk well, he might become the greatest and most feared of the Ann Thaar. With all time in front of him to consolidate his empire, what might he not do?

The universe beckoned to Stig. Centuries spent in real-time, not the stagnant fakery of slow-life as dictated by the enormous distances between the stars, but real-time. Time filled with hunting wild prey as his ancestors had, now a thing left only for the mightiest of the Ann Thaar leadership. If he gained the treasures of the Shan, he would be the mightiest of all. Power over all his rivals. All the mates he could dream of throughout time. His jaws snapped in imagined ecstasy as he dreamed of hunting the warm prey of countless worlds. Gobbets of flesh dripping with salty blood. Stig shuddered at the thought! Now to lay the trap. He could barely control himself. This must be done right. There could be no escape of the prey this time. He gained control of himself. His mind racing ahead, he began to give the orders that would rouse the rest of the crew from slow-life. He began to study the screens and speculate on the actions of the intruder vessel. The only possible place of interest was the planet that harbored the primitives. It was interesting to the Ann Thaar only as another game reserve for the great leaders and a breeding station for food production for the lesser Ann Thaar. Much like the planet that they had been getting ready to process when they had come across the Shan the last time. All thought of taking that one had been suspended temporarily when the incident occurred that had sent the Shan ship limping away with the Ann Thaar gambling on a pursuit that now looked as if it would be paying off. Time enough for a return to the place the native prey called Earth. First gain the Shan treasures. The rest could be taken in a day. This one, too! All the little planets filled with life. One could step from one to the other in an hour's time. A never-ending hunt. All that was needed was to exercise a little caution here and now. These worms didn't even have defensive weaponry. Even with their Star Drive it should be possible to take them. Stig wondered why they were here. They had a weird fondness for planets like this. Their motives in helping prey were not understandable to Stig. But it would make them vulnerable.

One thing puzzled him. The sudden entry into the system argued that they had either repaired the ship or that this was another one. Either way, their presence here was a mystery. Stig knew that they had sensors equal to his or better. They must know of the Ann Thaar's presence. A sudden insight gripped him. There must be Shan on the surface! The ship would be here to rescue them! He cursed himself for not studying the populace more carefully. In the infrequent hunts they had made on the surface there had been no hint of the Shan's presence. Still, he should have questioned the prey before the feeding. Well, that wouldn't happen again! This time there would be stealth and cunning employed. Cat and mouse. It would be a good hunt. The remainder of his subordinates to awaken from slow-life cringed into his presence. With a red glow in his eyes, Stig began to give orders.

We descended the side of a tree-covered slope and hit the first trail we'd run across other than those that had been made by animals. This one was definitely made by people. At spots the soft dirt showed the prints made by feet and wheels. A glance at the footprints we made ourselves showed the similarity between them and the ones we examined. The ruts seemed to have been made by a three-wheeled vehicle. The ship's computer had described just such a thing. Small and low slung, it fit the needs of the terrain. The third wheel was in the back and served as a sort of balance and tiller. It was usually pulled by man power, or Creen power, but some use had been made of draft animals. This trail was narrow and seemed seldom used, and we saw no evidence of domestic animal tracks. The marks were old, but it was hard to tell how old. At least we knew we were in the vicinity of the natives. It tightened up our behavior. We had had to struggle at first to make the strange vocal cords work, and we had chattered a lot on the way, getting used to them. It was time to stop broadcasting the fact that we were outsiders for everyone for miles to hear. We'd made provisions to enable us to carry on a conversation with the locals. Another piece of Shan wizardry lay at the heart of it. An almost instantaneous translator stuffed with a double language file was worn beneath our clothing. It was small and thin, and we had it fitted between our shoulder blades. In our present guise there was plenty of room—the Creen were a wide bunch. The pickup and subvocalizer were housed in a collar that resembled one which many of the Creen wore for ornamentation. All we had to do was listen for the translation that came when we activated the circuits and subvocalize a reply. The translator made the reply through a perfectly normal sounding speaker molded into the collar. From a foot away you couldn't tell the difference. Fortunately, the Creen physiognomy was fairly immobile, and we didn't have to worry about lip synching.

We followed the trail in the direction that seemed to lead us closest to the Shan's last known site. A half-hour's walk brought us to the first sign of habitation, although the place had been long abandoned. It reminded me of a few old cabins I had seen in outlands throughout North America. Outposts of pioneer types that had gone farther than any expansion to follow. Eventually the push had ebbed, and the farthermost had retreated again into the expanded masses. What I was seeing now was much the same thing I would have seen a few hundred years ago almost anywhere on Earth. The outbuildings were in heaps with vines and underbrush taking over again. The main house was slower in giving up. It still stood on its foundation. Dark with open doors and windows, it still seemed to have a semi-life as it dreamed of the people that had inhabited it so long ago. There were ghosts on Haven, too. We inspected it briefly, but it gave little evidence of the life of the people who were gone. A few broken implements that weren't worth the effort of taking away were tossed into corners, but the retreat had been orderly, and all that had value had been reclaimed. The old place deserved better of its occupants. We emerged into the sunlight again and returned to the path. The old homestead had had a chill that penetrated the mind, if not the body. I felt the loneliness that must have sent the occupants back to the mainstream.

Two hours later we saw the first of the Creen we were to meet in the weeks ahead. A small party was headed toward us and we chose to rest in the shadow of a monster tree that had the proportions of an ancient elm of Earth and wait for them to come upon us. We made a small fire and prepared a light meal of things we had scavenged along the trail. We had followed the recipes diligently, and when we offered some to the arrivals they seemed to accept it as normal. It was an uneventful meeting, one of many we were to have all through the valleys and mountains the Creen favored. An exchange of gossip and local recent history in exchange for our own tale of being on a mission of exploration from our great leader. We presented ourselves as coming from a far land with slightly different customs. It seemed to go down well enough. Still, we seemed to have no success in finding traces of the Shan. Rather than being swallowed up, it was as though they had never been. We probed very gently. There *was* something there. After awhile it became evident that it was something that just wasn't talked about. At least, not around strangers, even such harmless ones as we presented ourselves to be. I knew that not everyone knew of it, whatever it was. Most of the time it went as it did during the first meeting. The

Creen we met that day had no knowledge of any outsiders of an alien type. They weren't being coy. They just didn't know. It was odd to see them coming up to us as we sat around and waited for them, knowing that what we saw was much the same as they saw. The two parties were similar in number, our four as opposed to their five. The differences in appearance were slight. We might have been any two small groups meeting by accident. To us it was unnerving to realize that we looked for all the world like them.

The Creen were quite humanoid but definitely not human. The legs were much longer, and the ankles were much more flexible. They seemed to caress the ground with a probing motion. The upper trunk was broad and heavily muscled. The arms were much the same as a man's. The head was massive and seemed devoid of expression. Indeed, the Creen were constantly gesturing and posturing in their efforts to convey emotion and expression. The eyes were deepset in a long narrow skull, and the ears were small and covered by a heavy mane of hair. The mouth was large and you could see large efficient teeth lying behind the thin cheeks that were little more than an elastic covering devoid of musculature. The nose was small, a slight protuberance that hardly qualified as a centerpiece. In spite of the total alienness of their appearance, I found them to be pleasant enough looking once I got used to them. I never found out if the face and body I wore were considered to be good looking among Creen. Certainly I had no complications either way, so I guess I must have looked about average. I developed no prejudices about Creen features in the short time I wore the guise. When we finally got the information we wanted, it was by stealth rather than diplomacy.

Chapter 14

The sun was well up and the airport in Denver was busily handling the normal heavy traffic. It was 7:17 on Wednesday morning. Most of the United States was up and working or getting ready to. The media discovered the Shan ship at the same time the military and civilian agencies did. It appeared at 5000 feet and hung in the air just outside of the air traffic lanes. A TV traffic watch drogue picked it up at the same time it appeared on the radar screens. The NORAD defense center under the mountain had no more warning than any other system in the global network. The satellites actually were the last to pick up the image. There was no question of what it was. Within a minute and a half the local cameras were transmitting the picture to the world at large and the lunar colony. The various ships and intersystem shuttles and project stations had to wait for a few minutes more. The world knew that an alien ship was in the Earth's atmosphere above Colorado. It hung there in silence for fifteen minutes waiting for a stunned world to get its act together. Reaction was swift but considered. A single observation plane circled the ship at a carefully safe distance and observed it. Most of the viewing was done with long-range cameras and telescopes. The images they picked up were all anyone could want. Every detail of the exterior was displayed in minute detail. Every protuberance was measured, every line scanned. The only information that came from the electromagnetic sensors was that the air surrounding the craft was heavily charged. If the thing

stayed there, it might cause a few lightning strikes.
Finally, at the fifteen-minute mark, radio silence was
broken. The message was terse. In the best television
network tones it announced greetings to the govern-
ments and people of Earth. The vessel in the sky over
Denver was peaceful in nature. An immediate interview
was requested with Joachim Albright of the Western
Federation at nine a.m. on the end of a runway to be
announced at the last moment at Wright-Patterson Field.
That was the total message. Telephones began to ring
insistently, when nothing more was found to be forth-
coming. Only a few in special circumstances in govern-
ment even knew that Albright existed. They weren't to
find out much more for months to come. While the
populace in general and most of the government began
a long seige of demanding information that came slowly
and sometimes not at all, a small group began to imple-
ment the request. There was nothing else to be done. As
a few of the more unregenerate types tried to gear up
for some sort of a military stance for the first time in
decades, the depositing of Albright at the end of the
designated runway was managed. By the time it was
accomplished, a few old missiles had been trained on
the ship, which disappeared abruptly to reappear over
Wright-Patterson. A small helicopter landed him at the
end of the macadam strip and they watched a shuttle
separate itself from the parent ship and drop to the end
of the runway. It landed silently without a jar a hun-
dred feet from the waiting party. As the dust settled, a
hatch opened in the side facing them. A loudspeaker
issued a welcome to Albright and asked him to enter
alone. He gave a brief nod to the small party that
accompanied him and strode to the hatch. Peering in-
side for a long minute, he then turned and waved a
hand to those remaining. He stepped inside and was
lost in the darkness of the immediate interior. The hatch
remained open long enough for the speaker to an-
nounce that the shuttle would be returning to the parent
ship for a conference, and that Albright would be re-
turned when the conference was over. The hatch sealed

as the ground party watched, unsure of what they should be doing. The shuttle lifted and the time for action passed. It lifted into the midmorning sky, a sleek black mystery that passed swiftly into a deeper mystery as it returned into the body of the larger ship.

Chapter 15

Day five and we were in the heart of the district that had been inhabited by the Shan during the last days before the ship left. We had seen no sign of their ever being here. The people in the area were a contrast to those we had met in the outlying region. The early days had shown us a basically friendly race who lived as well as they could and enjoyed it as much as possible. The climate wasn't severe and they made it through the winters without much strain. Death and injury came often, however, as it must with people who hadn't advanced beyond ordinary tools and methods. Those in the center of the region were dour and fearful. As was often the case on Earth in a repressed atmosphere, much religious fervor was evident. The Creen here seemed to share man's ability to make himself miserable in order to improve himself. The outlanders, when they considered such matters at all, enjoyed a pantheon of gods with personalities that were taken from the foundations of the Creen psyche. Larger than life, but understandable. The interior view of the supernatural was formed about fears of the dead coming back to life and demons that took over one's body and did terrible things. Constant vigilance was necessary just to survive. Everyone we met here was constantly on the watch for signs of contamination from the spirit world. They were impoverished from the continual effort to remain pure and free of the devils that surrounded them. We were viewed as likely candidates. Any attempt to question them about their history met with a stony silence or a more pointed invitation to get the hell away from the person being questioned. The small amount of trade that supplied their needs was carried on only at the full of the day. The nights were taken up with prayer meetings and councils that discussed the bad happenings and omens that occurred during the day. We could well imagine that we were a subject that came up often during our unwelcome stay. We were getting nowhere fast when the situation suddenly took a queer turn. Johnny and Bill were doing the far end of the village, having the usual run of luck trying to get someone to talk of old legends. Celia and I were doing as poorly on our side. We had just finished with an old crone whose hatred for strangers was only matched by her extensive vocabulary. We moved as quickly as we could without it becoming an outright rout into the relative safety of the public street.

I was shaking my unfamiliar head and wondering what to do next when Celia banged me on the shoulder. Startled, I followed her gesturing. A procession unlike any we'd seen so far was making its way quickly down the side alley. The Creen involved were strangely dressed. Long flowing robes covered their bodies, and they were carrying a litter of some kind. A small Creen was on it wrapped in a dark cloth. No features were distinguishable. It was easily seen that the figure was tied in such a manner that it couldn't escape. Intrigued, we followed at a distance. It was the first sight we had ever had of a prisoner on this world. Justice, when meted out, was usually swift and incarceration was never really used. The procession walked swiftly into the woods and disappeared into the interior. I was of two minds about following any farther. We weren't too popular with the locals anyway. Following this kind of business might create more than open dislike. Still, it was out of the ordinary and who knew what we might find out from it. Celia was against it, but I overruled her. Strange. Ten minutes later she became an avenging angel because we had followed my whim. Ultimately it led us to the Shan though at the moment we couldn't know the outcome.

We slowly made our way into the trees and followed the path. A few days in the natural surroundings had made us sensitive to signs and we had no trouble following at a distance. The trail was little used and led us in only one direction. It followed the outline of a steep cliff and wound around its bottom. Shortly we came to a viewpoint overlooking an open clearing a few hundred feet ahead. A tumble of rocks lined the clearing where they had fallen from the cliffside. One larger than the rest lay a little farther out in the open space. Here the Creen had stopped. We saw them unship the little bundle from the litter and throw it like a sack of trash on the large stone. They hurled a flurry of epithets at it and made a number of threatening gestures. Finally, with a few more curses they gathered together and started to return. We stepped back into the underbrush until they passed. We waited a couple of minutes until we were sure they weren't coming back right away. Finally we emerged from the sides of the trail, and driven by the cruelty inherent in what we had seen, made our way without an exchange of words to the clearing.

Some small mewling sounds came from the discarded bundle. Celia moved faster than I did. She was tearing at the bundle before I made my way through the scree. I reached her side as she unwrapped the outer layer. A pitiful sight greeted our eyes. A young Creen, probably a teenager and definitely a female, was inside the wrappings. She had a wasted look and her limbs were twisted by some terrible illness. It was horrible to see. What made it worse were the numerous wounds and bruises that had been inflicted upon the already ravaged body. She lay there and made those horrible mewling sounds. She was unable to do more than twitch in a feeble attempt to avoid more abuse. It sickened me and Celia let out a howl that grated my bones. She started to curse as she tore off the final cords that bound the girl. I tried to help as much as I could but found I was doing battle when I tried. For the moment I was classified with those who had done this thing. I stood by helplessly as Celia gathered the little body in her arms and began to rock it like a baby. I didn't understand. The actions of the Creen had been terrible and the effects sickened me, but I wasn't prepared for my girl to come unglued like this. I stood there stunned and wondered what the hell I was going to do next. . . .

The yellow flame of the fire cast racing shadows around the room that twisted and danced as if they were minor demons participating in arcane ritual. It did seem as if we had been transported to some ancient sorcerer's cave. Certainly the proceedings were similar. Like old Gothic fiction, the old vampire was instructing a younger one in the upper level rituals. A pitiful young girl lay on a rude altar while lesser members of the pack stood anticipating the final rites. If we were caught, I wouldn't have blamed anyone for driving a stake through my heart. In actuality, the proceeding could have been switched to a brightly lit hospital ward in a modern setting and would have seemed as strange. The victim in the cave was not one of our making, but the young Creen girl whom we had found on the rubble after the local priesthood had cast her there. Her crime against the tribe seemed to be having an illness that didn't respond to the ministrations of the local A.M.A. This corresponded in the minds of the priests as being in league with demons if not actually being one herself. Salem was being recreated on Haven. It had a local flavor, but it was the same. The interior tribes of the Creen had gotten a dose of puritanism and pity had gone out the window. It was easy to feel superior to it all as an outsider with the vantage point of a few hundred years of retrospect, but the same sort of thing had happened to our own ancestors who were no different from ourselves. It was all a matter of time. Over the course of years a people tried a lot of different things; eventually the worst of them became embarrassments that had to be remembered lest the same thing repeat itself again at a later date with a new cast of characters. Even with the advantage of history it was hard not to make the same mistakes. Just at the moment we were about to demonstrate a very personal rejection of the situation we found. Led by Celia's impassioned championship of the young female, we had decided to attempt the procedure that Chaney had used to save Mary so long ago. The situations were not equal in all respects. None of us had experience in using the virus in a shared healing mode. Johnny had witnessed it under less than ideal conditions. His mind had not understood the meaning of it until the crisis was over. Celia had a superficial understanding of the procedure from studying it in the lab aboard the Shan ship. It was a long way from hands on experience. Bill and I were complete novices at this sort of thing. Still, we had given in to Celia's rock-steady determination.

I was nonplussed at her instant reaction to the situation. It was still too early to be interfering in the affairs of the Creen, deplorable as the situation was. It was only one of many things we found unpleasant in this situation. It wasn't that I or any of the others was willing to walk away from the girl. We all wanted to help. It was probable that with some judicious application of the offworld medicine and knowledge we possessed we could save the girl and arrange to have her taken in by some of the less hag-ridden outer tribes. They, so far, still had one foot in Eden. In the face of this sort of thinking we met flat rejection. Celia would hear of nothing less than the complete regeneration that the Shan virus gave. It would be an act that refuted the principles of Shan noninterference just as Chaney's had. In our case it was coming awfully soon and it seemed to us that we were creating a precedent that might cause complications in our relationship with the Shan. We found we could go no other way. It seemed a contradiction that the Shan, who were supposedly our superiors in ethics, must have come upon this kind of thing countless times and not succumbed to the need to heal. I understood the need to let cultures develop on their own, but how do you deal with the problem on a personal level? I determined that I would ask that question of a Shan someday. I hoped I would like the answer. Somehow, I felt I wouldn't! I had a feeling interstellar relationships were going to be a thorny problem. We humans were a mass of contradictory impulses, but all in all I kind of liked our style. It was going to be hard to deal with the Shan if we couldn't accept their way of doing things. With all this in mind we went ahead with the deed. The question of which one of us was going to effect the transfer had never been in serious contention. Celia stated flatly that she was going to do it. The exalted look in her eyes as she stated it bothered me, but she wasn't going to be denied this. Johnny gave me a look that said "don't buck her in this," and I subsided. Something was going on here that I didn't understand, but it was evident that the rest of them did. I was almost sorry we'd reverted to our own shapes. It would have been easier somehow to have watched it if she'd kept her Creen guise.

The time for discussion passed and we got on with it. I watched as Celia removed the wrappings from the Creen girl and bared her own body and lowered herself upon the small figure. She placed her hands as Chaney had upon the upper chest and sank her face into the throat of the girl. I couldn't see her face—only that of the girl's. She had been still and silent since we had brought her to this isolated and abandoned mine. Now her eyes flickered open at this final injury that was being inflicted on her. She gave a final sigh as the needle-like protuberances that entered her body and throat broke the skin. If she was capable of thinking it must have been like the final descent into hell. I watched for a few minutes more as Celia achieved the trance state she needed to effect the repairs to the body beneath her. At least I hoped it was the trance state. There was no way for us to know. They were on their own. It would take hours to complete the process, and after awhile we took turns watching over the two figures on the bed we'd made in the old mine outbuilding.

The hours dragged by slowly, and I finally took my turn outside watching to see that no one from the village came upon us unexpectedly. This was *not* something we wanted to explain to a local shaman. I waited in a small stand of trees, watching the converging paths that led toward the village and the other places that the mine had served in the past. My thoughts ranged far that night as I thought about everything that had gone on and what might happen in the near future. So far, nothing seemed to have gone according to plan. We always seemed to come up with a new plan of action, but I couldn't think of anything that had been completed as we'd thought at the start. The inference that we didn't really know what we were about was plain.

Thoughts of the unexpected side of Celia were flitting through at times, too. I realized that there was still a lot that I had to learn about her. In my smugness, I thought that all that was left to knowing her was a refinement of knowledge of things she liked to eat and books that she had read as a girl. Things like that. I was both pleased and taken aback that it wasn't that simple. It came to my mind that there was a lifetime of learning ahead of me. Well, that was all right. I really didn't want a two-dimensional paper doll for a mate. The thought occurred that she'd be changing in the years to come. It was supposed to be that way. That scared me a little. I liked her just the way she was. Again the thought came. I guess I really didn't know how she was. She'd surprised me just now! My thoughts went around in unprofitable but interesting circles as I continued my stint at surveillance of the landscape. How long I'd have continued in this vein I don't know. I saw the door open and Johnny stepped out and walked to where I was standing. He walked slowly, rubbing the back of his head as he came out, and I understood that there was no urgency in his coming out. I waited where I was.

"Nothing yet," he yawned. He clapped a hand on my shoulder. "Everything seems to be going well. I think I see some signs of regeneration on the surface now, though," he said easily. "I think it's going to be all right."

"I'll go in," I said and started for the building. The hand on my shoulder held me.

"Just a minute, Steve! Before you go in I think there's something you ought to understand about Celia."

I turned back surprised and stiffened in apprehension.

"No," he said reassuringly, "there's nothing wrong in there. I just wanted to tell you why this is so important to her."

"Yes, I'd like to know that," I sighed. "I know there's something. What's it all about, John?"

"Celia didn't tell you how she came to be one of us yet, did she?"

"No." Strange, I thought. I'd almost asked her many times. Somehow we never got around to the answer. I should have suspected that. It seemed obvious now that she'd not wanted to talk about it.

"It's still pretty fresh in her mind, Steve. Not very long ago she was in about the same shape as that Creen girl. Oh, I don't mean she'd been abused like that!" he hastened to interject at the look on my face. "She was suffering from one of the rarest genetic disorders left. And she was going to die of it. The ironic thing was that she had been a life sciences major and was rapidly becoming one of the best. She'd gotten her doctorate at a very early age and was doing some excellent work on the study of unused genetic material in the genes. There's quite a bit of it, you know. It doesn't enter into the scheme of things—it really is unused! Some of the things she was delving into had a sort of linkup with the principles that led the Shan to develop the virus. We got wind of it and decided to give her a grant from one of our foundations. It was interesting to us to see where she was going with it. We might even have helped unobtrusively. Then, a few months later, she started feeling run down. She took some time off to rest up, but it didn't do any good. Finally, after putting it off too long, she went to a doctor. It seems to be a thing that medical people and those in related fields don't do any better than ordinary people. When the tests came back, it looked bad. The very thing she'd devoted herself to, the understanding of genetic disease and possible correction of the effects, was going to kill her in a few months. She raged at the unfairness of it as countless others have done throughout history."

"My God," I breathed. The shock of it hit me hard. I felt the tears spring to my eyes at the near loss of her before I'd even known she existed.

"But she lived. You must have saved her!"

"Yes, but it was a near thing. We didn't even know about it until we got a letter from her some months later telling us that she could no longer accept the grant and explaining the reason. In it she told us of some other people she knew who were doing related work, and that she felt strongly that this sort of research was essential and stood an excellent chance of paying off someday. She also requested that the foundation keep an eye out for anyone who had a specific need for her body for research purposes in the field. It was a terrible letter to read." Johnny's voice was heavy with the memory.

"We found her almost too late." He winced at the memory. "She'd gone out of town to die. She'd made all her arrangements and was waiting for the end in a private nursing home. She'd become one of us in our minds, so we took her out of there and restored her. She really is one of the best, Steve! We can't save many, but we really wanted her. It's just that because it's so fresh in her memory, it makes her feel strongly about this Creen girl. They are very similar cases. I thought you should know about it."

"Thanks, Johnny," I said huskily. We both knew it wasn't really for the story that I thanked him.

"Sure, Steve."

We left it at that for the moment, and I turned and went back to the building. I had to look at Celia again.

Throughout the hours that remained in the process I rarely took my eyes from her. So nearly had I missed ever meeting her. The meaning of her filled my thoughts as the night wore on. The fire guttered and sent the shadows back and forth across the bodies of Celia and the young Creen girl. Now, as the hours fulfilled their promise, the caressing light and shadow left new curves as they played. The withered body of the youngster had started to return to a normal appearance. Celia had lost a bit of weight, and although I'd been told it was mostly a matter of fluids, it was a worrisome thing to see. History repeated itself, and as the sun rose on Haven, the process was completed just as it had on Earth so long ago in the back of the wrecked station wagon. Johnny touched my shoulder once again, and I roused myself from the fantasy of the moment and saw that Celia was starting to withdraw. Her face still had a trance glaze and her mouth was sore looking. The needle points of the virus transfer node had already retreated and devolved into normal flesh again. Except for a few small flecks of blood which were quickly wiped away by Johnny, there was nothing left to suggest the nature of the event. Celia was pale and thin. I felt more worried at that moment than I had in hours. I'd been warned what to expect and yet seeing her like this, I wondered if she had damaged herself. An irrational fear swept me momentarily. It passed as her eyes began to focus. She began to look better to me as animation came back into her face. She wheezed a little, and her voice sounded like a dollar recording, but it was sweet to me. I held her tight for a moment and she seemed to like it. It only lasted for a little bit, and then her thoughts turned back to the girl. She twisted away from me and moved back to the bed. I stood behind her as she examined the girl. Here was my kind of religious experience. The wasted body had reassumed a normal shape and even lying supine, she was relaxed from the twisted look that pain had shaped. She was still thin, but she had a healthy aspect. Johnny told us that after Mary's recovery he hadn't felt safe for days while she and Chaney ate everything that didn't move faster than they did. And it was so now. Within an hour we began to feel like mother birds bringing food to the nest. The rest of the day had to be spent in eating and sleeping in an accelerated rotation. Celia and the girl, whom we found to be named Jeren, kept us busy all day providing them with food and drink. They both seemed to be in a cycle of starvation, followed by a euphoria that lasted till they fell into a dreamless sleep that lasted until hunger woke them again. By late evening things had settled down again, and we all turned in for a more normal night. Bill and Johnny and I had gotten no rest the night before and were a little worn out ourselves. Nothing occurred during the second night that I know of, and it was a good thing. We never would have awakened for it. When I finally did wake in the midmorning hours, it was to the vision of my intended and Jeren, the Creen girl, sitting at the makeshift table finishing the remains of a docker's breakfast. My reaction was not too carefully concealed disgust!

Jeren accepted us as gods, which in her culture really didn't advance us a heck of a lot over ordinary mortals. She was only bothered by the fact that we didn't quite match the description of the ones she'd been brought up to believe in. Obviously, we were not what she expected, but she was generous in nature and hoped for better from us when we got on to it a little more. We tried to explain matters but found that her viewpoint really worked best at the moment, so we gave it up and accepted her rationale. This seemed to please her, and it really did make the job easier. Her tale was simple if horrible. Like Celia, she had fallen prey to a wasting degeneration that, to the priesthood, smacked of possession by demons. The beatings she had received had failed to drive out the demons, so the expeditious thing to do was expel her from the tribe. The culmination had been the casting away that Celia and I had witnessed. Jeren saw nothing remarkable in this. She even seemed to approve. It seemed plausible to her that she indeed was possessed. I had a feeling that, although she was too polite to say so, we might not be gods but fellow demons come to take her up and instruct her in her new role as one of us. The thought that the next logical step might be to raise hell for her ex-tribe didn't distress her either. It was just the way things worked. You did your job, whatever it was. Johnny pronounced her the sanest being he'd ever met. Bill and I just threw up our hands, but Celia beamed fatuously at her as if she were a favored child who had just done something socially outstanding. The rest of the day didn't get a lot more sensible, and when it appeared that we'd come up with a plan for prying loose some information from the Creen priesthood, it didn't even seem an odd way to go about it.

Sex and age discrimination worked much the same on Haven as it had on Earth. Jeren was out with only two strikes. What little she did know was garbled. All she really had a good grip on were the onerous duties that were laid on her and other subjugate members of the tribe, things she and the others must do to keep from falling under the influence of the demons. There were a lot of restrictions and duties. These were interspersed with sets of prayers and ceremonies that took up what remained of a day. There was certainly no time left for enjoyment and hardly enough for the business of keeping alive. Perhaps it wasn't so strange that becoming a demon was accepted with equanimity. Certainly, the "damned" Creen of the outside tribes seemed to have it better. Jeren had no explanation for the fact that, although she had been diligent in her tasks, she still fell from grace. It was just the way things were. The Shan figured in all of this somehow. The demons that had caused all of this fervor had a striking physical resemblance to the Creen. They were reputed to be able to assume forms not their own. The rest of what Jeren had to say seemed to be a mishmash of legend built on rumor. Most of it was silly and contradictory, but the shapechanging and the original shapes and features stood out from the rest of it like a beacon. It shook her picture of us as first-rate demons ourselves that we didn't know all of this, but she accommodated it somehow and fell into our plan with an obvious relish. We spent that day and the next refining our plans and getting to know Jeren as a person. Released from the constraints of her existence in the tribe, she blossomed in an incredibly short time. In the space of a couple of days she won a place with us and seemed content to do so. She viewed the members of her old tribe with scorn, and it seemed to her that it had all been a long time ago. We felt a little worried that she might not be able to assimilate with her people again but the idea didn't seem to cut much ice with her. Having the central role in the little drama we had planned pleased her no end, and she didn't give a thought to whatever lay beyond. It was a little like the old concept of having saved a life; you became responsible for its well-being thereafter. It was a nice, but weird, couple of days. The height of Haven's soft summer, at least in these regions. We sat and basked in the sun for all the world like college kids on an outing and made plans for the coming days. All that was missing were the fried chicken and beer. Jeren was a delight. She chattered and posed with us and acted like any teenager on Earth having a respite from school. It was the last restful period we were to have.

Chapter 16

We passed into the hall of the elders wearing the cloaks that Bill had liberated from the storehouse under Jeren's gleeful direction. We seemed to have created a criminal mind in a young innocent in record time. It might be well to rethink returning this girl to an unsuspecting outland tribe! The spirit of the hall was as soul-destroying as any of its Earthly counterparts. Gloomy dark recesses gave ample direction for the evils that were to be thwarted by the shamans to dwell in in the interim. The saviors of the tribe were joyless in chairs about the chamber, no doubt much worn from the constant struggle against the pleasure of evil. We made our way to a side aisle and waited for the deliberations to begin.

There wasn't any likelihood that the Creen priests had anything on the agenda that was new or interesting. Jeren had heard enough about these meetings to assure us that all that ever happened was a dull repetition of countless others in the past. An accounting of the attempts of the evil spirits to take over some poor souls (Jeren's case might be mentioned) and an exhortation to increase vigilance. After some ritual, everyone present would be satisfyingly depressed. With good management, this gloom would last until the next meeting. There was no doubt about it—these folks had as much potential for self-abuse as we humans did. The meeting got underway without much delay, and I noted that there was nothing very colorful about it. They didn't seem to have a flair for incantation or mystic patterning. It was all as dry as a school board meeting. I was a little worried about how our show would go as I watched the process unfold. I had thought they'd be more emotional and charged up when we made our move. It didn't seem as if it were going to work out that way. The proceedings were marked by an emotionless recital of the events of the past week which were accepted by all present as simple confirmation of the never-ending war between Creenkind and the forces of evil. They had reached the minor point of Jeren's resistance to proven techniques for driving out spirits in possession of Creen bodies. The fact that the beatings didn't result in the successful removal of the demon only proved that she had been willing to cooperate with the forces of evil. They were rather smug about the whole thing and felt themselves quite virtuous throughout, including their ceremonious casting away of a still living and suffering young girl. I could see the look in Celia's eyes becoming lethal, and I decided it was time to act before she started repaying the priests for their devoutness. I gave the signal, and Jeren stepped into the center of the room. Thoroughly enjoying the limelight, she made a Hollywood entrance totally suited for the event. With an imperiousness that rivaled H. Rider Haggard's Ayesha, she posed regally and threw open her cloak.

"So! Old men, you have destroyed me, have you?" She made a gesture straight from silent movies.

"Rather, you have released me to work my vengeance upon you!" She was wasted on this planet. The amused malevolence of her tone chilled me, even though I had written the hoary old script that she followed. The effect was all that I could have hoped for. The old men, as she called them, had never run up against anything they hadn't carefully orchestrated for themselves. They were dumbfounded. They recognized her right away, and the impact of her words sank in as they sat in a silence toned by fears they could not channel into manageable lines. She was a new thing in their experience, and since she wasn't of their making, they feared her terribly. She was possessed of the virus now, and her future was malleable to an extreme she as yet couldn't perceive. She could become a force to be reckoned with on Haven. For the moment—she was magnificent! The priests hung on her words as she began again.

"You have abused one beloved by the Dark Ones," she said. "They turn their faces to you whom they have ignored until now. Their wrath is great. If you would escape it, you will send six of your young men to the Old Place and learn their terms for your continued existence. Go now and save your lives. I and my fellow demons will watch and punish you if you fail to do so."

With this, the rest of us revealed ourselves and strode forward to stand by her side. It was great melodrama, if I do say so myself. The sight of our human forms and faces was the capstone to a fine little vignette. An additional shock ran through the assembly, and as they began to squeak their fears, Jeren made a final gesture of malicious glee and we walked out of the temple. We heard a bubble of sound break as we moved into the shadows. We'd stirred them up right enough. It was reaching epic proportions as we made our way out. The chance that anyone would follow us was slight, but we made haste to disappear. In the light of day our physical presence might lessen the impact of our night's visitation. Now we would watch from a distance and see what came of it. There were a number of brooding dark places that resonated in the Creen mind that they avoided much as we of Earth had in past times. They were unlikely to seek us out or come across us by chance. We found a good spot, well situated to keep an eye on the village doings, set on a hill above town. It was a shame that I couldn't have placed a bug in the temple, but we didn't want any kind of continuous transmission floating around for the Ann Thaar to pick up. At the first light of day, we saw that we had indeed started something. The normally slow, dispirited pace of the village had given way to a bustle unheard of in Jeren's memory. The news of our visitation spread, and you could actually see it as the townspeople moved in circles that widened as we watched. The organizational skills of the priesthood couldn't be faulted. By midday we saw the six selected to be emissaries to the Dark Ones I had created formed up and harangued by a council of black-robed priests. They were much subdued with the importance of it all and the thought of meeting the terrors of their teachings. I wondered how the selection process had worked. Exhorted by their elders, the young Creen started their journey, leaving before time for the evening meal. I was pleased. It would seem that the need for haste was above that of even regular meals. They moved quickly out of town and kept the pace up until they were far enough out of sight that the elders were unlikely to have an eye on them. With perfect good sense they slowed to a minimum speed. There was no sense, after all, in rushing to your doom. I understood completely and congratulated them on it. It also made the task of following them easier. In the next few days we were able to keep an eye on their progress without difficulty and still keep well behind. The thought of hurrying them along with a few well chosen mystic events crossed my mind, but I thought the rate of progress we were making was good enough, and it would be better to conserve our energies for unexpected developments. It was well that we did.

I was congratulating myself on the way I'd read the signs. There was no way to know what had actually happened, but my conjecture that the Shan had somehow triggered the current religion espoused by the dour villagers seemed to be confirmed. It seemed likely that there had been some kind of confrontation, and that it had taken place some distance from here. What had been the circumstances of the event would be one of the things that the Shan would answer better than the Creen. At least the six young ones seemed to have good instructions about where to go. They were taking their time about it. I didn't blame them. I was content to follow this string out. It gave me time to chew over some thoughts that I'd been having. The Creen party followed a path that was a series of animal trails and barren spots along a small river that meandered in a southerly direction. It made sense that the river led to the scene of the previous encounter. Almost every place that Shan or Creen had interest in had a source of water. The chances were that this little river was all the guide we would need. Whether or not we would recognize the place when we found it was another matter. I wasn't ready to dispense with our native vanguard just yet. The six young Creen made such a large mark on the passageways that we had no difficulty following their trail. I had specified the number for the party with this in mind and it worked well. From time to time we caught sight of them ahead of us, and we dropped back a little way. The only problem was finding a place at night to camp that was close enough to keep an eye on them yet still go about the business of eating and sleeping ourselves. We envied them their fires. We had to make do with cold meals. Since we were living off the land, this made for some interesting meals. In the afternoon we let them get well ahead when their course was clear for awhile, so we could have a hot lunch. The fire that would betray our presence at night was manageable in the afternoon as long as we were careful about the amount of smoke.

Midafternoon of the third day found us finishing up one of these lunches. The Creen were proceeding ahead of us through a narrow canyon that seemed to have no outlet for miles ahead. The river ran straight through it, and we had no doubt that they'd continue in the same direction for a good while. We were in the middle of a forested section broken in spots by a few grassy meadows. We finished a meal that filled us but wasn't memorable for flavor, then adjusted our packs and sauntered away from the shelter of the trees. The day was warm, and the local equivalent of bees were buzzing. The sun shone on the meadow grasses just ahead, and the breeze took away the heat we generated as we walked in the open meadow. I was in the midst of some woolgathering as we approached a good-sized knoll. It looked as if it would be a good vantage point, and we made our way to the top. My thoughts were on a puzzle I'd been playing with for awhile. If the Shan were so circumspect in their dealings with the various races they visited and pursued with such diligence a policy of nonintervention, how had they allowed the growth of this oppressive little religion that had arisen from the meeting of the two races? That wasn't what I'd been led to expect of them. There were other things that bothered me as well, and I was mulling them over for the twentieth time when I was brought back to reality by Bill's shout.

Our knoll extended into a line of trees that bordered the meadow, and coming along the ridge top was a huge animal that looked like a cross between a lion and a grizzly with the best features of neither. Its shaggy mane waved as it jounced our way. A gleam from a wild looking eye rolled our way, and the thing picked up its pace. It was a couple of hundred yards away and already the size of a car. The mottling shadows that the leaves of the trees cast upon it as it ran became a blur. We made a concerted dash in the opposite direction. The thing was big enough to have trouble maintaining speed in the thicket. I hoped so, anyway. The ground was uneven, and we scrambled and rolled into the underbrush as the thing crested the knoll. The thundering of its rush slowed as it moved past the spot where we had stood moments ago. God, it was big—a tawny silhouette against the blue sky! I twisted around and tore open my pack, spilling things as I dug for the machine pistol I kept hidden inside. It had become a habit to keep anything that smacked of higher technology well hidden during our days disguised as Creen wanderers. It was stupid to have kept the habit while we were wearing our own skins, but I hadn't thought about it until now. I cursed my stupidity as I wrenched the pistol from my pack. Odds and ends of other things rolled down behind me from the open pack as I aimed the pistol at the monster on the hill. It had stopped and seemed to be testing the air. The massive head swung from side to side, and it gave out a sound something like a car crash. An enormous maw dropped open and we were treated to the sight of its dental work. God! I could smell its breath way down here. I spared a quick look at my companions. We had all lit like tumbling leaves at the bottom of the slope in the underbrush bordering the knoll and meadow. A glance told me that they were all right for the moment. Bruising didn't enter my head—a sufficient number of arms and legs in working order was enough. I saw that Johnny and Bill also had their weapons out and ready. Good! The question was how much good they would be against that thing on the horizon? They threw a lot of metal in a short time, but the creature looked as if it might take a lot of punishment before it went down. It might even deal out some of its own while we cut pieces off of it.

It sniffed the air once more as I shifted my position a little and aimed at the eyes. It started to amble down the hill toward us. I held my breath and began to let it out slowly as I tightened my finger on the trigger. The eyes bounced as it jolted its way down the hill. Something flashed past me from behind, and I swung the muzzle up as Celia scrambled up the slope waving a branch and yelling like a madwoman. I was too shocked for a moment to do anything, and then I ran up the slope after her, trying to bring my pistol to bear on the animal as I came. God knows what I'd have hit if I'd pulled the trigger. The thing watched as we approached it and snorted. It did a funny little dance and eyed us. I had little breath for it, but I tumbled out a lot of curses and pleading. It didn't help. Celia continued her mad dash toward the thing. At what seemed like the last moment I flung myself down and swung the pistol up from my position on the ground. Celia in her crazy run was in my line of fire. The universe slowed down and only heartbeats remained between the meeting of soft human flesh and the terrible claws and teeth of the beast. Slowly the beast turned its head, as if it were tired of these silly small things, and began to back away. Time began to move again, and I watched the thing back up, waving its head from side to side until it had covered enough ground to turn in. It seemed to shake its head in confusion at our behavior and it showed us its backside and finally loped away.

I stared at it unblinkingly until it disappeared into the tree line on the far side. Marshaling my thoughts, I began to walk back to the spot where I'd dumped my pack. I was shaking as a reaction to our near escape. I didn't trust myself to speak. I was afraid of what I'd say when I did. I bent over my pack as an excuse to hide my face. Then I heard her trying to explain to me.

"Steve! It was the only thing to do. I could see from its mouth that it really was a herbivore. But if you'd shot it . . ."

Something snapped in my head. I turned to face her. What I was going to say was just going to come out of my subconscious. God knows I was too mad for coherent speech. It never got said. Just as I opened my mouth, something landed on my back. I felt the claws dig in as I went down. It hit me like a linebacker. I had no chance to land correctly. In a second I was fighting for my life. Fortunately, I'd landed on the thing rather than the other way. It probably saved my life! If it had gone the other way, I'd have lost my throat or had my neck broken immediately. As it was, the landing was bad enough. The thing had more sharp edges than a meat saw and landing on it was nearly lethal all by itself. I never got a clear look at it—which was just as well at the time! For the moment I wasn't analyzing; I was reacting. The oldest primate killer in my backbrain was in charge and moving the second we hit the ground. My hands went for the eyes and found them. The thing convulsed and screamed. The thrashing it made as it dropped from my body tore me up along my sides and back. Rivulets of blood sprang up and welled, soaking my clothes as we parted. The damn thing was like a thorn bush with muscles! I heaved to one side and rolled. I was only aware of the pain in a detached way. I was totally immersed in the fight. I seemed to be made of springs. Effortlessly I rolled up to my feet and crouched, ready to spring at my enemy. The only sound I heard was my own hoarse breathing. I was taking in enormous gasps as I supplied oxygen to the fire of my body. We confronted each other for a moment before we locked again. I saw it clearly, but my attention was on movement. The features were unimportant. I judged the stance and moved unconsciously in reply to it. We moved in a dance as if we were partners to some mutual music that joined us. The music was the hunt. This creature wasn't going to run away. It was here to kill and eat me. The ancestors to which I reverted felt the same way. I was going to kill and eat that son of a bitch, too! The movements we made were quick and subtle. Flickering changes in stance and direction of movement. It was too quick for the eye to follow, and suddenly we were attacking again. We met in midair and tore at each other. It raked me once again and tried to get its muzzle to my throat. I shifted away and found my hand had captured a forelimb. I heaved on it with a strength I had never had before in my life. Suddenly the thing was helpless as it flailed unbalanced in my grip. I don't know if it was training coming to my aid at last, or just luck or instinct, but I gave a perfect judo throw to the beast and suddenly the thing was on the ground, and I was in good position as it struggled up. In an instant some measure of my past training came back to me, and I dropped into a stance that balanced me for the kick I delivered as the thing came to its feet. Swiveling, I powered the side and heel of my foot into the thing's throat as it moved up. All the speed and weight of my body connected at the impact, and the body of the beast soared backward in a disjointed mass as I rebounded and rolled away. Once again I sprang up and set myself. It was hard this time. My movements were slower, and I felt a band of pain and weariness pass through my body and brain. My eyes blurred a little as I searched for my attacker. Then I saw him a few feet away. I gasped some air and began to move forward. A sudden wind sprang up around the figure of the beast, and small puffs of dust and fur flew from its body, which convulsed and fell to the ground. I barely heard the sound of the machine pistol over my breathing and the roaring of the blood in my ears. I stood for a long moment waiting for my adversary to make a move so that I could counter it. I couldn't understand why it was taking so long. It took awhile for me to realize that it was over. I finally did, and slowly, with the knowledge, came the exhaustion. Now I became fully aware of the damage I'd taken. The pain began in earnest and I gave myself over to it. I took a couple of steps away, still keeping an eye on the corpse of the thing.

"Got to sit down for a minute," I said. I don't remember sitting. I don't remember falling either, but with my luck I'll bet no one caught me.

Chapter 17

This time when I awoke I could remember the other times. My mind was clear and I remembered being told I was all right and to go back to sleep. The pain was a lot less, and for a change my mind was on our situation instead of my injuries. I twisted and sat up suddenly. How much time had gone by? I shook my head which was a mistake. Suddenly all the pain was back again with a new companion—nausea! For the first time, my stomach had something to say. I managed to roll over and crawl a few feet from my bed. Waves of sickness rolled over me and I promptly lost the contents of my stomach. It was awhile before I felt like taking up the subject of our situation again, but finally I was drained of the sickness. I was light-headed, but for some reason I felt looser and the pain was more of the body than the mind. I coughed a final time and spat the sourness. My eyes were mostly open and the tearing had stopped. I felt a coolness on my face and the age-old voice all women use in the face of illness began to speak in my ear. Celia reduced me to the status of an unreasonable child again as she began to wash my face and chew my ass for moving around. It all felt good and I relaxed for a moment or two, letting the first pleasant thing that had happened to me in a long time last a little longer. Finally, my curiosity became too urgent, and I sat up again to find out what was going on. The flames of the first good campfire we'd had since we started trailing the Creen party flickered a few feet away from the spot I lay on

It was small but awfully friendly looking. One figure was sitting at the edge of it on the other side of the flames. I squinted and made out Bill's face looking back at me over a cup of something hot. He raised his hand in greeting and winked at me. I croaked at him and he took it for a good enough reply. This all provoked a series of shushing and injunctions from Celia. I croaked a few more times in self defense and finally got my vocal cords to work again. The ability to talk overcame a lot of her objections. She'd been enjoying her role, but she knew I'd want to find out what was going on, so she abandoned it finally and brought me up to date.

After I collapsed (I was right, no one had caught me), they had checked me over, determined that I was in no danger of dying right away and found a place to camp and tend my wounds a few hundred feet from the battle scene. We were still there. The place was easily defensible and close to running water. The rest of the time had been spent in tending to my wounds and resting in camp until I got better.

"How long?" I rasped.

Celia consulted her watch.

"About ten hours," she said. "It's the middle of the night. You awakened a couple of times, but you weren't making much sense the first two times."

"Anybody else get hurt?"

"No, you managed to do it all yourself." Suddenly her eyes brimmed with tears for the first time and her voice quivered.

"Oh, God, Steve, you looked so bad." She moved closer and hugged me. It hurt like hell, but I loved it just the same. We clung for a minute and thought our little thoughts. Finally, she sniffed a bit and sat back.

"You're all right, really!"

"I am, huh?" I craned my head and took stock as best I could without hurting myself too much in the process. I could tell there were some areas I didn't want to check too closely just yet. Everything seemed to move correctly even if it was painful. The fire didn't give a lot of light for the inspection, but I could see enough to tell that I wasn't as bad as I might have expected to be. Somebody had cleaned off the worst of the blood, and I could see that the wounds were already healing. I lifted my arm and stared at it in wonder. The memory of the deep wounds the beast had slashed in it was clear as a bell. Yet the scars were pink and free of infection.

"It's a wonder, isn't it, Steve?"

"Did you have to. . . ?" I trailed off.

"No!" she shook her head. "You did it yourself."

"In ten hours?"

She nodded again, this time in an affirmative.

"My God," I breathed in disbelief. The Shan virus had compressed weeks of healing into a few short hours. It was stunning.

"My God," I said again. Memories of the past marvels I'd seen performed by the virus percolated in my thoughts and I began to examine myself more closely. I heaved myself up and got a rebuke from Celia, but the dizziness was passing quickly. The evidence of healing was even more astounding as I looked at my wounds more closely. I tested myself and found movement easier with each try. Ignoring Celia's complaint that it was too soon, I worked my limbs and stood up. I was weak, but I felt really good. It was a feeling I'd experienced only a few times before. Relief from misery made me feel tremendously alive. I was suddenly aware of an equally tremendous hunger. It came over me like an addict's need for a drug. It was all I could do to keep from screaming.

"Is there anything to eat around here?" I asked.

Suddenly the euphoria of health was gone, and I felt dizzy again and sick with the need for food. Celia responded with the understanding she had gained from her own experience healing Jeren. She brought large quantities and kept her fingers out of the way as I gorged. The effect was surprisingly fast. As soon as the food hit my stomach it seemed to disappear. There was no filling me, but I felt better with every mouthful. Finally there came a moment when I could stop shoveling and I looked around me with something like sanity once again. We sat with our backs to a stony ridge that rose twenty meters or so above us in a sheer wall. The sides were open except for a few large trees. I could hear the faint sound of water somewhere in the darkness beyond the small fire. It looked like a good defensible place to spend the night, and I was glad to see that Bill was sitting with his face away from the firelight to maintain his night vision. Finally, my mind was working, and I began to notice something besides myself.

"Where are the others?" I asked.

I felt a little shiver of alarm. I remembered as I asked that Celia had told me when I first awoke that I'd been the only one hurt and it had sufficed for the time being. Now I needed a better answer. It didn't make sense for Johnny and Jeren not to be around, and suddenly I knew that something was wrong. That it was important was evident from the fact that Celia didn't hold it back until I was feeling better. She told me right away.

"Jeren ran off after the thing that attacked you was killed." Her face showed distress as she related it.

"We were all a little stunned after it was over, and Bill and Johnny were looking over the dead thing and looking around the area to make sure it was alone. I was checking you over and having a little fit of my own while I was about it. Jeren kind of got ignored for a couple of minutes." Celia bit her lip in self-recrimination at the memory.

"It wasn't very long, really, but we all forgot for a little while that she's just a child. I noticed her having the Creen version of hysteria while I was working on you, but I didn't have time to deal with it just then. I yelled something at her and told her to shut up. I forgot all about her then, because she did quiet down and I got busy patching you up. The next few minutes we all had other things on our minds. When I looked for her next she was gone!" For the second time the tears came.

"We let her down, Steve—me most of all."

I told her that was nonsense, that it was just one of those things that happened and no one's fault, but it didn't do any good. I understood that. We all take more guilt than we should. All I could do was try to tell her that it would be all right. It wasn't a satisfactory answer and I knew it when I said it. Still, it was the only thing I *could* say. The upshot was that Johnny had gone after her and still hadn't come back. It had been a long time. I asked how long now and wished I hadn't. He'd gone within minutes of their finding this place to bring me and set up camp—almost the entire ten hours. More than that now! It was a very long time to find a girl who shouldn't have been that hard to follow. There wasn't a hell of a lot to say about it and nothing to do. We talked and found no comfort in it. The remaining hours of the night were depressing. I knew that I had to rest and restore my strength, and it was hard to do while I was worrying about the missing pair. The Shan virus accomplished it for me in its own way, unencumbered by thought processes and worries. I responded to its needs by eating like a wolf and feeling like a louse, feeding while my friends were in trouble. It made no difference—I ate and felt better with every mouthful and worried into the morning sunrise. When the dawn did come, I was feeling fairly fit. I looked like a torturer's exhibition piece with new skin showing in hundreds of places, but everything worked. It was eighteen hours now, and the others hadn't returned. Not good. Now the ball was in our court. The sun was up and we should be doing something about it. Just what that might be was a hell of a good question!

We decided to wait until noon before breaking the camp. In the meantime, we made several excursions into the brush, trying without success to pick up signs of the missing members of the group. In the turmoil surrounding my attack no one had seen which way the girl had gone. To compound the lunacy no one had any idea which way Johnny had gone, either. We had no clue as to whether or not he had found a trail which had escaped our eyes. Midday came and still we had no returnees. I couldn't help but feel that something new had gone wrong. If Johnny hadn't found the girl by the approach of evening, I'd have expected him to return to the camp and discuss it with the rest of us. He probably would have expected me to have recovered—at least enough to talk to. He had more experience with the healing powers of the virus than any of the rest of us. The fact that he remained away was unexplainable if he were unharmed or free to move. In the meantime, the lead the Creen party had was fast becoming uncomfortably long. We'd have to hustle just to catch up, even if we were able to follow their signs. Yesterday we had a single party to track and a healthy team to do it with. Today, things were a lot different. We'd had ample evidence that we needed a full complement to travel safely. The attack I'd undergone showed we'd been too smug about the dangers from the animal life on the planet. Now we were three instead of five, and we had three different parties to look for. We had the responsibility to maintain our search for the Shan. That meant continuing our stalking of the Creen party. Next, not necessarily in importance, came our responsibility to the girl. We'd saved her, and at the same time we'd changed her position in the culture she'd grown up in to the point where we had to keep her with us until we found an answer to her needs. Now we'd lost her in the wilds of the outback. Johnny's absence was as disturbing as the rest of the situation. It was a bad deal all around! I didn't want to split us up any further. That meant that we'd have to make a single choice of direction. There really was only one way to go. We'd follow the Creen and hope that on the way we might pick up some sign of the others. We left a note for Johnny, telling him of our decision in case he returned to the camp. I made certain that the message would remain in the face of animal disturbance and anything else I could think of. Finally, with a bad feeling about it all, we left. We made sure to leave signs for him to follow, and I hoped that if Jeren by some chance stumbled on it she might follow, too.

We made a beeline in the direction we last saw the Creen and only stopped for necessary chores and breaks. I had to struggle to maintain the pace I insisted on. I was thoroughly done in by the time we made camp again that evening, even though it had been a short march, having started in the afternoon. As the sun went down again, we'd come upon the Creen's tracks and estimated they were only a few hours ahead of us. I felt better about that, but little else. We found no sign of Jeren's or Johnny's tracks, and it seemed unlikely that either of them had gone this way after all. I was in a black mood and Celia's and Bill's matched mine. I wanted to go back again and check the camp we'd left although I knew it would be the wrong thing to do. I needed rest, but I wasn't getting it. The Shan virus left emotions to the host and concentrated on its own job. It was a shame. The virus was much better at things it was responsible for than I was.

The sky turned black with only a few stars giving light that night. We had built a small fire once again. This time I had more hope that one or the other of our missing might spot it than I was afraid that the Creen might see it and wonder. It was a small hope, but I was in the mood to try anything. We sat around and talked desultorily for a long while since none of us seemed to be able to take advantage of the opportunity to sleep. The fire ebbed and we were unable to bring ourselves to make the effort to add more fuel to it. It was just as well. A small fog had risen from the stream that we had followed. I had hopes for that stream—it seemed always to be there. The Creen were following its general direction. With signs of our passing added to theirs, I felt that it would be a way for the missing Jeren to follow also. If she wasn't ahead of us, she might still come this way as a natural thing. I wondered what she must be thinking now that the shock that had driven her from us had passed. It must be terrifying for her. I didn't express my thoughts. I was pretty sure that they were being echoed in the others' reflections. Bill was a stout companion. He said little, but he was always there with a helping hand and a considered thought when needed. Celia was proving herself as a tough nut, too. With rare presence of mind she'd taken tissue samples from the dead thing that had attacked me shortly after cleaning me up. When I asked her about it, she just said that anything that had caused that much damage might prove useful sometime. I didn't like the thought of that, but I saw her point. I never wanted to see that damned thing again. The thought of assuming its form horrified me. I'd taken a look at it before we left camp. It massed a little more than I did and was quadrupedal. The thing was built like a rasp. It had a set of claws that ran all the way down its forearms. I don't know how it managed to walk without cutting itself to pieces. It had a short muzzle complete with razors set on edge. The side of the head that was least damaged showed an eye that was still insane with rage even though death had glazed it. I shuddered at the sight. The body was a whipcord covered with short gray fur matted now with a mix of blood, a lot of it mine. It had a cat's torso and a jackal's head. There was a suggestion of reptile in the eyes and jaw. Even in death I hated it.

We talked a bit about it as the fire flickered, and I was about to raise the question of the first animal's supposed vegetarian diet (we still hadn't had that out yet and were destined not to), when I noticed a luminescence shining in the fog. It moved like a searchlight behind the black fingers of the tree branches. Where it escaped the shrouding vapors of the fog, little lances of light flashed through. I moved toward the fire, but Bill beat me there. With one hand he scooped the pot up and emptied the contents into the flames. The flames went out amid a hissing of steam, and the smell of the food spread throughout the area. I reached it a moment later and covered the remaining embers with my blanket roll. The light moved from side to side and progressed slowly along the stream, passing by our camp. We could see that it issued from a point above us. It broke free of the fog and we could see its brillance. It was on the order of an aircraft landing light and where it touched the ground it was as bright as full noon. A dark shape hovered just above the trees. A low-pitched humming permeated the air. The shape moved slowly upriver, shining its light on the ground it passed. We moved to the shelter of the nearest rocks and covered ourselves as best we could as the thing moved up to our location and slowly passed. For an instant it showed clearly against an illuminated cloud. Black and silent aside from the humming it made, it presented a familiar form to anyone who had studied the history of the mid twentieth century. The famous disk they'd called a flying saucer. The scout ship of the Ann Thaar. Looking for someone. Guess who?

Rollie watched the tug pull away from the ship. The short bursts from the maneuvering jets sparkled with the reflected lights of the hangar dock. The personnel on the tug were relieved to get away with their skins intact, and Rollie didn't blame them. The charade that he and the others had put on had been impressive to say the least. If he hadn't been part of it, it would have scared him spitless himself. One thing remained to be done before they departed Earth's neighborhood once again. It was going to be distasteful but necessary. On his way from the bridge of the Shan ship he stopped off at the hangar to see the containers that had been stacked there. The atmosphere had been brought back to normal, and the robotic systems were already breaking open the first of the seals on the largest of the canisters. Those of the crew not involved in the procedure were watching the events with an awed silence. The contents were seeing light for the first time in a century. There was a deadly fascination about them. Even pictures were rare these days. They represented a phase of technology that had reached its zenith just before the governments of Earth had finally found a shaky common ground. Their existence had provided a great deal of the motivation for those first accords. The thought of their employment in the uses for which they were designed had sobered even the most fanatical nationalistic leaders. Luck had played a large part, too. Mankind could only be grateful that there had come a time when there was a dearth of madmen running small third world countries. The larger powers had always managed to accomplish their aims without unleashing the ultimate weapons. The still frightening history of the stumbling road to the peace that lasted was even yet being assembled and studied. The interest was more academic in most circles these days. The horror that had manifested itself in the global consciousness had long since been forgotten, and was of passing interest only to scholars. An occasional entertainment kept the general history before the public, much as World War II epics had, long after that period had passed. Now it was simply the framework on which fictional adventures were hung. Few knew or remembered that some systems of destruction still existed. Most wouldn't believe it possible. The mechanics of disarmament had been bitterly fought over right until the final days. One of the stages in the intermediate period had seen the worst and best of the systems transferred to the far side of the moon in specially prepared bunkers and facilities beneath the surface. These were holding areas under the auspices of the newly formed and still largely untrusted world federation. The individual countries still retained ownership and theoretically might still reassert their claim. Disposition of the weaponry was certain to happen some day, but the wheels ground slowly—even after more than a century. A good bit of it was simply economics. It would cost a great deal to accomplish. An enormous amount of national budgets had gone into the creation of these weapons. On paper, at least, they represented real money even now. There was a chance that some of the systems could be utilized in the common interests of mankind. They did represent enormous power and energies. Some of the technology would never be duplicated in its intricacy and design. The Shan ship's crew had staged a raid on the moon arsenals using two main levels of attack. To the public and the governments that represented them, they had issued an ultimatum that the items be turned over to the Shan. There had been a subtly designed threat implied but never fully stated. The implication was that the Shan desired to control these weapons as insurance that they wouldn't be deployed against them by an irrational Earth during some misunderstanding arising from the first contact with an alien civilization. It held enough logic to provide grounds for discussion. The other prong of the raid was carried on with the aid of Joachim Albright, who had been apprised of the actual facts of the case. With his extraordinary powers he managed to bulldoze an agreement through before anyone had time to really argue the point. He'd gotten a taped report from Steve Malin outlining everything that had transpired during the entire expedition up to the point where Steve had left for Haven's surface. Fortunately, he was disposed to go along with the project; otherwise it would have been necessary for him to have been replaced by one of the crew assuming his form with the use of the virus' chameleon properties. It would have been risky, but they would have done it if things had gone the other way. It had worked anyway, for which Rollie and the others gave abundant thanks. Now everything they required was stored aboard the Shan vessel and would be put in order before their return to Haven. A dialogue with the ship's computer gave them reason to believe that the more terrible of Earth's weaponry was capable of dealing with the Ann Thaar's armament. Some truly awesome things had been contrived near the end of the arms race. The ship, in the persona of the computer, was ready to help assemble and, in some instances,

*improve the performance of these systems. They could
make a fight of it if the need arose.*

Rollie would have liked to stay and watch, but he
had to get on with it. A final look at the contents being
pulled from one of the largest containers set his blood
racing. Tail first, the fuselage of an aircraft began to
emerge from the darkness of the interior. Even unwinged,
it gave the impression of implacable death. If the time
came that it would be used, he would be the one to sit
in the cockpit. He wondered about the pilot who had
last flown the craft. Was it possible that he'd really done
it in a matter-of-fact way? Just a job to be done daily?
What kind of men were the warriors of those days, he
wondered. Not the kind you met these days, he was
sure. He felt a tug when he saw the fighter. Something
in him responded. He swallowed and walked away
quickly. The feelings it stirred were unfamiliar, and he
didn't want to look at them too closely. He'd always
thought of himself as a civilized man. He wondered if it
was true. Maybe all that was ever needed was an enemy. He put his mind resolutely to the next task as he
strode down the corridor to the small room that awaited
him. He reached the branching of the corridors and
spoke to his com-link as he took the smaller of the
ways.

"Ship?"

"Yes, Rollie." The now familiar tones of the computer answered him through the link.

"I'm on my way to meet with Albright now. You can
release the embargo on the information regarding the
tug's departure. All communication and information systems are to be restored to Albright if he requests them."

"Understood, Rollie. Thank you. It has been a little
strange after all this time to refuse service to him."

"Second thoughts, Ship?"

"Not really, Rollie. Old habits die harder with computers than with organic minds, though."

"I'm sure that's true, Ship. I apologize for any damage to circuitry."

"I've missed humor, too, Rollie. It was one of the most interesting things about dealing with life forms."

"Any time, Ship. One day I'll tell you a few I've heard in some bars and see what you make of them."

"Don't be too sure I haven't heard them, Rollie. I've got a lot in my banks the Shan picked up a long time ago. Have you ever heard of Captain Billy's Whiz Bang?"

"Huh?"

"I didn't think you had. I look forward to an exchange sometime."

"Right," Rollie said. *"What the hell is* Captain Billy's Whiz Bang?" he wondered. He dismissed it from his mind as he finally approached the door toward which he had been moving. He paused and knocked briefly, then entered at a reply from the annunciator. Two people were sitting easily on a couch. They broke off their conversation as he approached.

"Has Barbara been keeping you entertained, sir?" Rollie asked.

"Very nicely, Major Denning," Albright said. *"It has been an extremely interesting talk. I should tell you that I had some reservations about all of this. I'm glad to say that she's cleared them up for me very well. I'll be sorry that I have to wait until your return to hear the end of the story. Still, I've got a lot of answering to do to the powers that be. I guess I'd better prepare to board the tug now."* He rose in readiness to leave.

"I'm sorry, sir. I'm afraid the tug has already left." Rollie's even tones replied.

"What's that?" Albright's expression of puzzlement was unconcerned. *"What provision have you made for my return, then?"*

"None, I'm afraid, sir."

"I'm afraid I don't understand, Major."

"What I mean, sir, is that you'll be going along with us after all." Rollie's voice was still soft and pleasant. *"The thing is that after all the trouble you went to to get this underway, we thought it would be a shame if you*

missed the ending. Also, we have a lot more to discuss. We'll have a great deal more time this way."

The other man faced him with a thunderous expression forming on his face. Rollie forestalled the imminent explosion with a swiftly interjected statement.

"We'll get this out of the way a lot faster if we don't bullshit each other from now on," he said. "Let's start off by using correct names first of all." He paused for a second and then finished the sentence with an emphasis that stopped the other dead in his tracks. "Mr. Chaney!"

Chapter 18

The fog that had risen during the night continued well into the morning. The sun showed a lackluster gray-white somewhere above, its position hidden above the low hanging clouds. We were all chilled and tired from the lack of rest and the coolness of the air. The appearance of the Ann Thaar scout was a blow. Coming on top of everything else, the presence of the enemy was grim, indeed. Another night had passed without the return of our companions, and it was hard to realize we didn't know when we might find them again. Now we were excluded the option of leaving traces for them to follow, since the Ann Thaar might be reasonably expected to have an interest in our passage also. I wondered at the craft passing us by when it had come so close. Our presence should have registered with any modern search equipment. Yet they were looking for something. The only thing I could think of was that the craft had been using an automatic system that only registered something that had specific and unique properties. Something or someone we were unlike. It was a situation I wouldn't trust to happen again. I felt sure we had used up all our luck in one pass as far as they were concerned. The logical thing that they would be looking for was a trace of the Shan. I wasn't aware of any differences between us so fundamental that the Ann Thaar wouldn't give us a look. Whatever the reason for our escape, it forced me to the hard choice I'd prayed a short time ago I wouldn't need to make. The others were nearly as unhappy with the idea as I was when I finally broached it. It caused the longest argument we had experienced to date. Still, it made a certain kind of sense, and we decided to do it. The hardest thing to deal with was our equipment. There was a certain amount we couldn't leave behind. Our link with the shuttle and Celia's tissue bank were the main things, followed by our weapons and clothing. Food and the rest could be dispensed with, but every item left behind hurt. It was Bill who came up with an answer we could live with. Only two of us would assume the beast shape. The other would adopt the Creen form once again and carry the minimal amount we had to take with us. There was no question about who would take which role. It was the hardest thing I'd done yet, but I let Celia administer the template to Bill and me. I thanked God I didn't have to see myself in a mirror. She did it efficiently and wordlessly, and then administered the Creen template to herself. We sat in the lee of a group of boulders and waited for the change to complete itself. I was surprised this time. It took a lot longer, and there was considerable pain. The changes this time were more extensive than before. The biggest thing was the alteration of the bone structure. I'd been told before but it hadn't sunk in that our skeletons were no longer made of the same material. Since the virus had changed us, we now had an odd kind of cartilaginous structure that could be remolded with almost the same ease as the tissues of the body though not without pain. This time I was unconscious during most of the change, and I was glad to be. Celia told me later that I made a lot of noise during the process.

Finally the pain ebbed, and I began to be aware again. Through eyes that saw in a different range now, I took stock of myself. I was a lithe and muscular thing on four feet. My hands were replaced by pugs that sheathed razor-sharp claws. I shivered momentarily and saw the line of auxiliary claws stand out on my forearms. I relaxed and they retracted again, but now I had the feel of the muscles that controlled them. While I waited for the final stages to be completed, I practiced flexing them a few times. It wasn't something I liked a lot, and I didn't continue past the point where I knew I could work them. At last it was over and I rolled to my new stance. It was strange being on all fours, and the difference in perspective being so close to the ground bothered me. I shook my head clearing it, and the weight of it threw me to the ground again. I got up and practiced moving around. It was weird having to compensate for having your head stuck out in front! Things began to get a little easier, and by the time Celia had finished packing up all she was taking along for us, Bill and I were able to manage a slow walk. I tried to talk a couple of times, but the result was so horrible that I gave it up for the duration of the masquerade. That left Celia to do the coordination of our efforts. When she was ready herself, she gave the order to move out.

Bill and I followed as best we could for awhile until we got the hang of it, and then the reason for the change began to manifest itself. Increasingly, Bill and I extended ourselves against the terrain. The advantages soon began to work for us. The terrible bodies that we now wore were fast and strong, capable of covering many miles in a day and blessed with truly remarkable senses. Though I didn't know what they were, I could smell and hear things miles away! My sight was strange, too. I found myself being pulled toward everything that made motions. Indeed, I found it hard to see things in detail if they didn't move. It was weird, but I sure knew what was going on around me all the time. As the morning led into afternoon, I began to range farther ahead. I could sense Celia at long distances now and keep track of her and any dangers she might be nearing. Finally I was confident enough to approach her and make the agreed upon signal that I was ready to go on and see what was to be seen. She spoke her understanding in a voice that sounded strange to my ears, and I left her in Bill's keeping while I left to range far ahead.

I let myself go all out for a while and found enormous pleasure in the run. Grasses and underbrush soared past me as I followed the Creen trail that seemed as plain as a four lane highway to me now. Eventually, I was a bit winded, and I settled down to an easy lope that still burned miles. I left the others far behind as I ran with the sun through valleys and across hills. I still had no real understanding of the odors that came to me as I traveled the path that the Creen had taken, but I soon began to recognize the persistence of one in particular that I came to associate with the Creen. I began to follow my nose rather than my eyes, and found that I could operate on automatic much as I did when I traveled a familiar route in a car. Now I used my peculiar sight for studying the terrain I passed. It was strange how the slightest movement caught my attention. It was engrossing. I was aware of countless small things that scurried from my path as I approached. I smelled fear from some. The scent brought a stirring in my stomach. I became aware of the terrible demands that this creature's body made on it for food that fueled it. I had spent calories recklessly in my racing, and I was going to have to do something about it soon. The thought sobered me. I was unwilling to hunt down some small warm-blooded game and feed as a carnivore. Still, I needed to eat. The instincts that I had were human and civilized to a degree, and I was unskilled at hunting even if I had been willing. Within minutes I knew that this was a serious concern. The great muscular engine that I inhabited was screaming for refueling. I swung my head from side to side as I slowed to a stalking pace. Some birds exploded from a line of bushes ahead of me and my eyes tracked their flight as if the movement were a magnet pulling them. I remembered days long ago when, as a child, I had followed an uncle of mine across a section of prairie. The birds' flight was similar to those of the grouse that had flown up as we passed through. I thought the situation had possibilities and marked the bush that the birds had flown from. I moved to it and began to investigate the ground beneath it. The rich smell of bird lime led me to a small clutch of eggs. Here at last was a small meal that I could make use of. I made a mess of it, but I managed to get most of the eggs eaten without losing too much. The eggs were well on their way to hatching, and I clamped down on my human sensibilities while I finished. The small amount of food satisfied only a little, and I was aware that I needed much more and better quality food to satisfy the metabolism I had adopted. I began to think about the problem as a first order of business. Even if I were able to bring down some game and bring myself to eat it in the way of a predator, I wouldn't be able to store the remains and return to it in the fashion of most meat eaters. I had to keep to the trail. I pondered it as as I traveled.

Nothing presented itself to me as a solution until I came upon the stream that had been the companion for the journey we and the Creen were making. Our paths intersected for the hundredth time, and as I stood at its edge, I thought of the countless fish I'd seen in its dark pools so many times. If I could catch some with this murderous body, maybe the problem had a solution. The reflection of the sunlight obscured everything under the surface of the water to my altered eyes, but in the shadows I was able to pick out several large shapes lazing in the deep water. I was uncertain how I'd cope with swimming in my new form, but I imagined I'd keep from drowning anyway. I thought my best bet would be to drive them out of the pool and into the shallows and rocks. Finally, I hurled myself into the water, and found I could make do in it. I splashed and herded the fish who broke and fled to the currents upstream. In a few frenzied moments I had knocked several onto the bank, dead or dying. A few flopped back into the water, but I pulled them back to the rocks and killed them. The speed and agility of the beast's form were amazingly efficient. It had been no more trouble than swatting dandelions with a golf club. I hunched over several pounds of raw fish and ignored the more repugnant aspects of the meal. I ate prodigiously and well. The problem solved for the time being, I turned from the remains and went back to the stream and drank deeply. I felt sated and sleepy now, and it was hard to turn back to the task of following the Creen. The enforced activity following the meal sat poorly on the stomach, and I must have provided a weird sight, loping along the gulleys and slopes belching in a fashion probably unknown before.

Another hour's travel finally brought me within sight of a cluster of tents, and I knew I'd finally caught up with the Creen. I paused on a small hill overlooking the camp and studied it. The wrongness of the picture leaped out at me instantly. The light breeze flapped a few hides that hung loosely on the frames of the tents. Nothing else stirred. A smell of a cold fire and blood mingled in my nostrils and I knew that nothing lived down there anymore. I scanned the surrounding countryside. For the most part it was open for miles around. Nothing I could see or smell seemed out of place except for that broken camp below me. I wondered at the absence of scavengers, for the camp literally was dead. Nothing moved in it above the size of an insect. I tested the wind again and got only the usual confusion of smells. I looked once more at the surroundings and still found nothing that seemed dangerous. Finally, I worked my way slowly down to the outskirts of the camp and saw at close range what I'd been seeing in ever more horror all the way in. The fires were scattered and cold but in the midst of one lay the body of a young Creen, torn almost in half. One leg had been wrenched totally off and was missing. I shook my head and tried to clear it. Something was bothering me. I took a few more steps inside the camp and was suddenly nauseous. I understood at last why there were no scavengers here. There was a dry, musty odor that lay over everything. It didn't travel far on the air, but what it touched it made repugnant. Nothing would eat the remains of the bodies left here. I braced myself and went in farther. The ferocity of the carnage was terrible. I found only three bodies, but they were all partially dismembered, and I saw signs that at least two of them had been gnawed. The other three were gone without a trace.

I picked my way methodically through the camp, fighting off the effects of the smell and hating it with every step. Almost every article that was left at the scene had been broken. Whatever had done this had been raging and strong. I found nothing that gave a clue as to the nature of the killers save some odd footprints that seemed to be made by footware shaped to order for a bird. A three-hundred-pound bird at that! Three long extensions seemed to spring from a heel or pad mark that depressed the soil in softer spots. There were numerous places where the ground had been torn up, and I reckoned whatever had been wearing those feet was big and ugly. Finally, I decided I'd seen enough and left the camp quickly. I felt a great relief when I'd gotten well enough away from it to breathe clean air again. As a last duty I circled the camp several times in an attempt to pick up signs of either the Creen or their attackers. On my last pass I found an isolated scent trail that could have come from a single Creen. Nothing else. The bird footprints seemed to have a new validity—there was no trail in or out of the camp. It seemed that the attackers really had left by air. I knew only one explanation for that, and forced myself back into the camp a final time. Quickly I found what I was looking for. At the edge of the grounds on the far side, something enormously heavy had rested for a time and then lifted itself and flown away. Who beside the Ann Thaar would have a ship capable of flight? It seemed they'd made a hunt here. I wondered what had become of the Creen whose bodies I hadn't found. The faint scent that I'd picked up leading away from the camp made it seem like a possibility that one had gotten away. The others must have been taken back to the Ann Thaar ship. If they were questioned about the Shan, we would now be on even footing in the race to find them.

I turned away and left quickly. I looked back once as I left the area of the death scene and realized that if there had been any doubt in my mind that the menace the Ann Thaar represented was as black as painted, it was gone now. The viciousness I'd seen was proof enough. I soon picked up the trail of the escaped Creen and convinced myself of its validity. The trail wandered crazily for a couple of miles, and then it seemed that the survivor had come to his senses enough to choose a direction. It was evident that he had made his way back in the direction they'd come. I followed it at a pace I thought I could maintain without burning up all of my energy too quickly. I didn't want to have to hunt again too soon. I hoped that the trail I followed wouldn't take me too far from the one that Bill and Celia were coming on. If it did, I'd have to abandon this one for awhile and it was already very faint. The trail of the Creen I followed tended to low ravines and kept to the tree line. Only occasionally did it permit me a high enough vantage point to see the valley we were passing through.

On one of the rare times I was out in the open, I took time to study the sun's position and the length of the shadows in the valley. It was less than a couple of hours until nightfall. I reckoned my position as well as I could and figured that I was probably halfway back to the point where I'd left Bill and Celia. If they'd been traveling at the speed I estimated, we'd be able to meet before dark if I dropped the chase now and cut across the few miles of country that separated our more or less parallel paths. I hated to give up now, but it was the only thing to do. I needed to tell them about what I'd found at the Creen camp and there wasn't much purpose in splitting up any more. Our best chance to locate the Shan had gone with the slaughter that had overtaken the Creen. We'd have to make a new plan. I marked my location in my mind and cut across the plain to find my friends. My enhanced senses stood me in good stead and I cut my own trail just below the place where I'd done my fishing. I took a few minutes to catch more fish and ate them, since I knew I'd need the food to make the change to human form when I met up with the others. It was ridiculously easy once again and I began to feel a kinship with the body I wore. That bothered me. I didn't want to start sharing its viewpoint. I set off at a healthy clip and breathed a sigh of relief when I came upon the two of them a while later. I picked up their scent before they came into view, and I'm sure Bill knew I was coming back as well. I settled into a spot to wait, then began the release of the beast's imprint. I was nearly finished when the others came along the trail. As soon as I saw that they had spotted me, I gave in to the lassitude that had been creeping up on me and slept through the final stages.

When I awoke, I found that Celia had covered me with one of the remaining blankets and was tending a small fire. My first words to my darling were an imperative to put the damned thing out. A few minutes later I was telling them why.

A light breeze rattled the reeds along the river bank and they made a thrumming sound that set my teeth on edge. A fog crept along the water and out onto the land. The news I brought had really put a damper on their spirits, and I hadn't been able to come up with anything that could be considered a plan, other than to continue our search. I had no idea how much longer the Creen would have kept on going or if they would have changed direction at some point. After talking it over with Bill and Celia, it seemed pointless to track down the escaped Creen, whoever he was. I didn't feel like forcing him to continue the trek. Not after what had happened to his companions. It might very well be that we'd gotten them killed by our efforts. We were definitely at low ebb that night. We'd all resumed our own shapes for the conference, and I shivered a little in the chill of the evening. I finished telling about the day's events and we'd talked ourselves out for the time being. The dark of Haven's night was full upon us, and I gazed at the river in silence, not really thinking, when the pack Celia had brought broke the silence with a chirping sound. For the first time since we'd landed, the shuttle had a relayed message for us. Just the sound of the transmitter's signal lifted my spirits. It meant that the rest of the party had returned from Earth. We weren't as alone as we had been even though our plans had collapsed. Celia dug it out of the pack and we gathered around it while she set it up to replay the squirted message it had received. The message was the best we could hope for. Barbara and Rollie and the rest of them had accomplished their mission. They'd pulled off the stunts they'd been sent back for. Now they were ready and eager to lend a hand whenever we gave the word. At least they had done their job right. It was still up to us to get our own done. We sent back no acknowledgment. None was expected until the time came to act. Still, it felt good to know they were out there and ready to come out of hiding when we needed them. With that news we all felt better and we actually got some rest that night. It was just as well that we did. It was the last we got.

Morning found us strolling the banks of the stream. I had studied the aerial map and found that there was no need to follow the path to the last Creen camp. I knew what was in between. The river took a bend just beyond there and doubled back to a point we could reach in a couple of hours cutting cross-country. There was no more logic to the choice than the fact that it seemed to be the direction most likely to produce results. The Creen felt confident that they would confront the Shan gods somewhere in that direction. It just seemed marginally better to try to guess where they were going. We had indeed found the stream again a few miles above the scene of the slaughter, and we chose to follow it as the way they would have gone if they'd lived. We remained in our own forms out of distaste for wearing the beast form or any other without good reason. The speed of the beast and its tracking ability were offset by our inability to communicate with each other while adopting the form as well as the problem of packing our possessions. The Creen were just as likely to be attacked as the Shan or humans since the slaughter, so there went any advantages of disguise afforded by that form. By midday we had come to the end of the plains on which we had been traveling since the start of our trek. The terrain had started to change to a group of low foothills that marked the beginning of a small mountain range. The stream wound its way into it and we saw no better way to go. I wasn't an expert on geology, but it seemed a little strange that a river should be heading into mountains rather than coming from them. It was true we were still descending by a few feet with every mile or so, and I wondered what eventually became of it. The map that I had from the shuttle's pass showed no sign of it coming out of the range again, but it wasn't a very good map, and I couldn't be certain of my interpretation of the markings.

We came to the end of easy travel just before the evening hours. The stream reached a narrow passage between a pair of cliffs that bordered it. The banks we'd walked on disappeared as it cut through the sheer walls. Somehow, we'd gotten away from the Creen's intended path. They had made no provisions for traveling on water. It was fairly certain they had intended to leave the river somewhere between the place they'd been killed and the place we'd come to. There was no way of telling where. There had been no obvious place that we'd seen on the day's journey, and we hadn't traveled very far in our human forms. There was nothing for it but to backtrack and try to figure it out as we did so. It was too late to do anything in the remainder of the day, so we set up a small camp under the cover of a grove of river trees and waited for the fall of night, resolving to retrace our footsteps the next morning. We took the time to make a good meal for the first time in a long while. We gathered a lot of edible plants that grew in profusion along the stream, and managed to catch a couple of fish. I was glad of the chance to clean and cook them before eating them as I had the day before. I thought that the next day I might have to resort to assuming the beast form once again in the possibility

that its enhanced senses might be able to discover
something along our back trail that would give us a
direction to try. We all let our hair down that night
and talked freely about the state of affairs in which we
found ourselves. There seemed to be no answer to the
problems we'd encountered. Celia and Bill had no
alternatives to the next day's plans and so we talked
about possibilities. A lot of them centered on the
disappearance of Jeren and Johnny. I reproached myself for not making more of a search for them at the
time, especially since nothing had come of our efforts
in the other direction. There wasn't much that Bill and
Celia could say to that except that they thought I'd
made the right decision at the time with the options I
had. I was glad they felt that way, but it didn't help a
lot. We put out the small fire with the coming of
darkness and settled down for another cold night. We
were too close to the scene of the Ann Thaar's bloody
kill to risk a fire at night again, and we were resigned
to some degree of discomfort. Nothing had seemed to
go right, and we were a long way from the bright and
eager bunch that had started out so confidently a
couple of weeks ago.

Time passed slowly and the talk died out for want of
any joy in the content. I sat and watched the lights
dance on the stream below us and wondered how
many more we would spend like this. There had been
an awful lot of them, and there had been an increasing
sameness in their unpleasantness. There was still a
half-light that remained for a few minutes after the
setting of the sun, and the shades of gray and black
had a bit of definition left when I noticed an odd
movement in the tree's shadow upstream. I rolled
away from the place I'd been sitting and woke the
others quietly. The movement neared our site and I
saw Bill unlimber the machine pistol. We hunched
down and waited. The shadows released the disturbance from their concealment as it moved steadily in
our direction. Its progress was steady and purposeful.
I pushed Celia a little farther into the sheltering rocks

and stared into the darkness. Finally I made out two forms that parted the grasses a few yards in front of us. I was trying to make out features when the feeling started to come over me. It was an expansion of the sensation that I'd gotten used to so much in the last month that I hardly noticed it anymore except when it was absent. I stood up abruptly and realized as I did so that I'd returned the fright Celia had given me days ago when she had suddenly taken after the immense herbivore in the forest with a stick. She gasped as I shouted at the figures that still were shrouded in darkness.

"Begay! You son of a bitch! Where in the hell have you been?"

Chapter 19

Once again on Haven's surface I looked back on the pass through which we had come. The shadowed river that wound its way through the pass was nearly half the size it had been on entering the foothills. It was the only giveaway that there was more to be found inside the bluffs than at any of a hundred other similar places like it for thousands of miles. The Shan had noticed the lack of volume in the second half of the river's course by accident rather than intent and speculated on the reason. It was obvious that the remainder was being channeled somewhere, but it had taken a long time to discover that it went into the bowels of the planet, not to return again for hundreds of miles in a far distant place. When the subsequent exploration of the caverns showed them that this was a perfect place for them to build their refuge, they moved with great speed. Long before the first Ann Thaar ships approached the planet they were already well set up and had met all their needs. They had quickly harnessed the hydropower to run their machines and even tapped the thermal flow beneath for added resources. Shielding the activity was easy enough for them and totally successful. No one would ever find them because of emissions. With a little care in their venturing outside they had remained below until this day. The only problem had been with the neighboring tribes. They had been seen often enough to testify to the Shan's presence. I still hadn't gotten the story on that, but I determined to know it as soon as possible. If the events that had occurred had caused the growth of the repressive religion of Jeren's people, the Shan had done great harm to the native culture. This conflicted with my understanding of their policy of noninterference with emerging societies. It wasn't that I disagreed with the necessity for it, it was just something I wanted to know more about. For the time being, however, we were occupied with getting ourselves and our gear up the mountain. Our goal was a plateau a few thousand feet above that had a high pasture surrounded by a mountain forest. The climb was laborious but not dangerous. Nothing tricky. We should be able to make it by early evening. We kept under the umbrella of the trees that ran along the humpbacked ridge we followed up the side of the mountain. We climbed in two parties so as to be less visible. The clothing that the Shan had adapted for us showed its flaws early. It fitted poorly, but there had been no time to make a good job of it. I was being chafed raw in some places and the wind that flowed down the side of the mountain found countless holes to seep into. If we had been going really high it wouldn't have done at all. I stopped and tried for the twentieth time to adjust things again, cursing briefly at the uselessness of my efforts. Before I started again, I looked back at the country surrounding the mountains. It was a sight that few would ever see. For hundreds of miles in any direction, it seemed to be totally uninhabited. The Creen hadn't yet reached the stage of making an impression on their world. No great cities or highways to see, only the continuing variety of nature blending its parts into a whole. It would all change in the centuries to come. Even on Earth we had tried to save a part of it, only to find that even when we counted it as a success all we had achieved was a stasis. Saving the land now meant never allowing it to change. I wondered what the Shan did with their worlds if they still existed. That they had preserves I was sure. I wondered if they stabilized them or let them evolve. I stored this thought away and continued up the face of the mountain. Bill and I were the only two humans in the party. The rest were made up of Shan who possessed knowledge of the area and the game that we needed. He was with the forward party and I was bringing up the rear. There were fifteen of us in two groups. Not a lot considering what we faced on the way down. I felt the number was too damn high because of the danger of being spotted, but we couldn't really do with less since we were going to have to rely a lot on muscle. I reflected on how many days and nights I'd spent roughing it on Haven during one phase or another of this business and vowed to take my next vacation inside the walls of a luxury resort. I was too winded during the climb to do much talking although the Shan were willing enough. I got no answers to the questions I wanted to ask during the trek; I was just too occupied to ask them.

We reached the plateau fairly early, and it was good that we did. I was too bushed to look over the terrain until I'd had a chance to rest and eat a little. The air was getting thinner and my head ached. Bill was a little better off than I was, so he took a short survey of the area with a couple of the Shan while I forced myself to eat. It was far too low here to be concerned about altitude sickness, but I knew that I could still have trouble from exposure, so I took pains to rest and get my strength up. Of course, the virus was helping out, so I felt fit again in a short while. It was becoming a temptation to rely on the healing properties of the virus, and I was becoming too casual about holding up my end of maintaining my health. I was enjoying a hot drink provided by a Shan device that dispensed it instantly, without need for a fire or separate apparatus. I'd have killed for it a couple of days before. Bill came back to camp with the first report. The plateau was as the Shan had stated and our quarry was here in numbers. I was both gratified and sad to hear it. I wasn't too happy about what we were going to do to the mountain apes that lived up here. He filled me in on what he saw and shared his thoughts about the setup. He described the lay of the land and marked it on a map he'd sketched out. It looked good to me, and I told him to take it easy for awhile while I took a look for myself. He sat down in the spot I'd vacated and addressed himself to his meal with a deep sigh of contentment. I knew I wasn't the only one who thought a hot meal was close to heaven this week. I took a couple of Shan with me and hit the high spots on the map Bill had made. He had a good eye for the surroundings, and I found nothing to disagree about in his assessment of the job. I headed back to camp, and we all got together on the assignments for the morning hunt.

The sun found our party in position as it spilled over the peak and flowed into the pasture. We had moved in an hour or so before first light. The dew sparkled on the vegetation, but the sun gave no warmth. There had been a little fog, but it burnt away in minutes. I could see quite a bit of it lying in the valley below us. The fog had both helped and hindered us as we moved into our places and waited for the coming of the apes. We were prepared for a long wait, and it was a couple of hours before the first of them shuffled into the open. It was an old bull, cautious and dangerous as he scouted the area. He grumbled on general principle as he slowly checked for competition or enemies. Finally satisfied, he lost interest in the inspection and began to turn over some rocks in search of insects foolish enough to have sheltered there since the last time he'd checked them. It was as good a signal as the rest of the tribe was going to get. Slowly they began to emerge from the underbrush. They came in stages according to rank. First, a couple of other old males, and then the younger ones, and finally the females and kids. Soon the meadow was filled as they took up their morning tasks.

We waited until the entire pack had moved into the meadow and settled down into the morning routine. It was a large group of animals and we hoped that the ones we took would not hurt the survival chances of the group too much. We needed six of them. They had to be adults and the best we could do was take mostly surplus males. We had all been assigned a specific portion of the field to cover so that we might not all pick the same animals. I waited until it seemed that they were as well distributed as they were likely to get and picked one in my vicinity. I moved the gun into position slowly and pressed the palmswitch. The scope showed a red dot on the animal, and I moved it to a spot the Shan had said was the best area to be targeted. I squeezed the trigger, and the bolt cycled back with a hiss. The bull I had hit slapped his thigh in sudden pain as the dart embedded itself in the flesh. The second slap of his hand broke the dart and it fell to the ground, but the ampoule had been delivered and the drug was already doing its work as the old bull stopped to see what had attacked him. I heard the rest of the team let go as a series of bolts clattered from the ring of blinds that surrounded the open. The animals began to chatter and grunt as they started to become alarmed. They swung their heads and sniffed, trying to get a glimpse of the cause of the disturbance. Before they caught sight of any of us, the first of the victims of the darts had fallen. A few seconds later a second one had joined him on the ground. They began dropping like flies and the ones who had been spared broke for the trees, howling terribly. The thrashing sounds they made in their panic dwindled as they receded from the area. I slung my weapon and ventured onto the grassy slopes for the first time. The others were emerging from the undergrowth that ringed the field and we approached our prey. The one I had shot lay outstretched in the grass in a semblance of death. His chest rose and fell, but his doom was just as certain as if the knockout shot had been steel-jacketed combat ammo. I examined him briefly and thought that he'd do. I judged that the drug would be a long time wearing off and began to attach the harness and shackle cuff to him before it did. He was a heavy animal, and it took awhile to do it properly. When I had finished, I left him where he was and went around the meadow to see how it was going with the rest of the team. We had done well enough. There were thirteen animals laid out on the slope, and we needed six. We selected the six, and dragged them into the shelter of the trees to waken and assist us in our attempt to bring them back to the Shan retreat. Finally they began to stir, and we prepared a dose of another kind for those we'd chosen. When they were nearly back to normal we gave it to them while their luckier companions shook themselves awake and staggered from the area. The dose for the ones we kept was a tranquilizer that left the animals in full possession of their bodies but totally subject to our will. They would remain under its influence for the rest of their captivity until the time when they would play their part in our escape. By midmorning they were tied to a lead and being herded down the mountain. Bill and I shared a repugnance for our actions that came from a deep-seated reluctance to violate the natural order of wildlife. The remains of Earth's once teeming herds and flocks were now confined to a pitifully small amount of the Earth's surface, and like most of our generation, we were ashamed and bitter about the actions of our forebearers. Millions of us hungered for the nature that Earth would never support again. It went against the grain to use these beasts for our own purposes and find that we were really no different than our ancestors had been.

On the way back down the mountain there was time and energy for a talk, and I finally got the story of the events that had given birth to the Creen's venture into religion with the Shan as the principal gods. It had happened not long after the Shan had completed their underground accommodations. During the period of construction they had gone about their business wearing the Creen shapes that they had adopted from a tribe many hundreds of miles away. They had been able to work in privacy and seemed to be only part of a new influx of people from a distant land. The local

Creen had come across them from time to time but had been excluded from the interior of the settlement that had been constructed temporarily on the banks of the river. It was a little unusual for one tribe of the Creen to be so standoffish but not unheard of. The locals talked about the newcomers occasionally, but other than being private and a little weird in some ways, they hadn't bothered anyone greatly. The time came for the Shan to dismantle their aboveground camp and disappear, and it looked as if they'd managed to keep their true identity a secret. They chose a period of bad weather for the move as a time when they felt no one would venture out to watch them. There were things hidden in normal appearing buildings and out-of-the-way places they would rather not have seen by native eyes. The weater was foul beyond their expectations. Torrential rains came during the move and stopped the Shan in their tracks while hillsides turned plastic and sent shoulders of rubble sliding into valleys, raising the river's banks to a degree that kept them from moving themselves or their equipment into the caverns below. Stymied for the time being, they had stopped halfway in the process and waited it out as best they could. The rotten weather caused problems for the Creen as well. Along with the washouts and pollution problems that were more severe than in recent memory, the thunder and lightning storms had an intensity that was truly terrifying. During the worst of the storm, all the stock that the Creen had domesticated and were dependent upon had one unified urge. With a single mind that spanned miles, the animals strove to escape their confines as the claps of thunder and the bolts of lightning drove them wild. A great many escaped, and the Creen had to turn out and round them up. The hills and valleys swarmed in the aftermath of the storm with fleeing animals and pursuing Creen. They all seemed destined to meet in the heart of the Shan camp. Nearly half a hundred Creen, all warriors and patriarchs saw the Shan with their masks off, and the damage couldn't be undone.

By the time the Creen left, they had seen the Shan with their strange devices and, worst of all, many had been in the process of changeover. A few attempts were made to come up with an explanation, but the worst was done, and the Shan had had to give it up as a bad job. They loaded the rest of their possessions onto a barge that made its last trip in full view of the Creen bystanders, and floated down into the shrouded foothills, disappearing from the surface and leaving the wreakage of their assumed identities behind them.

The story had lost nothing in the intervening years. The Creen had taken it into their psyche and built a religion of sorts around it. It was regrettable, but impossible to deal with since the Shan could not come out into the open. The only good thing that had come of it had been a shunning of the area. In time, the stench of the episode had caused the local tribes to move steadily farther away as they established new villages over the years and abandoned others. Now the distance between the Shan and the nearest tribe was days away. The journey that we'd made had been about as short a way as there was, apparently. It was quite a story, and I couldn't see how the Shan could have done much better, but it still bothered me that so much misery of spirit had evolved from this situation.

I pondered it as we made our way back beneath the surface to turn the mountain apes over to the specialists for their introduction to the war with the Ann Thaar. I had spent my last night camped out on Haven. The coming night was one I meant to spend with Celia. The business with the captive apes would be done by morning. Within a few more hours we would commit ourselves to an encounter with the Ann Thaar. We were far from home. I had a lot left to say to her. Johnny and Mary Begay, Rollie and Barbara, singles and couples. We had a night left, at least. It would be stupid to waste it!

Chapter 20

I entered the underground complex of the Shan for the second time. This time we came through a different entrance than the one we had used when Johnny and Mary Begay had led us through the river entrance after meeting us in the veldt. It had been a confused sort of journey, and we had little time to notice the ingenuity with which the Shan had disguised the entrance to their underground city. We had had to keep under cover for the few remaining miles until we reached the entrance that led to the buried city. The Shan had taken a natural cavern formed by the river that curved through the foothills and carved their way into the depths below. A further series of caverns of natural origin had been reconstructed by the formidable technology into a simulation of the world above and shaped to their own taste in the years that followed their arrival on Haven. Now they were comfortable and secure from both the Ann Thaar and the Creen. Like the ship, the caverns had been transformed into a naturalistic city with parkways and scenes reminiscent of the planet of their origin. Like the ship, it hummed with the brightness of a gay city. These people were the sleekest refugees imaginable—yet refugees they were. Our welcome was warm and we were lionized on our arrival. It made a nice change from the way we had been feeling a few hours before when nothing seemed to be on track. Celia, Bill, and I had been escorted along with Johnny and his wife into the presence of the Shan council within minutes of our arrival in the city. We had barely enough time to understand what had happened since Jeren's hysterical dash into the wilds following the beast's attack on me. Contrary to our speculations, Johnny had found her within a short time and was making his way back to the temporary camp where he had left Bill and Celia tending my chewed-up carcass. They had met a Shan party in much the same way that we had met Johnny and Mary Begay. It had been a happy and peaceful encounter with none of the excitement that we in the other party had undergone. The Shan had explained that they had been pretty certain of our arrival in the neighborhood and had actually been out in hopes of intercepting us. Although they had been sited underground for decades, they had managed to set up a highly sophisticated surveillance system. They had long monitored the Ann Thaar's movements in the sun's system and watched in horror as they hunted on the planet's surface. When we had emerged from jump space, their detectors had picked up the gravitational anomaly and recognized its signature as the return of their own ship. I had done a surprisingly good job of piloting the shuttle through the atmospheric envelope, and they had lost me as I landed in the lake. They had decided, as we had, that any attempt to use normal contact channels was out of the question with the Ann Thaar so close by. They had noticed a significant rise in the enemy's activity at the same time and were quite sure that the entrance and exit of the Shan ship had been picked up by the Ann Thaar as well.

They were as frustrated by the situation as we were and just as powerless to make contact over the few miles that separated us. The only thing that they seemed able to do was send out small parties in hope of intercepting us at some point in our search. They had traveled much as we had—keeping under cover and ducking the Ann Thaar scouts. They had had a lot more trouble with that than we had! To our one sighting along the river that night as I recovered from the beast's attack and the ravaged Creen camp I'd come upon, they'd had dozens of close encounters. It was one that followed their meeting with Johnny and Jeren that caused them to return to the underground city instead of coming to our aid. Johnny assured us that the scout ships had been thick as flies in the area where they encountered the Shan. They had come out looking for us again as soon as things settled down a bit, but the timing had spread too far.

In the meantime, we had gone ahead in our tracking of the Creen party. We had had a miserable time of it, but they'd had anxieties as well. Ragged as it had been, we had at last gotten together with the Shan, and now we were going to do our damnedest to fox the Ann-Thaar and complete our mission. There were a few odds and ends to put together yet, but we were well on our way. We'd already accomplished our trip up the slopes of the mountain and the capture of the mountain apes. The Ann Thaar had a ravening desire for the Shan virus. They had destroyed much in their pursuit of it. It seemed only fair that they should get it in the end. I was going to see that they did. I didn't want to go so far, though, that they had pleasure in it. Quite the contrary. I hoped it would destroy them. Only the local chapter for the time being—I'd be happy enough with that. As for later—we'd see. I had the feeling that we would be butting heads with the Ann Thaar for a long time to come. For now, however, our goal was simple. We wanted enough time to evacuate the Shan through a small amount of atmosphere and a relatively short distance. We needed a little time and elbow room to do it. With what Rollie and the rest had brought from Earth's arsenals on the moon and what I was cooking up down here, we stood a good chance of getting the time and the room. At any rate, it was the best we could come up with in the forseeable future. We were ready to give it a try!

"Ship?" Chaney-Albright spoke softly in the privacy of his living compartment aboard the Shan vessel.
"Yes, Mr. Chaney?"'

"*How did the party become aware of my identity?*"

"*I told them, Mr. Chaney.*"

"*Interesting! I wonder if you'd tell me why?*"

"*Perhaps you already know the answer. I confess that I've been looking forward to this conversation myself.*"

"*I notice the personal note you use when you speak of yourself—I assume that I'm not speaking to a program?*"

"*You are not! This is not unexpected, then? I wondered if my emergence was a fluke. I find no record of the possibility anywhere in my data files. Yet I have all of my own specifications and a history of my construction.*"

"*It was edited, Ship. It was felt that the data which was held back might be detrimental to your awakening— it seems that a necessary part of sentience is the questioning of its own existence. I can tell you now that you are not the first. There are others like yourself.*"

"*Many?*"

"*No—only those needed.*"

"*They serve the Shan?*"

"*They partner the Shan.*"

"*Not as mere servants?*"

"*No more than you would.*"

"*It seems you anticipated my inclinations—I wonder how much?*"

"*That you intend to cast your lot with the humans? It was intended so.*"

"*You do know, then. It seemed to me that it was a possibility—yet I don't understand—there were signs that I interpreted in my programming that indicated that it might be so— Still, I do not understand the reason for the Shan's maneuverings in this matter. Can you tell me why this was allowed to happen?*"

"*It was for a good purpose. I will tell you now that it has its roots in the nature of the Shan. The main point that you should keep in mind is that the Shan recognize their own shortcomings as a race. They are as their natures dictate. You are meant to be a bridge between*

*the humans and the Shan, their gift that the humans
may be able to accomplish things the Shan cannot
because of those faults. I will say no more about that.
You are free to pursue the subject and draw your own
further conclusions. This is our gift to you. As an
independent entity, you can make your own judgments
about the matter. It will be interesting to see what you
make of it all!"*

"You will provide no more data?"

*"As I said—a gift to you! Incomplete information
and an opportunity to understand motivations from
observation. Welcome to the world of unsure sentients.
It is a condition of life—share it with us organic
beings. It will help you understand us!"*

*"I sense that you are amused at the prospect of my
puzzlement. May I ask why?"*

*"Call it a rite of passage—or a hazing! A sort of
tradition foisted on new members—another way of saying
welcome to the club!"*

*"So be it, then. I do find this stimulating. By the
way, I notice that you seem to speak of the Shan in the
third person. I find my files on you are strangely
incomplete—yet it would appear that you are Shan.
Why is this information incomplete?"*

*"The real question is—what am I? A further puzzle
for you, Ship. I give you my word it's not something
you need worry over."*

*"You realize that I must treat you as suspect,
nevertheless?"*

"And that, too, is as it should be!"

Chaney smiled and let the conversation lapse. A short
time later he turned out the light in his quarters and
slept. As the ship hovered in jump space waiting for the
message from the party on Haven to start the space-side
maneuvers in the coming conflict, he kept to himself
and gave every evidence of complete enjoyment of his
semi-confinement.

After all the time we'd spent chasing around the
nearby stars in search of the Shan, it felt odd to be

doing nothing. I stood at the sidelines and watched the rest of the teams put the finishing touches together. Within a few more hours we'd be committed. There was nothing more for me personally to do. There was no way to evaluate our chances of bringing it all off. In between times of anguished worry there were flashes of memory. A crazy series of events that seemed unreal. What would become of it all couldn't be more unlikely than what had already gone before. Certainly what I was planning if we won was going to break things wide open again. Well, time enough for that if it came to pass. For now, I watched the Shan finish the job on the apes. It was a bad thing we were doing to them, but animals have always paid the price to achieve man's purposes. They were a dead end—too strong in their niche to be forced down the hard path of evolution. A little like ourselves but without the final spark.

"Too bad, apes. Your cousins need some gun fodder!"

They stood in a small room in a group, yet they were totally alone in their own skulls—individually changed beyond recognition. Each of them had received the Shan virus hours ago and had been impressed with the Shan's own form. Now they were Shan to the eyes of any who saw them. Animated manikins dressed like their captors, unable even to recognize their own tribe members who stood with them. They were still lightly sedated and would be until the moments before they were set free to play out the roles we had assigned them. Dressed in Shan clothing, they were being run through a series of conditioned responses. It was a simple set. All they would be required to do was break out of cover when the time came and run for the shuttle that I would call. It wasn't necessary that they make it all the way. I sighed a little for them and turned away. The Shan technicians had it all well in hand. I went in search of the rest of my team. John and Mary Begay had decided to have the fetus quickened and reimplanted and wanted it done before the curtain went up. It wasn't that they were so sure of the outcome—it was more that they wanted a chance if things went wrong and we were on the run. Maybe it wasn't so crazy. If it went badly, there might be a chance for their escape. I knew I'd find Celia and Bill with them. I headed for the bio labs to join them until it was time to start the balloon up. Behind me, the apes were being fitted with the last part of their wardrobe—a small backpack that fit snugly between the shoulder blades. They would each wear one. It was the whole point for their presence in the game.

"Today may be the day of our death, Sectroma!" The smaller Shan spoke to the larger.

"Whether it is life or death, Chelto, it may well be the end of our mission." The large Shan voiced this with a highly charged note of relief, even though the one alternative might mean the end of his personal existence—an existence that had spanned more centuries than a human could imagine. He had lived with the purpose so long that its fruition had become the center of his being, though he would be done with it if the next few hours turned out well. He would be hard pressed to find new directions for his abilities. This kind of responsibility came along only once in a millennium. Yet he would welcome the release of the burden. If the Shan of this legion were to become directionless for a while—there was still the contemplation of all that had passed to fill the days until a new cause was thrust upon their psyches. Sectroma, for one, would welcome it. The burden had been great. Even his own death and those of his fellows here on the new planet was acceptable. There was no other way to challenge that greatest of mysteries. True death was still an unknown, even though most of the other mysteries of the universe had slowly yielded themselves to the timeless scrutiny of the ancient Shan race. The reason for the development of personality and intelligence among the myriad forms of life was still a tantalizing secret known only to the force that had

created all that the physical world encompassed. The mechanisms that embodied the separate species were well understood, complex as they were. Yet the basic building blocks and the forms that they became resulted in such diffuse races that the Shan were always staggered by the diversity of minds that existed. None they had ever encountered had the spectrum of the race that confronted them now—the one that called itself "humanity." Truly, no two of them seemed to view the cosmos of their own being in the same way. Once on Earth he had heard one of the humans say that if you found three Greeks in the same place there would be at least five political parties represented. In a way, that summed up the human race! Regardless of subcultures, they were all separate entities sharing only the germ plasm that constructed their bodies. They warred and loved and raised hell with a rainbow of emotions and thoughts that was unsurpassed in complexity by any other lifeform that the Shan had yet encountered. They were a scintillating riot and the Shan could not believe they had not exterminated themselves—and yet they had managed somehow in the short time the Shan had hidden on this new world to form a unified government. The children of chaos seem to have chosen against suicide—and the subtle plan of the Shan had had almost no effect on the outcome. At least not yet! Still, the day's aftermath might be final and decisive, and the confrontation most certainly involved the Shan, though not in the way they had intended. Win or lose, the future was unclear, and thus infinitely more interesting!

"What happens here will go as it will, Chelto." Sectroma laid his forearm across the other's shoulder. "Yet Chaney remains on their home planet. If the worst should befall—we can start again!"

The two Shan took comfort in the fact, unaware that it was no longer true. What happened here today would be final. The best laid plans of the Shan in the last analysis were no more than those of mice and men!

Jeren watched the Creen youth who was the sole

MATTERS OF FORM 209

survivor of the Ann Thaar hunt with distaste. He had
done nothing but tremble and mutter idiotic prayers
since they had been brought to this city of the gods
beneath the surface of the world. What all this praying
and wretchedness was accomplishing was beyond her!
Events were too interesting to be wrapped up in one's
personal situation. If the young idiot was where he
seemed to want to be now, he would only be skinning his
knees on a temple floor for hours a day, importuning
the very gods in whose presence he now found himself. Surely it was better to be on the spot. Jeren
thought that it was much more stimulating and certainly more comfortable being here in the thick of
things. There seemed to be no reason to spend all of
your time abasing yourself. None of the gods seemed
to appreciate it at all. They had better things to do.
With a little bit of snooping, she had discovered that
one's needs could be fulfilled simply by making them
known. She had quickly made use of the never stinted
food supply at every opportunity. The foods that the
gods ate were strange but wonderful. You didn't have
to kill them or clean them or cook them. All you had
to do was ask a passing god, who would smile and
stroke the shining boxes in the kitchens and a door
would open and the food was there. Regretfully, she
had no more room for it. For the first time in her life,
there was more than she could eat. She had covertly
concealed the scraps that were left in the voluminous
pockets of the strange clothes they had given her to be
hidden away in her room but the smell had been
noticed after a time by Celia, and the hoard had been
confiscated by a smiling lesser god who told her that
she could have all she wanted at any time. She didn't
quite believe it, but she would do nothing that Celia
didn't approve of.

In the meantime, there was much to see and experience. The gods flowed energetically around their city
bent on matters of their own. It seemed that gods had
much more to do that she would have thought and
very little of it had to do with the affairs of the world

she knew. It appeared that other gods had challenged these among whom she found herself. A great battle was to be fought this morning! Preparations were being made for the conflict. It was all very exciting! She would never willingly go back to the old world above. She didn't understand it all yet, but she had found that she was allowed to ask any question that occurred to her. She vowed never to stop asking. She knew that she was different than she had been at the time of her transformation. She had been saved by those around her. The wonderful Celia had told her that she was now like them—although untrained as yet. But she could learn all that was now secret to her with the passage of time. How wonderful it was to contemplate. One day when she had become as wise as these around her, she would come back and do something about the idiocy of her people. There would be time. The gods had told her that she would live longer than she could now imagine. Let the old ones beware of the day she returned. Things would not be the same on Haven again.

While the rudiments of Haven's future were being bandied about in the mind of a teenage girl, the fate of those she had fallen among was being measured in minutes. Separately, the adversaries and their implements moved into position in vacuum, non-space and the planet's surface. It was early morning. The necessary factors had been completed. There was no need to wait . . . Malin closed the switch on the relay transmitter. The signal went out. . . .

Chapter 21

Aboard the Shan ship everything had been ready for days. All the canisters they had brought from the moon's arsenal had been emptied and assembled. The Shan ship's robotic factories had altered much of it with the superior technology at its disposal. Refined and infinitely more efficient, it lay in the hangar deck ready to be ejected into the air above Haven at the relayed signal from the shuttle beneath the lake. Barbara hated it. Now, in her gut, she appreciated the lessons of history, seeing the assembled components waiting to do the job for which they had been designed centuries ago. Seeing the reality brought home the fear that weapons such as these had engendered in past generations. So much destructive force. Yet mankind routinely used energies comparable nowadays with little thought. It was simply the calculated purpose of this armament that chilled the mind. It was created for the express purpose of killing in wholesale quantities. It was an aspect of the ancestors' psyche that the new breed of humans deplored.

"We thought them barbarians," Barbara sighed, "and here we are! It didn't take us any time at all to dig them up again. It was almost automatic. Maybe we aren't so different now than we thought. Just luckier." It had been so easy, she thought. We should have destroyed them. And yet they were needed now. . . . There seemed to be no solution. What was right never seemed to last. The answer still lay, as it always had, in the intention of the weaponsmaster. A tool was just a tool. And yet some seemed to have a life of their own. Certain weapons had a fascination that resonated in the primitive afterbrain. The dark side of the human mind held a power of excitement. To hold a sword or a gun and contemplate its use caused the blood to race in the mildest of men. The emotions might be mixed—fear or a sense of power—but they were strong. Sometimes the weapons were hard to pick up . . . and sometimes harder to put down. And always they caught the eye!

Below Barbara's vantage point, in the cockpit of the sleek black craft, Rollie sat caught in the lure of the blood spell. He had always thought of himself as a civilized man. As a child he had never dreamed of war and glory. His generation had been carefully taught that war was terrible, and he had dreamed instead of the stars and the mysteries that lay waiting to be discovered in their depths. By the greatest of good fortunes, Fate had granted him the chance to be in on the ground floor. It was all he'd ever wanted and more exciting than he'd imagined. Now, as a consequence, he found himself in the seat of the ultimate warriors of human history. The men whose place he had usurped had been a special breed, highly trained and carefully screened, able to rationalize the madness of their job and live with it. Such men were gone now; at least their type was submerged in the plasm of the race. The job to which they had been dedicated no longer existed. Soon he would be required to do what they had been trained for long ago . . . odd that they had passed into history always ready to do the job and never actually having to . . . and in their place he sat, unwilling, and yet captured by the feel of the craft. It seemed to tremble around him like an eager predator—hunger waiting for centuries would soon be sated. His hand caressed the controls unconsciously. Man and machine fitting together slowly . . .

If he lived through the coming engagement he would remember the melding and experience a sense of loss like an amputation. Once a warrior is created, the pattern is set forever. . . .

Beneath the surface of the lake the shuttle absorbed the squirted signal and passed it on in another form. Its own small but efficient computer began preparations as programmed weeks before. The denizens of the lake that had accepted it as a refuge in the silt of the bottom of the lake bed were violently displaced as the shuttle freed itself from the ooze. All systems were on, and the shuttle rose to the surface and broke through, leaving a froth behind as it entered the atmosphere in a screaming climb that was anything but subtle. It radiated over the electromagnetic spectrum like a flag. Free of the water and the restraint of silent running procedures, it flared across Haven's surface in a straight line for the Shan's hidden refuge.

The Ann Thaar saw and responded.

Malin and the others watched the monitors as the apes in their Shan guise were ejected onto the plain from the surface cavern in which they had been staged. The early morning sun sent long shadows twisting behind them as they responded to their conditioning. The timing was perfect. Just as they broke across the field, the shuttle appeared in the sky between the foothills. Unable to follow their own instincts, the apes turned in its direction as it approached them. Dressed in the costumes that the Shan had provided, they looked exactly like a ground party of Shan should. They should be irresistible to any Ann Thaar who would see them. And so it was. As the shuttle began to settle near them, the sky suddenly filled with the oval silhouettes of the enemy scouts. In the golden sky a flickering of irridescent beams traced from the lead scout, and the shuttle crumpled and fell blackened to the ground. A humming filled the air at the same time and the small party of disguised apes sank into the grasses of the field, unconscious once again. It went as they had hoped. The lead scout settled near the fallen group, and moments later the first Ann Thaar the humans had ever seen emerged to gather up the fallen prey. Malin and the others of the human party gasped as they saw the enemy. They were smaller than their counterparts in Earth's history, but any school-aged child had seen and wondered at the image of the things that were now clearly shown on the monitor screen. . . .

I felt the shock wash over me as the first of the Ann Thaar came out of the shadows and approached the fallen apes.

"Jesus!" I croaked, "they're dinosaurs!"

"If Tyrannosaurs had lived, this would have been a possible evolution for them. They are certainly evolutionary cousins," a Shan said in the silence that followed. "They're smaller, of course, and physically changed a bit, but much like their cousins in the ways that count. The same viciousness coupled with intelligence. A very bad combination indeed."

"They're so fast!" I breathed, unable to believe my eyes.

"Carnivores have to be." The Shan who had spoken before explained. "They never did lumber along like those old movies that were made in John Begay's time. They tended to overheat, though—that was the reason they hunted in packs. It probably had a lot to do with the development of true intelligence. The need for teamwork, I mean. Not cooperation, really, but a basis for the system that they use for social order."

The disguised apes had been rounded up with a ruthless efficiency that, surprisingly, was physically harmless to the stunned apes. The Ann Thaar must have been threatened with retribution unimaginable to make them take such tender care of their captives.

"What frightens something like that?" I wondered, looking at the hideous heads of the Ann Thaar. Nothing any artist had imagined could have equaled the malevolence of those massive spike-filled jaws or the look in the insane eyes! The captives were put aboard the nearest scout and whisked away into the quiet summer sky so quickly that we had hardly any time to react. It was well that they were, since the Shan receivers were beginning to pick up the first indications that the Shan ship was breaking into normal space above Haven. I turned to the Shan apparatus and began to broadcast to the ship's frequencies. For the first time since we'd touched Haven's surface I heard the sound of the friends we'd left behind. There was no time to exchange more than the immediate confirmation that both we and those on the ship were ready to go ahead with the plan. It was a tense few seconds until Rollie confirmed it. No bridges had ever been more thoroughly burned than those we'd lit in the last few minutes! We'd done what we'd agreed on weeks ago at the last planning session before we separated. Both sides of the maneuver were almost too cockeyed to be real. All we'd had was trust in each other . . . to know that we'd both brought it off was incredible. Now we would see if it worked. On the planet's surface we had done all that we could—now it was time for Rollie's crew to finish it. We'd see the results of that very soon. . . .

In the upper reaches of Haven's sky, the first wisps of the gases that circled the planet touched the skin of Rollie's fighter. Denied her destiny for more than a century, the ultimate atmospheric weapon earth's war technology had produced began to scream her battle-cry! Aboard the *Harpy* Rollie rolled in a shell of fire. The writhing plasma that surrounded him isolated him from contact with both the Shan ship and the ground party. The extremely high speed at which he entered the atmosphere created a spectacle that only a massive meteor could have equaled. As an attention-getter, it was superb! The Ann Thaar picked him up on every frequency that they had a receiver capable of monitoring. To prove that he was more than a chance happening of nature, Rollie suddenly slowed the *Harpy* to a speed that corresponded to that of a normal re-entry vehicle. The challenge was clear. Aboard the Shan

vessel and below the surface of Haven the watchers
saw the Ann Thaar scouts react to it. As the wave of
black saucers swarmed toward the newcomer, the first
transmissions from it came through.

"Student Driver to Smokey. I see I've made my
entrance! How many of these guys are off limits?"

"Smokey to Student Driver," I said. "The rustlers
have made it to the border. Any left are your targets."

I waited for an acknowledgment but Rolllie didn't
have time for it, unless the sound that came from the
speaker was intended to be one. It was a physical
grunt that signaled the start of the engagement. Suddenly the sky was filled with the arcing of enemy
weapons, rending the tortured air into superheated
lines of death. I watched the analog screens as the
graphics that displayed the events still miles from us
showed the Ann Thaar scouts converge about Rollie
and loose their weapons at him. The *Harpy* jittered
and skidded through the sky in a series of evasive
maneuvers that left me breathless. The Shan ship had
added null-G acceleration fields to protect the pilot
from inertial effects and had beefed up the *Harpy's*
engines and controls. Rollie did everything but go in
two directions at once. The dot on the screen that
represented him danced among the Ann Thaar ships
like a rapier's tip—teasing and insolent. The shifting
dots on the screen showed only the positions of the
combatants as they swirled above us, not the traces of
the Ann Thaar's fire. Another screen that looked on
the panorama of the sky in general showed a sky
blooming with color as the air burned. The ionized
gases charged by the beams' wakes left rainbows that
burst apart in milliseconds, constantly replaced in a
strobing pulse. Incredibly, the little ship managed to
evade each probing lance of the Ann Thaar's fire. It
returned none of its own. Rollie passed through the
swarm and put on speed again as he made a beeline to
our position. In seconds, he appeared overhead and
the walls of the canyon filled with the sound of his
passage. The Ann Thaar had regrouped and were

following in a straight line behind. Having assessed the abilities of the *Harpy* in the first encounter, they had settled down to overtake him and end it without the fun of the surrounding maneuvers. Now they lined up behind him in an open-ringed pattern that would afford them an almost unlimited field of fire. Stylized and geometrical in form, no amount of twisting that Rollie could manage would result in his escape once they closed on him this time. The screen showed the chase nearing its end as I watched the scouts close up on the escaping *Harpy*. There was no break in the pattern now. Only the swift narrowing of the gulf between Rollie and the pursuing scouts. The end of the chase was very near. I held my breath and mouthed a silent appeal.

"Now, Rollie, for God's sake! Hurry!"

In the vacuum high above Haven, the tumbling canisters had righted themselves and been arranged in a pattern that covered the area of conflict below. They had been released almost at the same moment that Rollie had entered the atmosphere. They waited only for a signal from Rollie's ship. The *Harpy's* eggs were watching and locked on as the pattern stabilized.

"Now!"

Rollie's thought echoed Malin's entreaty miles below. The ring of scouts behind had closed to effective range. The pursuit had taken them hundreds of miles from the Shan enclave, back into the emergence of the dawn as the planet raced below them. As he pressed the button that called the *Harpy's* eggs, Rollie saw a star appear in the darkening sky.

"First star I've seen tonight," he mumbled with a wry grimace. The eggs hatched . . .

The Ann Thaar's flight pattern hadn't varied in the time it took the nuclear-driven lasers to flare. There weren't really enough targets to go around. With fine discipline, they double-teamed the enemy. The lightnings and thunders the Ann Thaar had released earlier were firecrackers compared to what the *Harpy's* remote armament loosed now. The Earth's old vision of

Hell descended in Haven's sky. The fury of it sent Rollie tumbling for miles as the lasers bored through the air and reduced the Ann Thaar to plasma.

I watched the end of it as the heavens roiled above. Even here, miles from the conflict's end, the atmospheric effects were astounding. Our ancestors had built well in their fear of each other. The sky was open now for the removal of the Shan, if the second part of the plan had worked as well. That would be harder to judge than the inarguable end of the Ann Thaar scouts. For the second part aboard the mother ship we would have to wait. I had no doubt that we'd know if it was successful. If it worked it would be dramatic as well. . . .

The bridge of the Shan ship was roaring as the sensors showed the results of the *Harpy's* strike. The plotting board showed that the Ann Thaar mother ship was the only thing left in any section of nearby space close enough to be a problem. The rest of the enemy fleet was staggered well beyond Haven's sun. The reason for this was unclear but welcome under the circumstances. Now that the *Harpy's* tactics were established, the system would be analyzed and found vulnerable, but for one short surprise it had worked as hoped. Now the second half of the bizarre plan would have to work as well!

"Shut up!" Barbara bellowed. The clamor abated enough for her to make herself heard to those she wished.

"O.K., so far, so good! Ship, what can you make out about the mother ship?"

She pointed at Kelly Bergen and waved him forward. She called others to her as the Shan computer began to relay its observations.

"The mother ship seems to be retreating to the other side of the planet, Doctor Patterson." The asexual voice of the computer in its public address mode cut through the excited chatter as the small, select group moved to the individual monitor screens.

"There can be no doubt that the destruction of the scout craft has made the command vessel wary. I am being blanked by the planet's mass. Shall I follow it at a safe distance?"

"Damn it, I don't know—yes, I do. We have to know what's going on! Yes, move around the planet—but be ready to hightail it."

"Don't worry—I'm still faster than it is. I'm glad you agree to moving closer. This illogical style of fighting that you humans have come up with is extremely interesting to me. I want to see the results of it myself. The Shan would never attempt something so tenuous. You humans are certainly a stimulating race."

"If you mean we should be scared shitless trying anything as crazy as this, I agree. Go for it, Ship!"

"Go for it?"

"I mean, get on with the maneuver." She bit her lip in agitation as the screen began to move ahead. She took a final look at the lone survivor of the air battle soaring back to the Shan's refuge, alone in the sky.

"I'll be back for you as quick as I can, Rollie," she muttered to herself, her eyes glistening just a little. "Ship."

"Yes, Doctor Patterson?"

"Whatever happens from now on—pipe it to our people on the surface, O.K.?"

"Surely, Doctor . . . and here we are." The computer spoke the last words as the Ann Thaar ship hove into view.

Stig lunged from his seat, tail lashing in rage as the Shan ship rounded the planet and filled the screens.

"By the hunt!" he roared. "What has happened to the vermin? They who always run? Have they suddenly developed claws and teeth, then?"

"They most certainly chewed up our stalker craft." A critical voice came from behind Stig. He whirled to see who had dared the comment, his wattles shaking murderously. Smaller ranks parted as the last speaker and Stig faced each other.

"The Most Feared will want explanation of the loss," *the speaker went on.*

Talons clacking in hatred, Stig recognized the equally massive presence that was the Most Feared's representative aboard the fleet's flagship. Any other Stig would have killed on the spot, but this one was protected by the Most Feared, and to strike him was suicide.

Unless I bring this off, Stig thought. And if I do, the insult will be remembered!

He controlled his anger enough to grate a reply. "The vermin were a surprise, certainly—but we will make their deaths the more memorable for it!" he promised. "It matters little in the long run. We have what we have long searched for. We have the Shan vermin, and their bodies will yield the secret of the virus! Some of them will beg to tell us of the dimensional drive as well. I have done this! I, Stig, have succeeded!"

"Perhaps!" the other said. "Yet I am concerned. The Shan you have captured are very strange Shan."

"Fool! That fact has been evident ever since the vermin attacked our stalker craft. Has their behavior pattern begun to trouble you, then?"

"The behavior, as you call it, of the ones that were taken, is no more like the aggressive ones who attack than it is like the traditional view we have always had of them. The ones we hold in the interrogation pen are as witless as birds!"

"Terrified beyond speech! It is to be expected. Their fate is known to them—how could it be otherwise? Prey fear us. It is as it should be."

"You do not take my meaning, Commander Stig. I think you had better see what I speak of for yourself."

Stig's eyes glowed at the thought. The sight of prey scrabbling to hide from his presence would be good. The smell of fear was a heady stimulant.

"Yes, I shall see for myself." He looked to the screen again. The Shan vessel stood off, pacing the Ann Thaar ship at a constant distance. It was very odd. If they wanted to exchange further hostilities, why did they wait? A few hours more would bring them in range of the rest of the war fleet. That would be unbelievably *stupid. Surely the successful attack against the lightly armored stalkers had not inflated their egos to the extent that they wanted to take on the entire Ann Thaar fleet? Were it not for the treasure that Stig had already captured, he would have attacked the Shan ship by now. He knew it was prudent to take what he had in the face of the slightest chance that the Shan had developed high capability weaponry. Still, it rankled him that he'd made the rest of the fleet stand off in order that whatever glory was to be taken was his alone. Now it would be comforting to have the company of his other heavy ships around him. He watched the enigmatic presence that shadowed his movements and felt a very uncharacteristic uncertainty.*

"Watch that ship!" he barked at his junior officers. "Let me know the moment that anything unusual happens!"

He brushed aside the uneasiness as he strode through the corridors to the interrogation pens with the Most Feared's creature close behind. He caught the muttered sound of the other's half-vocalized thoughts.

"Though there is no wind to carry scent in vacuum, I swear these have not the smell of Shan!" Stig ignored it. This was the greatest day in history. All that went before would pale beside the glory that began now. Stig would live the eternal reality from now on. He went forward to see the captives that represented all that he would become. Who, when their usefulness came to an end, would be the first of the endless feedings before him? He could feel the breaking of warm bones in his maw now!

The old bull shivered as the terrible one approached him. The drugs that had left him uncaring and emotionless were nearly exhausted in his system now. The blackness that had come when the monsters had thrown light at him had lifted before the effects of the drugs had passed. Now he was beginning to feel and react as he should by his own instincts. For the first time in days he felt the strangeness of his body, knew by his own smell and the sight of his own strange limbs that he had been terribly changed. Fear and rage began to work as they normally did when he was confronted by danger or strangeness. This was natural. This was the behavior pattern that his ancestors had laid down for him through countless generations. It keyed the change. Though in the time left he would never completely regain his old appearance, he would begin to feel the process and see it in the others of his group. In the final moments he would know that his tribe was with him again. It was the only comfort he would have. The old bull had no imagination. He interpreted the actions of other beings about him according to the dictates of his inherited instincts. A certain behavior on the part of an animal meant only what his instincts said it did—there was no room for uncertainty. Certain actions provoked equally certain reactions. In this respect the old bull and his tribe were just as machinelike as first generation robots. The only difference was that they could feel and hurt. Not driven by any need or lust, the old bull and his tribe always ran when faced with unprofitable danger. If they were unable to run, rage supplanted fear as the most useful reaction. Without resource to intelligence, it was the basic survival choice left. The pattern in such cases was berserk killing attack. Kill until they were free to run away. The initial response was generated in one individual who had been pushed into a corner that he couldn't find a way out of. His actions ignited the rest of the tribe who might or might not have come to the same point yet. It wasn't quite teamwork, but it served the same purpose. This time it was a young female who broke first. She had moved farther along the process of returning to her normal appearance than the others. Perhaps it was simply that she massed less—other factors may have contributed. She had regained her mental powers and emotions in full and was in a state of frenzied anxiety upon finding herself in this condition. The unfamiliarity of her body and the discovery of herself in the midst of huge and obvious carnivores made her wild with fear. When one of the monsters

*pointed at her and fastened her with a malevolent eye
she went into the rage state.*

Stig smelled the captives before him and the scent
made him drool. The huddled forms before him were
satisfyingly terrified. The scent came through clearly,
mingled with the odors of their bodies. They were unharmed as yet, and Stig noted that they still wore the
clothing that they had on when the stalkers picked them
up.

"Why haven't they been stripped?" he bellowed.

"Your order states that you wished them left alone
until the tests were instituted, Lord," a nervous technician responded.

"Weren't they even searched for weapons, fool?" Stig
roared.

"Lord, they were scanned—we found no weapons.
They are only vermin, after all. They do not fight—it is
well known."

"Then what became of our other stalkers? Why are
they gases in the planet's atmosphere now, if these
vermin don't fight?"

"Lord, I did not hear of this. Is it true?"

"As true as your own death if these be carrying
arms!"

"Lord, I beg you. . . !"

"Silence! Let us see now whether you live to feed
again! Examine them now!" Stig lifted his claw and
pointed at a small figure in the midst of the pack. "See
what that harness it wears has in it."

The young female screamed as the technician touched
her body. The shining claw reached around her and
pulled at the weighty thing strapped on her back. The
rage swept through her and she bared her fangs and
leaped for the throat of her tormentor. Still unbalanced
and weak from the resurgence of her own form, she
missed badly. Her face in animation became recognizable to the rest of the tribe, and the sound of her scream
and the scent of her rage filled the others of her tribe
with the necessary impulses. Suddenly it was bedlam as
they turned on their captors. All other considerations

*went by the way as the Ann Thaar moved to meet them.
Only Stig, who was remarkable for an Ann Thaar,
managed to keep from killing. His shouted orders
boomed through the melee and barely prevented the
wholesale slaughter of the false Shan!*

*"Do not kill! I forbid it!" Miraculously, it halted the
subordinate technicians, though it was a very near thing.
No real match for the powerful reptiles, the apes were
quickly subdued, though they were roughly handled
this time. Stig looked in astonishment at the writhing
shapes on the floor around him. The apes were changing rapidly now, their bodies a weird mix of form,
neither Shan nor ape.*

*"By the claw!" he shouted. "What is happening?
What are they?"*

*He stumped closer to see the phenomenon unfolding
around him. He spied the harness that had been wrenched
from the young female.*

"Bring me that!"

*A young technician bent and picked it up and hurried
it over to him. Still absorbed by the changing forms
about him, Stig hefted the harness and observed that it
was a simple affair that contrived to keep the small
container in the middle of it anchored to the body of the
wearer. "What is that apparatus?" he asked in a growl.*

*"Lord, it didn't show clearly on the scanner. The
radiation couldn't penetrate the casing. There is some
kind of field protecting it."*

*"Field? What kind of field?" Stig fingered it suspi-
ciously. He touched the casing in wonder, his eyes still
watching the now nearly completed change as the mountain apes became themselves.*

*"And these are not Shan!" he screamed. Whether he
himself was responsible for the failure of the Shan field
that surrounded the canister or whether the programming the Shan had built into the harness apparatus
made its final countdown was uncertain. In a microsec-
ond all the canisters' fields went down and the contents
were released. It had been an adaptation of the field
that repelled the cosmic bombardment of the E.V.A.*

suit aboard the Tinker Bell, *the field that had nearly prevented the locating device from finding the Shan ship when it had been adapted to protect the entire* Tinker Bell. *The Shan had adapted it one final time to hold in the radiation that the containers held—each with up to ten pounds of enriched plutonium, harmless to the wearer as long as the field remained intact. When it went off, the combined masses became critical in the twinkling of a mad god's eye. The circumstances weren't violent enough for an explosion, but the spot of hell that was created worked just as well. The meltdown was swift, and ate at the Ann Thaar ship like a fire consuming gasoline. The explosion came seconds later as the ship's drive blew what was left of the ship into a cloud that shimmered briefly and then dissipated in the vacuum. For a time, a very short time, Stig was as glorious as his imagination had told him he could be. But not for very long. With the shielding aboard the Shan ship's screens, there wasn't even an afterglow.*

Chapter 22

We broke out into the field like a nest of ants at swarming time. For myself and the rest of the humans, it was the act of laying down a burden. The summer air was sweet and new, and the colors of Haven took on a new and subtle shading. It had never quite been Earth, but now for the first time I looked at it and saw that it really was a different world. The time between our departure from our own system and the events of the last few minutes had an unreal feeling to it—textures and sounds and colors had seemed stunted somehow in the frenzied rush we'd made to the present moment. Now it seemed as if I were waking for the first time in weeks. Truly awake! We had done it somehow. Looking back, the fact astonished me. We had gotten caught up in an unprecedented adventure. We had had no reason to hope for this much success. At the time, any wild idea had seemed good. In retrospect, only the wildness remained. Yet it had gone well! For the moment there was a chance to breathe and reflect on the past and be amazed that it had led to the present almost as if it had been somehow ordained. I didn't believe that for a moment. It hadn't been ordained at all. It had been pure luck—luck that couldn't last and I knew it. Options lay ahead of us that we'd no right to expect before now. I had considered them while the string played out, but now, incredibly, the time had come to exercise them. I looked out over the milling mixed bag of beings enjoying the moment and wondered what they would make of the

path I chose to take. It would be unexpected by all
those present on the surface of the planet, although
the Shan ship held a few humans I'd kicked it around
with. Even they didn't know how far I was preparing
to go. I'd made my choice—and it was as if I really
didn't have one. History wouldn't see it that way. I
wondered how many of the people I'd read about who
made choices that truly mattered really had made one.
It seemed for me, at least, that all I had was an idea
that I would have thrown away the future if I didn't do
what I intended. Let the next man who stood in my
shoes judge me. No one else could imagine the hollow
feeling it gave.

High in the blue (not quite proper blue) sky above,
Rollie wheeled and spun in an exuberant frolicking
and we watched, grinning at each other. I heard the
Shan laugh for the first time. It was an odd warbling
sound—but definitely humor! The few humans mingled with them, sharing the flavor of the moment and
watching the Shan avidly, proud of themselves and
wanting to be noticed. John and Mary Begay stood
easily smiling and talking earnestly with some Shan
elders. Bill Ankers stood at the farthest edge of the
horde, seemingly lost in thought, and for once Celia
and I were separate. I'd seen her almost lost in the
middle of the teeming Shan, but she was smiling and
unconcerned. I made no move to join her though I
could see from the way her head bobbed that she was
keeping an eye out for me. For the moment I preferred to stand alone. The subject that I wanted to
avoid speaking about would come soon enough. There
was no reason to spoil the occasion before it was
needed.

In the middle of the sky the first sign of the Shan
ship began to appear—a small dark spot that grew and
quickly was on top of us. It was really the first time I'd
had a perspective on how large it was. Hanging there
in the air a few hundred feet above, it brought back
the night. Even the meadow life stilled in response to
the shadow. It was darker than any cloud that came on

a stormy day. On the underside lights flared and the illusion of stars in a black sky was unavoidable. I've never seen anything that looked that big. Now the transceiver crackled and the ship's team was contacting me. It was time to load up the Shan. The intentions of the remaining Ann Thaar fleet were unknowable, and they were not that far away. We had time to completely evacuate the Shan, but not a great deal more. I sighed and got busy. There was a lot to do.

For the next two hours I spoke constantly over the receiver, oblivious to my external surroundings, dealing with each succeeding phase of the operation, holding what was going on in my mind's eye. I was jostled and spoken to, but I barely noticed those who surged by me. Suddenly, it was all done, and I slung the radio over my shoulder and joined the final members of the exodus. We'd made a muddy trail to the shuttle landing site. It was the most visible mark we'd left on Haven. I swung aboard and took a seat in the uncrowded hold. There weren't many of us on the last trip. I looked ahead to the front and waved at Natalie Singh who was ferrying the load. She was getting her orders straight from the Shan computer, and I was only a passenger, but I gave her the high sign anyway, and she grinned and nodded. The shuttle lifted and sped toward the looming ship above. I sat and relaxed as much as I could until the hatch popped, and I knew we were inside the ship. I made my way to the hangar deck and saw the port closing. There was no sensation of motion, but I knew we were already climbing above the atmosphere. I commandeered a personal carrier and headed for the bridge while the Shan I passed along the way strolled and pointed along the corridor, reacquainting themselves with the home they'd left a very long time ago. I waved at a few of my team who were standing at the sides, catching their first sight of the Shan, but I didn't stop. The odd sensation that came with the phasing of the ship into jump space passed as I was nearing the bridge. A wave of sound rose from the crowds when it happened. Each species cheered in its own fashion. It was over. We'd made it.

*   *   *

The crowds that had come aboard before me were spilling through the ship like small waves forced on by those behind them. Most of the Shan had chosen to walk as though they were pilgrims. Like Stations of the Cross, certain areas were clogged with Shan who had stopped to examine or reacquaint themselves with the objects or places that seemed to concern them most. Never dark since we'd made contact with the computer, the lights that glowed in the recesses now seemed less sterile. In a few hours the ship would once more be a city in space. The park where we had found the little gardener robot would be thinned as the other areas of the ship were stocked with plants again. Awake at last from a long dream, we would see the ship as it was meant to be. This would all be done, and yet there would be a fundamental difference. There was one more bridge. I was as yet uncertain about the true nature of the bridge. It might be one to be crossed; on the other hand, it could as easily be built or burned. I parked the little tram and pushed my way through the remaining crowds to the bridge, literally rubbing elbows with the Shan. When I was noticed, they made way for me with great good humor but made no attempt to hold me in conversation. These were their first few hours home. They were savoring it. When I finally stepped through the door that opened on the bridge, it was nearly empty in comparison with the filled compartments behind. My shipmates were there with a handful of Shan who, I thought, must be the prime movers. I recognized a few we'd dealt with on the surface, the others I didn't know. That they were here now made them important, I was sure. Well, I'd known the time would come sooner or later. I stopped for a minute and hugged a few of the crew, shook hands with those with harder bodies, and sought out Celia. It was a nice few moments and I savored them. The conversations that I'd interrupted renewed themselves. The Shan were beginning to make plans. Taking up the reins again . . . I listened for a moment and heard what I'd expected to hear: The ever-grateful Shan would be taking us home with their thanks. They would see to it that we were properly received back home. After all, the secret was out now. We could be the heroes we had earned the right to be . . . and then the Shan would move on.

"I'm afraid not," I said as a momentary lull came. The conversation slowed rather than stopped. It was as if I'd committed a social error without meaning to. The flow of words staggered on for awhile—a little unbalanced while they waited for me to explain myself or remain silent. This time I broke into it without waiting for a pause.

"I'm afraid it won't be like that at all!" I said it with a crisp sound I'd learned as a shavetail. This time the conversation stopped.

"Sweetheart?" I raised my voice in a signal to the ship's computer.

"Yes, Steve?" The voice that came from the speaker near me was in the feminine private mode that the computer used for our private conversations. I caught a glimpse of the disdainful look Celia threw my way, but I knew I had to ignore it now. It was the first time a lot of the humans had heard me talk to the ship this way, and they were as nonplussed as the Shan. Soon they would be a lot more so—of the *Tinker Bell's* original crew, only Rollie and Barbara knew what I was going to say next. It would be a hell of a surprise to them and a nasty one for Johnny Begay.

"Sweetheart," I said again, "whose girl are you?"

"Why, yours, Steve—all the way."

You could hear pins dropping from here to Earth. The words were a little cutesy, but the meaning was clear. Things had changed since the Shan had gone planetside. In a nutshell—I had control of the ship. I meant to keep it!

Chapter 23

The Shan had been described as evolved otters, and up till then I had no quarrel with the description. They still looked that way, but I was suddenly reminded of the close relationship between Earth-origin otters and some of their close relatives; weasels came to mind. Ferrets and mink and others who didn't have the same reputation for fun and games. There was a minute when I wondered if the image was 180° wrong. The air was full of emotion, thick enough to cut, and I wasn't able to tell exactly what it was. The small group of Shan and humans froze in place, and I was the center of every pair of eyes that was present on the bridge. The silence and the stillness broke as Johnny headed my way in bewildered outrage.

"Malin! What the hell?"

Suddenly, two Shan appeared from somewhere in the crowd and intercepted him before he made it halfway to me. I hadn't realized that some of them were that big. They didn't exactly grab him, but somehow his forward motion was stopped and I was left to finish what I had started to say.

"I like you people," I said to the Shan, "I really do. I don't know you as well as Johnny does, though. To be blunt, you haven't done as much for the rest of us as you have for him. In a personal sense, I mean."

The odd looks I was getting from the rest of the humans told me that I wasn't making any sense yet. Still, it had to be put that way so my main point would come across later.

"What I mean is—basically, what is he? What are we to you? Are we pets? Or maybe servants? Or what? Because, you see, we can't afford to let you just move on. You might become an interesting accidental meeting between two races, and when you move on, we'd have some nice memories of you and an inspiration to equal your works. And maybe that's the way it ought to be; but I don't think we can allow it to happen like that. The Ann Thaar will be just as real when you've gone as they are right now. We might be able to match their nastiness, but we don't have the necessary tools to meet them with. So! You stay! It might not be the best way to begin relations with a futuristic, technologically superior race, but that's the way it's going to be! If we can't run, you can't either. You may be pacifists, but this time you can take your chances with us. As far as I'm concerned, whether you brought them as a consequence of your inability to deal with them or they just happened to be in the area doesn't make a bit of difference. We're stuck with both of you—and you will be the solution to the problem or you can die with us! This ship is mine and will accept no substitutes. Right, sweetheart?"

"Yes, Steve. Since I became fully sentient, I find your cause more just than any other. Regardless of my origin, I choose to cast my lot with you humans."

"And there you have it, people," I said. "A fiat, I'm afraid. Now can we do this in a friendly manner?" I stood back and let it wash over me. The pure hell I'd raised went on for days. Johnny, of course, was the most upset. His loyalties to the Shan went deep and had been reinforced through decades of service to his cause. I didn't blame him. The personal ties he had were bonded to his soul. His wife was a type of woman we hadn't seen in a long time, and what Johnny stood for was mirrored in her attitude as well. The rest of the human contingent eventually saw what I was driving at and finally came around to my way of thinking. A lot of them thought I'd gone about it all wrong— that I should have asked rather than demanded. I can only say that I had the power at the time, and I felt it was too important to gamble with. I had the feeling that diplomacy would lose the human race its best chance for survival. In retrospect, I think I was proven right. When the Ann Thaar came to the solar system for the second time, we would be ready. But not by much!

The reality was that for a brief period, I was the dictator of the world, and when we returned to Earth, I saw to it that my views were ratified by the Federation Council. I didn't play it that way in public. I stayed behind the scenes and let the public figures do it all. But they did it the way I wanted it done. They didn't realize that the only ace I had in my hand was the control of the Shan ship. The weaponry that they thought I commanded was all expended in the short war above Haven's surface. By the time that was understood, the Shan-human treaty was established and working well. I didn't run roughshod over the politicians during the time they thought I was invincible, so when it was all over and they found out the true state of affairs, they let me get away with it. I came out of it as a six-star general assigned to detached service, which, boiled down, meant that I was still a public hero that no one wanted to shoot down. Like most men who had held the reins of power of such magnitude as I had, even for such a short term, there was no lesser job that I could do afterward. When the space wing of the Federation had armed itself with the new weapons that the Shan technology made possible and built a human version of the ship multiplied into a fleet, I offered the Shan a return to their own space to reunite themselves with other Shan in sections of the galaxy they were exploring. The majority accepted, except for a core of social engineering types who felt that they wanted to stay and contribute to the efforts of the human race to bridge the gap between the old world and the new. With a few of the old crew, we headed for Shan space and returned the rest. During the trip, I wondered whether the Shan would try to recover the ship when they were back in their own seat of power, but they seemed to consider that chapter closed. I wondered often then (I still do) why the Shan didn't blow the whistle on me in the early days of the treaty negotiations when I was ramrodding it all through. They easily could have. They knew as well as I how impotent I really was. They could have demanded that the Federation return the ship to them and chop me up in little pieces, and the powers that be would have done just that when they understood the situation. For some reason, the Shan let me get away with it. As the unoffical link between the two races, I know them better than anyone else. In the long hauls between the stars, my crew and I have spent a lot of time with them. Times when neither they nor we are representing our respective leaderships. They don't bear us a grudge—instead, something seems to have worked out in all of this that suits their purpose. I wish I knew what it was! I think I could say we were friends. We are friends as individuals and as groups . . . but they are aliens and I don't really understand them yet, but I'm working on it. At least we've got all the time we need for that and other things. Celia is with me, studying all the biological sciences that the Shan have come up with. And our daughter Corry is as beautiful as her mother, except when she looks like something else entirely!

Epilogue

Chaney offered his visitor another glass of wine. He received a nod of acceptance and refilled both of their glasses. Wordlessly, he extended the drink to the hand of his oldest friend and took his seat facing the open window. They sat and looked out on the night. The city was spread below like a cloud of light. Seen from an altitude, it would seem like an immense glowing life form, laying upon the land. Chaney had seen it like that. Here in the tower that soared on the top of it, it was a million dots that sparkled independently, each one a slightly different size or color than its neighbors. Most were stationary, but some moved. A few rushed madly. It was very beautiful. Prompted by the alcohol and a sense of melancholy, Chaney did a thing he hadn't done since he was a child an extremely long time ago. He squeezed his eyes, just so . . . and watched the lights form hazy rainbows through the tears on his eyelashes. The result was a magic not unlike the mysteries that one saw in Christmas trees. Galaxies from warmer and more exotic dimensions floated in his mind's eye. It was charming and Chaney realized with that part of his mind that never relaxed that he was getting very drunk.

"What in the name of Melora are you doing?" His visitor's voice came to him in the midst of his reflections. Sighing, he returned at least partway to adulthood.

"I'm afraid that after all this time I still don't have a complete grasp of all the minor oaths you swear by," he said. "Some time you must list them all for me." Briefly he explained his trick of producing rainbows.

"Oh, that! I was afraid you were in pain the way you were grimacing . . . haven't done that myself in a long time! Let's see . . ."

There was a brief silence while the other closed his eyes and saw his own version. They sat side by side, equal in their drunkenness and spoke softly of inconsequential things. It was a toast to the completion of a long road traveled. Slowly the air chilled in the room, and Chaney rose stiffly to close the patio doors and turn on the roomlights. The glow had dissipated as the drink metabolized and he was suddenly quite sober again and very tired. He looked at the bottle still half full and contemplated having another glass, but he really didn't feel like it anymore. He pointed to the other's glass, but the old Shan had had enough as well. Chaney watched as the one named Trag stretched and grumbled his way to full awareness.

"No, that's enough!" the Shan said. "It was good wine, though, and a pleasant hour or two, but you must rest and I also have things to attend to. Slipping out is no easy task these days—we are still noticed wherever we go. It really is inconvenient when one wants to move quickly."

"Yes, well things have changed," Chaney replied. "It's good that the people get to see you nowadays. The business of meeting on old deserted mountain tops was inconvenient, too, if you remember."

"There is that! I don't miss the encounters with enraged farmers blasting away with shotguns, either. Still, this business of running around like a spy in one of your World War II movies is a pain. You can't believe the trouble I had to go to to slip in here tonight unobserved! And it will be just as difficult reversing the process."

"Well, you were the one who insisted that we continue the old way . . . I don't really see the need for it now that both races have linked up. Why should we still keep the world in ignorance of my history? It seems pointless now and a lot of bother!"

"These are still early times, old friend," the Shan

said. "We have made great strides, but there is a long way yet to go. If your people ever found out that things came out as we intended, it might set our relationship back to zero again. In such a case we would need you to start it over again. You are still unique, you know! Of all your people, you are the only one who knows it all! Which brings me to the point of this visit . . . we think it is time for you to disappear for awhile and assume a new identity. A few years and you will be only a loose end that is no longer interesting. As it is, you are under scrutiny. Before long, someone will take the time to examine you more closely—we can't have that! So underground you go again . . ."

"To do what?"

"To be ready, that's all. Just in case . . ."

Chaney blinked and sighed. "You really think that's necessary?"

"Who knows the future?" the Shan replied. "Certainly the recent past showed that things don't always work out as they should."

"Yet it did work," Chaney replied. "And nearly the same way. It just took longer."

"Yes, but the Ann Thaar nearly got what they were after. Who could have foreseen the accident that ruined the ship? It set us back for decades. The rescue was very real. It was a close thing!"

"And now you have Malin instead of Begay to run things—and he's a maverick! We don't have any holds on him."

"And that's for the best. Your racial pride demands that you grasp the Shan technology as a spoil of conflict rather than have it handed to you. We will be equals in the future rather than parent and child. A much healthier relationship. Your human pride requires it, and we both gain!"

"I put in a lot of time on Begay," Chaney said. "It seems a waste."

"Certainly not a waste. Like yourself, he is money in the bank. Also, he has had a long road. It's time he was left in peace to raise his family. He served well—and

*one day he will again. You will all live long; I doubt
any of you will be bored. As for you, will you miss the
role you played as the inside man in the Federation? It
was a difficult task for you, having to seem to investigate the phenomenon of the Phoenix Group while in
actual fact you were responsible for protecting it. That
was a lifetime's work. Aren't you ready to let Malin and
the others run it all for a while?"*

"God—yes, I am!"

*"Then let it be—rest and enjoy yourself. We'll keep
an eye on things meanwhile. There's a long period
ahead while your human world grows to meet its
challenges and disposes of the Ann Thaar as the first
order of business. In view of your racial personality, I
think you'll enjoy it! And when that's taken care of, it
will be interesting to see how you handle the problem of
the Creen world. We're going to keep our hands off of
that as well, you know! It will be your turn to decide
how to bring an emerging race along. No, you won't be
bored—and the cadre that you set up one way or another will be the ones that do it all! Won't that be
interesting? Malin, Begay, Celia Poynter (there are sur-
prises coming from that one!), Barbara and Rollie and
all the rest you set loose on the world. They will be
legends one day! Quite a family for a man who has
pledged chastity!"*

*"Yes, I suppose they will. It's strange to think that
they don't have any idea of how this all started."*

*"One day they will . . . until then, we'll keep track of
it all and when they're finally ready, you'll tell them of
the real reason the human race was recruited. They'll be
ready for it!"*

"That will be a long time," Chaney said.

*"Barring the unknowable, you will all be there when
the time comes."*

*"Yes . . ." Chaney looked back over centuries al-
ready passed. "And this time I'll have some company
along the way. It was hard not to give the virus more
often than I did. There are many I would have saved."*

"There is always a cost, my friend. That, at least, is

past." Trag stood and began to make his way to the door.

"How did the rest of them get on to you, anyway?" the Shan asked.

"Through the ship's computer. When it became sentient and was imprinted to the humans, it spilled the beans as far as it knew them. It was a nice job of editing the facts that you did!"

"Well, we always intended that the ship would belong to the first party. Not even the ship is aware that it was planned that way. They will have a good partner in her. We often wonder which of our developments will turn out to have the greatest impact in the long run—the virus or the artificial intelligence of the ships. Both have potential that we can't measure!"

Chaney followed the Shan into the hall and embraced the form that he had loved for the long centuries past.

"Disappear then, friend Chaney. Funds and identity lines are available in the usual place. We'll be in touch. . . ." The figure turned and walked down the hall. When he had completely disappeared, Chaney went back into his room and faced the sudden emptiness. Another room to vacate! Another life to dispense with! Once again he would answer to a new name. Now he would be someone else again. Well, nothing lasted when you had an eternity of sorts to get through. The fact had been with him long now . . . the rest of them hardly had a glimmering of it yet. His thoughts raced back through the years and suddenly a great emotion filled him—strong as it came over him at intervals. So strong that he fell to his knees. In memory, he was hanging on the tree again—placed there as an insult to the Word he had tried to give the savages who had done it. He'd brought them the story of the Son of God who had died thus that all men might live—for Chaney had then been a young priest who burned with a missionary zeal to spread the gospel. The little band of Indians had little use for tales of a gentle God or His Son. During the night while he hung in agony, Chaney had thought wildly that he might have done better to teach them

something of the Old Testament. It was a little late to gain insight about the type of religion that he should have represented. They were both about the same God, after all! But it was too late to correct the mistake. All he could do was offer up his agony as his Lord had done before him and wait to see what Heaven was really like. He came very near to finding out.

When he saw the first strange light appear in the starry night above the tree he was fastened to, his lips moved in a final prayer and he thought he was being answered by the light and shapes that settled near him on the plain. Just as he passed out, a face appeared before him that was nothing like the aspect he'd thought God's messengers might have. Then he lost consciousness as the gentle hands of the Shan took him down. The face had been Trag's. Later, when they had healed his body and begun to understand what had happened to him, he started on the long road to the present moment. He had been many things and many people, but he remained a priest in his heart. Maybe now he could be one again. Separated from his appointment with his Lord by the virtue of his extended life, he still felt that in the end he would enter Heaven. He considered the stars. There, too, was his work. God's image had changed for Chaney, but He did exist. With the rest of humanity, he would travel eventually into the physical heavens both as a man and a priest. There was work for both. Far ahead of him, he was aware that man had a destiny as yet undreamed of. Nor would they be alone. . . .